ALEX BEECROFT

CONTRABAND HEARTS

RIPTIDE
PUBLISHING

a PORTHKENNACK
HISTORICAL

Riptide Publishing
PO Box 1537
Burnsville, NC 28714
www.riptidepublishing.com

Contraband Hearts

Cover art: L.C. Chase, lcchase.com/design.htm
Editor: Carole-ann Galloway
Layout: L.C. Chase, lcchase.com/design.htm

ISBN: 978-1-62649-805-1

First edition
April, 2018

Also available in ebook:
ISBN: 978-1-62649-804-4

ALEX BEECROFT

CONTRABAND HEARTS

To all those people who waited so long for another Age of Sail book from me. I hope you enjoy this.

TABLE OF

CONTENTS

CHAPTER ONE

PERRY ARRIVES ON THE SCENE

July 1790

My dear mama,

I am finally arrived in Porthkennack. I have this moment alighted from the coach and come into a fine new inn by the name of the Hope and Anchor. You will be happy to know that I have secured a room here until I can find something nearby more commensurate with my salary. I may be corresponded with, therefore. Please write, and tell me all the small doings of the family. Even though the journey was short and it has been but six days since I departed from London, it has been ample time to realize that I miss you all.

Speaking of time, as soon as I set down my luggage, I sent my regards to Mr. Gwynn at the customs house, asking when he required me to report to him, so I am writing this with one hand, while with the other I attempt to shift my travel-worn coat and neaten my bedraggled wig in anticipation of a summons. I hope you can read the terrible writing! I—

Oh, that thunder at my door must be the man already. My apologies. I will pick this up when I return.

"Yes, yes." Perry put down the inn's spluttering pen and rose to flick up the latch on his door. His room was barely large enough to house a coffin—he had been writing with his travel slope balanced on his knee, sitting on the cot-sized bed—but he hoped not to have to endure it long. "I'm coming."

"Mr. Peregrine Dean?" The man at his door backed off when Perry opened it, his eyes rounding, and his face passing through a sequence of expressions that had become familiar to Perry over the course of his working life.

"That's right," Perry said, sternly. "And you are?"

The newcomer scratched a short-shorn head of brown hair beneath a brown leather tricorn. The fair skin that showed at his wrist contrasted with the deep baked tan of his face, which nevertheless glowed across the cheeks and the bridge of the nose, either with a blush or with sunburn. His figure was both large framed and plump, his jacket brown as his eyes. A red neckerchief was tied jauntily around his throat in place of a stock, and his stunned expression was already in the act of turning into a smile.

"I'm Jowan Ede, riding officer, and your partner." He held out his hand, and said—still grinning, "I didn't think you'd be a black man."

Perry sighed internally. No doubt Jowan hoped for an explanation, a pedigree even. He could go on hoping for it, or earn it the way any friend or colleague earned the intimate details of one's life. "I didn't expect my partner to come and fetch me. That was kind of you."

"Oh, well." Jowan shrugged a shoulder as if embarrassed. "We can be efficient as you like, up at the customs house, and it ain't every day we get a recruit come in from London. Lord Petersfield, taking an interest in little old us? It's obliging, ain't it? We've got to be obliging back."

Perry's back still ached from the constant jogging of the coach. His spirits were already oppressed from having been shut up in tight confines with five other people for six long days, yet now they took a further dip. He had hoped that the supervisor of Porthkennack would have had the sense not to mention to his staff that Perry had been sent not only to fulfil a riding officer's duties, but also to keep an eye open for corruption, on behalf of the authorities in London.

To cover his consternation, he attempted once more to brush road dust from the sleek black strands of his wig. But the summer had been hot, the coach had thrown up a cloud of choking dirt as it rolled, the windows down so they could breathe, and the pomade with which the wig had been dressed had been sticky. Now the wig looked like a mouse that had got into the flour bin. A punctilious appearance being ruled out, he would have to be friendlier if he was to present himself as an innocent colleague and not a snitch.

"What do you think?" he asked. "You must know Mr. Gwynn—will he be most insulted by a bare head or a dirty wig?"

"He won't rightly care." Jowan's grin had made itself so much at home on his face it had drawn pale lines in his suntan. A good-humoured man, then. One who could be talked round. "Though I wouldn't keep him waiting any longer."

"I shall pretend the colour is the latest fashion." Perry slapped the dirt from his coat and donned it, jammed his gritty wig back on his sweating head, and closed the door behind him. "Lead on."

A sharp scent of sea hit his nose as he followed Jowan out onto the stone sets of the street outside the inn, and the water's glister closed off the horizon on every side. A reek of oily fish joined the odour as Jowan led him between flowerless cottages whose doors were packed around with empty barrels. Women in greasy stays were hauling the barrels up with brawny arms, and piling them atop carts as their children danced in and out of the wheels.

"'Tis pilchard season." Jowan caught him staring. "The boats'll be coming back in an hour or so, and then there'll be a grand rush to salt 'em and pack 'em and get 'em sent over to Spain, where the papists do like 'em for their dinner."

At least Jowan did not seem like the kind of man to resent Perry for doing a job he had been sent to do. He might be obstructive, but would hopefully not be violent. Perry tried not to shout, though the racket of the wagon wheels and the clatter of empty barrels made it necessary to raise his voice. "All these barrels going to and fro must make it hard to distinguish contraband from lawful goods."

Jowan paused and gave him a slightly condescending laugh. "You've no idea. Oh you've no idea at all."

"I've worked five years at the London dockside," Perry protested—he would not be thought ignorant as well as prying. "I know plenty of the tricks. You are not getting a booby for a colleague, I can assure you."

Jowan snorted. "How you do talk." He chuckled. "Just like a gentleman."

Since it was Perry's ultimate goal to *become* a gentleman, the man's amusement rankled. "My patron made sure I had an excellent education," he snapped back, as Sangraal Street ran out ahead of him, leaving them both on the breast of a headland fraught with toothed brown rocks.

"Well, don't be too smug about it," Jowan replied, as they both contemplated the view, "the lads won't like that neither."

A promontory surrounded by jagged islands stood out against the foaming seas to Perry's left—though *islands* might be taking it too far. The largest would barely have supported a house on top, and was crowned with a bare two visible trees.

Beneath Perry's feet, the land tumbled down in shards where every shadow might be a cave. From the end of the headland, the sea stretched to the horizon, a wonderful blue green close at hand, and far off a dazzle of light blended seamlessly into the sky. Changes of colour showed currents and sandbanks. Shadows on the seabed suggested wrecks, and yet the surface of the sea was crowded with sails.

A naval second rate glittered at anchor far out in the bay, as slighter ships—brigs and cutters—slipped around her. Closer to, the harbour was filled with smaller boats spaced in precise measures from one another, linked with long nets that bulged and writhed with glistening silver fish.

"Them's the seine nets," Jowan volunteered, following his gaze. "On a good year, a man can make a fortune from pilchards—take 'em up by the thousand hogshead, in a season that lasts July to October. See the little hut?" He pointed out a small white building—scarce more than a roof over a seat—close at hand to them, at the top of the cliffs. "That's where the huer sits, searching for the shoals. When he spots them, he gives a shout, and all the boats set out at once. We get a bit of peace when the pilchards are running, mostly, cause all the smugglers that can afford it own pilchard boats as well."

"I'm grateful for your local knowledge," Perry offered, feeling somewhat guilty for his snappishness. He followed Jowan down the cliff path, to where the rocks gave way to the sands of Polventon Beach, and a hub of grand buildings indicated recent government interest in the doings of the town.

"No one's more local than me, my lad," Jowan agreed, guiding him to the customs house, a purpose-built modern building with its name on an arch between its pleasing bow windows. A single cannon stood in front of it, and in a courtyard within the arch, integral stables stood neatly empty. Jowan seemed to droop a little, relaxing, as he entered the shade of its walls. "Locals are wise to all the tricks and the characters from birth, right? That's why there's not normally a call for bringing in London boys. What do you know about this town, eh? About who's a villain and who's just got caught up in something 'cause they don't want no harm to come to their old mum or dad? You're like a newborn babe here. You need to listen to me."

He flung out this last observation as they passed through a door on the inner side of the customs compound, between the stables and a large building that must be a warehouse. Inside, the white walls and unvarnished wooden floors reflected their footsteps as though they were accompanied by drums, and when they passed through the main room, where three officers were filling in reports at battered desks, Perry felt the stares like the threads of a net closing around him.

They were at least no better dressed than he—two of them without wigs and the third wearing an obviously secondhand physician's bob. His practiced eye summed them up swiftly as grimy ordinary men—the sort that practiced ordinary forms of corruption and lasciviousness and thought themselves no worse than the rest of the world for it.

"So that's the snitch?" someone whispered behind his back as Jowan opened the inner office door.

"They'll have the very dogs reporting on us next."

Perry's face set hard. His pressed lips went cold as he fought the urge to turn around and demand satisfaction for that remark. It wouldn't do to start his career here with duelling or brawling. But his blood was still up as he walked into the supervisor's office, and he was pricklingly aware that Jowan had left the door open. Presumably so all the men behind him could listen in.

The supervisor was a corpulent red-faced man whose clubbed hair was thinning on top. He wore a flowered waistcoat that suggested he did little crawling around in ships' cargoes. "*You* are Peregrine Dean?" he sputtered, his eyes round and horrified as he got a good look at Perry. "No. Some wag is trying to pull one over on me."

"I assure you, that's not the case." Perry took his birth certificate and his letter of introduction from Lord Petersfield from his breast pocket and offered them as proof. Watching Gwynn pour over them, his nicotine-stained finger smudging the letters, skewered Perry's jaw with pain as he ground his teeth to stop himself from urging the man to be more careful. "I am here to take up the post of riding officer, as has been agreed."

"And to report back to Lord Petersfield as regards the corruption of my officers and department." Gwynn scowled at him as though he were a carcass crawling with maggots.

Perry's jaw gave another throb. "That, sir, was meant to be information confidential to you. Not to be shouted out loud with the door open and half your staff listening in."

"Do you criticise me already, young man, before you have had even one day in practice?" Gwynn rose, hands braced against his desk, and his face as red as Jowan's with humiliation, or rage, or fury.

Do not do this, Perry's inner councillor told him. *Your patron is relying on you. Be a man and keep it under control. Be graceful in comportment, gracious in manners, gentlemanly in the face of adversity.*

Perry unclenched his fists and took a long, deep breath in and out. "Forgive me, sir." He dropped his gaze. *Zeal is excellent, but be aware of the golden mean—if your passion gets in the way of doing your job, it is too much.* If he was going to be proud, it should be pride based in his achievements—in his ability to clean up corruption, to please his betters and prove that he belonged among them. That he could be trusted to handle great things with tact and discretion appropriate to the higher ranks. "I did not mean to imply that. I apologize for speaking out of turn."

Gwynn's ruddy face paled, though his eyes continued sour. "I'm glad to hear it," he said, taking his seat once more. "I have no need for a man so far away from his native haunts, so unfamiliar with the native dodges. But it just so happens that our local magistrate—with whom we cultivate the strongest of ties—requested yesterday that I put a man at his disposal. He can have you. Report immediately to Sir Lazarus Quick, and ask of *him* what use you can be."

CHAPTER TWO

A PRIVATE COMMISSION

Perry recognized the magistrate's house from Jowan's description. Jowan had come part of the way with him and had pointed out the tall white dwelling that stood at the entrance to the narrow headland from which the Merope Rocks stood out.

"I'll be in the Seven Stars coffeehouse if you need me," Jowan had said, and given Perry a nudge that he took to be sympathetic.

"Should you not be back on your rounds?" Perry muttered, more to himself than to the Cornishman, but Jowan's good-humoured face turned confiding, and he nudged Perry's shoulder again.

"There won't be no smuggling on a bright day like this. Storm and dark, that's the weather for the underhanded. But I might catch a rumour or two if I keep my ears open in the coffee shop. Many a plan goes a slip over a cup of chocolate and the latest papers."

Well, that might be true. Perry bid Jowan farewell as he resumed the walk up to the very top of the promontory. *But it also keeps Jowan indoors and off his feet, rather than patrolling the cliffs as he ought to be.* A certain amount of guilt attended this thought, since Jowan had been the most pleasant of the people he had met so far. Perhaps he knew his own business best. Perry should attend to his.

Like the customs house, the magistrate's dwelling had an official air about it. A nautical flair was apparent in the swivel guns installed front and back on the upper balcony. A flagstaff stood naked by the red-painted front door, and on the southern side of the square stone house, an orangery of many panes of green glass threw back the sun in a sheet of flame.

"Big house," Jowan had said. "Built by Admiral Quick nigh on thirty years ago. 'Tis his son lives there now, with the admiral's widow, and his two children. Sticklers they are. I don't envy you. You'll know the house by the telescope, if nothing else. He did used to like to watch the shipping, the admiral, and they kept his room as it was when he died."

Perry double-checked, and yes, the bulky wooden tube and round golden eye of a telescope protruded from one of the seaward windows, a suggestion of movement inside the room telling him he was being examined in turn. He made another attempt to thumb the dust from his wig—or at least to spread it more evenly so it would look applied by design—then straightened his stock, his waistcoat, and his cuffs and went round to the front to pull the chain to ring the bell.

The door opened a crack. Then it closed again sharply. Perry massaged the ache in his jaw with his fingers, sighing, and knocked a second time, more firmly.

"We're not interested," a woman's voice shouted. "Go away before I set the dogs on you."

"Not interested in what?" Perry asked—this was a new permutation of an old theme.

"You're one of them abolitionists, aren't you? We don't donate, and we don't want pamphlets. We're not interested."

You seem keen enough to profit from Africa, Perry thought, for there were pineapples growing in frames visible in the conservatory. The inner wood of the room appeared to be teak. Ivory was inset into the door handle and the pull of the bell. *But of course you have no desire to aid her.* He held his tongue on the hypocrisy, however—he was himself a freeborn Englishman, son of a free man, and if his mother had come out of slavery, well, that had been a very long time ago and she never talked of it.

"I am Mr. Peregrine Dean," he told the woman patiently. "I am employed as a riding officer, and I have been sent here by William Gwynn at Sir Quick's bidding. Just tell him I'm at the door and see if he wants me let in."

"How do I know you are who you say you are?"

He hoped it wasn't going to be like this the whole time. At least the capital was cosmopolitan enough to accept that Londoners came in every shade.

"I can show you my papers." He took them out once more, and when she opened the door a sliver, passed them through. Moments later and she pushed it wide, handing them back. His heart softened a little on seeing that she was clearly still a child—tall but gawky, all eyes and elbows, her nose smudged with boot blacking.

"I'm sorry, sir," she said, dropping him a courtesy, "I didn't know. You sit down here"—she indicated the row of chairs that lined the entrance hall's right wall—"and I'll go and get the housekeeper. It's washday and we're all at sixes and sevens."

The wait was welcome at first, helping him to calm down and taking the ache out of legs that had had a rude awakening to toil after a morning in the coach. However, he'd missed his chance at luncheon, and had begun to feel hungry and ill-done-by by the time the housekeeper arrived and ushered him into a glowing, rosy room adjacent to the orangery.

She stopped him just outside the polished teak door and whispered, "Sir Lazarus Quick, Mrs. Damaris Quick—that's his mum—and Miss Constance. Master Clement's out riding."

Then, taking a deep breath, she announced him. "Mr. Peregrine Dean of the customs service, sir," and he followed as if into a ball. There was even a footman into whose hands he could have thrust his overcoat, if he had been wearing one.

His first impression was overwhelming pinkness, as though his eyes were closed and a bright sun beat upon them, but by degrees the details became clear. The dazzling light of the sea burst through the many windows of the orangery and streamed upon a chinoiserie wallpaper on which salmon-pink dragons floated amid rosy clouds whose colour was echoed by upholstered chairs of pink velvet with gilded legs like curlicues of flame.

In this warm celestial setting, the Quick family themselves emanated a jarring chill. The old lady on the sofa in the centre of the room wore a sack-back gown of silver blue, paired with exuberant swan-patterned lace of an extraordinary daintiness, and topped with a long string of pearls like winter moons.

The man who stood behind her must be Sir Lazarus Quick. He was much more austere—all his garments as iron grey as his hair and his jutting eyebrows.

Only the young woman who sat by the window seemed to match the room's floating romanticism—a pink ribbon wound in her blonde hair to match the pink of her sash, a few ringlets en déshabillé around her delicate face, and her eyes rarely straying from the window as she petted the white cat in her lap.

"*You* are Mr. Peregrine Dean?" the old lady asked, thunderous. "I hope Gwynn is not practicing upon us."

Her voice was so sharp that Perry didn't dare sigh. These were people of quality—people it would benefit him to befriend. "I am, ma'am. Those who know me well call me Perry. I understand you requested Mr. Gwynn to send you one of his men—he sent me."

"Gwynn does not employ an African."

"Indeed, ma'am, for I was born in Hackney. Nevertheless, I am the man he has sent you. I arrived in Porthkennack from London this morning."

"Extraordinary." She raised her eyebrows at him and fell silent.

"The man who was sent was a particular protégé of Lord Petersfield," Lazarus Quick slipped into the silence left by his mother. Perry couldn't tell from the tone if he was being accused of a lie or not, but it seemed likely.

"I had supposed that information to be of a delicate nature, sir. Not to be widely spread about. Yet now I'm here, it seems everyone is aware."

"Do you call us 'everyone'?" Lazarus demurred. His voice had a whispering quality like the scratch of snake scale over stone. "Do you mean to suggest this information is such as should have been withheld from the magistrate of the county? Or that I am a person who could not be trusted with it?"

Perry raised both hands to his jaw and rubbed the hinges. He would break his teeth on his pride one of these days, but he had still rather have it than not.

"My apologies," he managed again, "that was not what I meant. Of course it was important for you to know. In that light, yes, I have been fortunate enough to gain Lord Petersfield's patronage. My father is a sailor on a London pilot boat. He saved Lord Petersfield from a gang of footpads at the docks—saved his life, indeed—and in gratitude Lord Petersfield took an interest in me and my career. I consider any debt to have been wholly reversed by now, such that I could never repay him for his kindness toward me. I am eager to show him that his trust in me is not in vain, and if there is corruption here, to unveil and end it."

Over the course of this speech, some of his anger had joined his passion and hope and made his voice ring. When he finished, even languid Miss Constance was looking at him, her fan tip pressed to the end of her nose, the peach silk standing out vividly against her dark-blue eyes.

Damaris huffed and rearranged the folds of her apron with ring-encrusted fingers. "I'm glad to hear you speak with such conviction," she allowed. "Our purpose in calling you here was to make you acquainted with the greatest ruffian of the town. A man whose involvement in large-scale smuggling goes totally unchecked. He is clever and ruthless, and we believe he is not only a wholesale smuggler, but a pirate and a murderer also."

"And he tarnishes our reputation." Constance rolled her eyes and offered this bored observation in a sweet mew of a voice. Her father's frown in return just provoked a tiny smile. "Oh, you can't claim our dislike for him is not personal. It'll be obvious as soon as you tell him the name."

"I'm not trying to claim I am indifferent to his insult to us in particular," her father bristled, drawing himself to even greater heights of rigidity. "But you should not pretend to know anything of this matter. Stick to your painting, my dear, and refrain from further interruption."

A fine watercolour view of Barras Bay as it might be seen from an upstairs window of this very house hung above the mantel. Perry flicked his eyes to it, wondering if that was Constance's work—the painting of which her father spoke. She was talented, if so.

When he looked back, Lazarus's eyes were trained on him, steely like the rest of him. "This smuggler we speak of has been so successful that the small independents of the town now contract with him. He has influence over the miners and the townsfolk. This is not a jug of spirits forgotten in the galley, nor even one or two barrels hidden among the mackerel. The man is making himself into a power to challenge the authorities. I don't think I need to tell you how dangerous that is, in this time where the poison of rebellion against all God's anointed leaders is also being smuggled over from France."

Perry nodded, letting his eyes fall closed on the confession that he had some sympathy with the ideals of the revolution himself. "The man's name?" he asked, gently.

Damaris scoffed again. "He calls himself Quick." Her thin face was all cheekbones, hatchet edged with the sharpness of her gaze. "Tomas Quick. He has not the slightest right to the name. He simply chose it to mock us and to bring our family into disrepute—that is what Constance meant by saying our dislike was personal. This man is traducing our good name. But our dislike is also rational. The rogue has his claws in everything that goes on in Porthkennack, yet he is as slippery as a handful of frogspawn and as impossible to hold—"

"If you could bring him to trial successfully, you would succeed in something the customs service here has been trying to do for the past ten years," Lazarus Quick urged, all the distance and superiority in his voice having burned away in favour of zeal. Perry recognized with a thrill that for this moment, the magistrate was treating him as a valued colleague, as an equal.

His thoughts took flight into a future where he also lived in a house like this, where his word was law, where his order kept the streets safe, and defended the honest citizens from those who would prey on them out of selfish strength.

He could not quite see himself with a wife, a daughter. But if he, too, could become a magistrate, he could reinterpret the harshest laws to defend those men like him, who only wanted to privately love another man. Hell, once he had enough power, high enough rank, he could change the laws from the inside. All through doing good and doing it excellently.

He was rather getting ahead of himself, though. One step at a time.

"What do you say, Mr. Dean? Will you take down this villain for us?" the magistrate asked.

Perry had to smile. "If he is as bad as you say, sir—and I have no doubt of it—I will be delighted to. You may confidently leave it in my hands."

CHAPTER THREE

THE ENEMY IS GLIMPSED

"You will, I think, need more tangible authority than your own word," Lazarus Quick had said to Perry later. Once he had pledged himself to their cause, the ladies had withdrawn, and Perry had followed the magistrate through to his study, a sumptuous room in shades of indigo and silver that put him in mind of a moonlit night. Here, despite the scorching heat outside, a fire burned in the grate and Perry's travel-worn clothes prickled on him, reminding him that he had not had a change of shirt for days.

Lazarus settled into his imposing chair and uncapped an ink-bottle in the shape of a schooner, pulling pen and paper before him and beginning to write. Perry did not tug at his collar, and if he found himself gazing wistfully at the firmly closed windows, it was easily passed off as a natural curiosity over the doings of the port. Admiral Quick's house commanded an excellent view of the shipping just approaching the point, and a better angle to see the rocks lying beneath the water than Perry had seen before.

"So here." Lazarus shook sand over his note to dry the ink, tapped it off, then passed it to Perry. "A note in my hand to say you are in my employ and are to be obeyed with the alacrity with which a man should obey me. If you need to take charge of the customs cutter, the *Vigilant*, in order to intercept the rogue at sea, you will show this to her captain."

Even his eyes were grey, as he levelled them firmly on Perry's face. "I hope I do not need to stress what a high degree of trust I am placing in you."

Despite being stifled, the flush of warmth within Perry's breast at this was pleasant—barely arrived and he was already in the confidence of the highest authority. Why would that not feel pleasant? "I am sensible of the great honour you do me, sir, and I will not fail you."

"Good." Lazarus's prim little smile looked out of place on his mouth. The worry his face fell back into seemed habitual. "I feel it only right to stress to you that the man is dangerous. I did not wish to urge this in front of the ladies and frighten them, but you should go armed, for Tomas so-called Quick carries both blade and pistol. Though we cannot prove it, I believe he has murdered upwards of a dozen men. Let your zeal be tempered with caution, therefore. It will not do to find evidence against him if it is only to take it to your grave."

Perry had cherished a somewhat ill opinion of the Quicks thanks to their chill reception, but this warmed his heart. To receive both trust and consideration so far away from home and so early in the process of proving himself was a boon. If anything, the caution just spurred him on. "I am equal to the challenge, sir."

"Excellent." Lazarus broke out the awkward smile again and rose to indicate the door. "Then I look forward to hearing from you soon."

Having arrived as a disrespected foreigner, Perry retraced his path into town as a trusted agent of the magistrate. He had been given no timescale but *soon*, so he considered returning to the inn to unpack a few things from his trunk, discover where he could have his clothes laundered, and perhaps take a bite of lunch. But all of that seemed tedious and time-wasting, and he wanted to get started on the important task that had been entrusted to him.

He could at least find out what this Tomas Quick looked like, where he lived, and who his principal friends and neighbours were. Which boats did he have a share in, and which was his own principal vessel? If Perry did nothing more today than learn to identify his prey by sight, that would be a start.

Down in Constantine Bay, the boats were landing pilchards by the hogshead. Pilchards in great sleeting mounds lay aflap on the sandy beach and in the hollows of the road beyond. The dazzle of them under the bright summer sun was dizzying, and the beach was packed like the commons of a popular play with the whole village out to process the catch.

Fishwives stood ankle-deep in the slurry of fish, their bare arms white to the elbow with salt and their hands red, chapped, and oddly delicate as they placed each individual small fish in a radiate design— each layer of pilchards a sunburst, heads to the centre, tails outward, beneath a layer of salt.

Perry stood next to a woman in a green skirt for some minutes, waiting for her to notice him. But in that time her focus never shifted from the fish, and at length he reached out and tapped her elbow, which was gritty with salt and slime.

"What is it? Can't you see I'm busy?" She shrugged her arm out of his grasp and turned her head minimally to put him in the corner of her eye.

"I need to talk to Tomas Quick," he said, trying to sound like he meant no harm. "Which is his house?"

"Phew!" She gave a long, tired exhale through her teeth and straightened up to regard him more closely. He hoped the news that there was a new black riding officer in town had not yet had time to spread, and perhaps it hadn't, because she smiled. "New crewman, are you? All right, then."

She tucked an errant strand of light-brown hair back beneath her yellowed bonnet and nodded to the cluster of cottages that rose from the stone on the other side of the beach—a mile of fine yellow sand and frantic fish packing in between. "'Tis beyond the bay over there. Blue painted door and a big glass lantern outside like something you'd see in church. You'll know it when you see it."

He considered trying to interrogate her further but she had already turned back to her work. So instead he said, "Thank you," and began to pick his way through the tumbrels, barrels, fishwives, fish piles, seabirds, thieving cats, gossiping sailors, children, and beggars of the beach.

On the western side, the ground finally regained its firmness. Perry struggled up a loose sand dune, barely kept in shape by pale dry grasses, and then to stone and saxifrage. Here a row of whitewashed cottages faced inward toward the land, the walls of their back gardens towards him. He found a cut-through between two of them, heat coming off its stones.

A black cat lying on the rounded cope of the wall to his left leaped down as he passed and disappeared into a yard full of white cloths—sheets, petticoats, shifts, and shirts—enough washing to clothe a regiment.

When Perry emerged from the cut-through, he found a pretty gate in a low fence in front of a yard full of laundry, and behind it a cottage with a blue-painted door, over which the incongruous shape of a moorish lantern—shards and stars of blue and clear glass in a lattice of silver—glittered in the sun.

The white fabric of the laundry clapped against the ropes on which it hung as the breeze skirled in from the sea. Used to London's grime, something in Perry exalted unexpectedly at the smell of distance and wildness, at all the blaze and gleam of light.

He pushed open the gate, coming through into a small front yard, bare but for the linen, with only a patch of yolk-yellow marigolds eye wateringly bright beneath the water butt. The cottage itself looked as though it had once had barely two rooms—one up, one down, but recent prosperity had led someone to build it outward in all directions. There might now be four rooms upstairs and four down. A particularly flat stone in the corner of the yard suggested to Perry's experienced eye the presence of a cellar also. But it was still not the fortress nor the palace he had half expected.

Perry wiped his palms on the skirts of his coat and considered whether he should have brought his pistols out of his trunk before coming here. No, this was a courtesy call, just to look and go away, just to let Quick know the game was on.

His knock brought light footsteps and the sound of two bolts sliding back—they locked up tight. The woman who opened the door made him step back a pace, his heart rattling as though a foreign queen had opened the door, terrible and beautiful. Tragic.

He blinked at his own flight of fancy, but even with his eyes cleared, the woman in this modest Cornish cottage was an orchid in a milk pail. She was as tall as he and extremely slender, her face so pale he could see the blood flush up into her cheeks, presumably because his speechlessness embarrassed her. She wore a bronze-coloured house dress, a tall turban of gold silk and earrings of gold and carnelian that were almost the same colour as her brows and eyelashes. He registered the creases around her blue eyes, the slight sag of her ivory throat, and the swollen knuckles of her work-roughened hands a moment later and was knocked again to realize she must be twice his age. A notable beauty once and still stately to the core.

Fortunately, she appeared to have been equally surprised by him. She recovered only a moment first. "Yes? Can I help you?"

Perry cleared his throat, inwardly congratulating himself that he was not a man to desire women, and fortunately his mind remained clear. "I'm looking for Tomas Quick? You're his wife?"

She laughed. "I'm his mother, dear: Zuliy. But you've just missed him. The tide's turned, the boats are floating. He's gone this very moment to the north steps to cast off the *Swift*. If you run like the wind, you may catch him."

He had followed the gesture of her right hand and was running up the street toward the tip of the promontory before he fully registered that she had not come into the sunlight, nor had she let go of the door—if he had kicked it, she could have slammed it in his face. Was that a personal modesty, or a perpetual readiness to delay the law long enough that her no-good son could slip out the back door?

Curiosity piqued, almost excited by the thought, he sprinted over the rough ground at the edge of the promontory and almost fell headlong down the stairs carved into the sheer rock. Throwing himself backwards as soon as he noticed the cliff, he tumbled—rather shaken—to his arse and had to scrabble up to hands and knees to peer over the edge, where the stair, cut into the cliffside, went down like a ladder.

Below, the sea was indeed coming in. Its waves already lapped the bottom step of the stair, so shallow as yet that the pebbles were visible moving beneath it.

A hundred feet further down the beach, however, a handsome cutter had been lying on its side, but it was already rocking itself upward as the waves lifted it. Green livery—a wide green-and-gold stripe beneath its gunwales. It wasn't yet upright, but already two men on the windlass were winding up its stern anchor.

A boy by the wheel, with wide voluminous petticoat breeches was— But no, that was a girl, barefoot and brown armed, apparently reading a chart. The aft main and top sails, above and below the gaff, were already lowered, helping to heel the cutter upright and the jib and staysail were ballooning out to catch the wind.

She would be under way in moments, and even as Perry realized this, he saw the man he had come to interrogate, breast-deep in the water below the hull. The man seized a rope tossed down to him and swarmed up the side, throwing himself over the gunwale with a glittering spray of water. He must have been barely fifty yards ahead of Perry, before Perry balked at the stairs. Now he was as out of reach as if he had been in Antarctica.

Almost as soon as her captain was on board, the cutter was upright. Quick balanced with practiced ease on the heaving deck, and—looking back—caught Perry's eyes to give him a contemptuous grin.

Perry's heart, so rattled by the man's mother, now stopped altogether. Someone had already talked. It was certain as death that Quick already knew Perry was after him, and this was his challenge.

Perry stared down the hot gaze as he would have stared down the barrel of a duelling pistol. He wished he was close enough to see better, and yet he already knew he would never forget this distant glimpse against the immensity of sea and sky: The man's vivid face and his flame of red-gold hair. The insouciant outright fucking mockery of his smile, bright under a slew of freckles, brown as pebbled stones. These things would always be with Perry now until he could wipe that grin off with the back of his hand.

You think you can defy me? His pride exalted, almost like joy at the prospect of the fight. This was to be personal was it? *Bring it on.*

CHAPTER FOUR

THE HUNT IS UNSUCCESSFUL

A sandy path in the dunes that bordered Constantine Beach provided a faster way for Perry to get back into town than fighting through the industrious crowds on the beach again. Someone at the magistrate's house must be in Tomas Quick's pay or confidence—must have overheard his conversation with Lazarus and slipped off to tell Tomas that Perry was coming. From there, Tomas's own guilty conscience had made him flee so precipitately, snatching himself out of Perry's grasp a bare moment before they could touch.

What a face, though! Dazzling gold like Lucifer newly tossed from heaven, still with the impudence in his eyes. Perry enjoyed the chase at all times, but with the prospect of this man being his quarry, he was abruptly deeply delighted with his new home, his new circumstances, and his life. It was with a bound in his step that he turned up the street where his partner had left him and headed for the building with a door over which hung a collection of rusted iron stars on a chain.

Seven stars, arranged in two rows—four above and three below— with flecks of gold paint still clinging to their interstices from a happier day. The door and sash window beside it stood open and pipe smoke wisped out of both. A scent of strong coffee and of cooked fish reminded Perry that he had not eaten since taking a little dry toast before being hustled onto the coach this morning.

Had that really been only this morning? Already he felt profoundly changed from the man who had arrived here. He had a purpose now, and it was one that filled his blood with passion.

Nevertheless, he still needed to eat. Kicking the sand from his shoes at the door, he dived into the fug of the coffee shop, his presence (and complexion) causing a brief silence before the conversations began again at lower volume.

The change of light from the brilliance outside to the smoky gloom within foxed him for an instant, and then he saw—as he had expected—Jowan Ede lounging at a table at the back of the room, the *Porthkennack Gazette* spread out in front of him, a mug of small beer by his left hand, a long clay pipe drooping from his right, his feet up on the bench opposite, his head reclined against the wall, and his eyes closed.

The proprietress, in a fetching gown of printed cotton that must have cost a fortune if the fabric were not contraband, rose from her perch in the corner to take his order, and sneered a little at his expression, as though she could tell he was measuring up the legality of her dress. He asked for stargazy pie—whatever that was—and coffee, and dropped heavily onto the bench on which Jowan's feet were resting, startling him awake.

"Busy at all times riding the area of your ward, alert to prevent smugglers by land or sea." Perry laughed. "Of course I've been partnered with the laziest bastard in the county—unless you're all like this?"

"I do my job," Jowan grumbled, rubbing his eyes and looking with disappointment at his pipe. Not only had it gone out, but as he'd slept, his hand had turned, and there was now a small pile of burned and unburned tobacco on the ground beneath the empty bowl. "'Tis no surprise I'd fall asleep the one time I get to sit down after patrolling the cliffs all night. Not like you. Barely arrived, you have and you're already off with your hoity-toity friends."

He got on his knees beneath the table, pinched up the spilled tobacco, and pressed it back into his pipe.

While Jowan was down there, the woman in the sprigged dress slammed a plate of pie in front of Perry and clicked a small cup of sludge-like Turkish coffee next to it with a firmness that made even the gloop seep over the top. The pie had fish heads baked into its crusts and their open mouths seemed to gape at his rudeness.

Evidently his attitude was not making him any friends.

"I'm sorry," he said, when Jowan was upright once more and struggling to light his pipe. "Sometimes I don't know what's going to come out of my mouth until it does. I should not have been so thoughtless, nor so cruel."

"Get yourself in trouble with that mouth, you will." Jowan glowered at him until the tobacco finally caught, and then he drew in a deep breath of smoke and his expression eased. "Well, nor you won't be the first officious bastard I've partnered neither. We'll learn to rub along, I'm sure. How did it go? With the magistrate?"

Neither pie nor coffee tasted as vile as it looked. Perry took a mouthful of both and felt strengthened for them. "He wanted me to investigate a man called Tomas Quick."

Even the name now made his breath catch in the back of his throat, and a thrill of danger course through his veins. "Which is apparently not his true name. You've mentioned that you are a fount of local knowledge. What can you tell me about the man?"

Jowan chuckled and took a long draught of his beer as sunlight slanted through the room's one window and lit the smoke within into a milky swirl. "He didn't lose no time, did he? No secret there's bad blood between Tomas and Lazarus Quick. I don't quite know the story there—no one does—but you ask around the town, and you'll find that Tomas is very liked hereabouts. Upstanding Methodist. His mother's a bit weird, but then she's foreign. Shipwrecked here she was, as a girl. It's amazing what the sea blows up. His da started as a sailor but drug himself up to become a lawyer. A good one too. Also popular."

Jowan laughed again, a little huff of amusement through his nose. "You're in trouble, mate. The town's not going to be happy with you coming after Tomas. The man's a gentleman, whatever his birth."

Perry's stomach lurched with something he wasn't sure how to identify. It should have been disappointment, but it oddly felt like hope as he imagined introducing himself to Tomas as a friend. That could be an altogether different pursuit—equally dangerous, perhaps, but with what a reward! "You mean he isn't a smuggler at all?"

This time it was a full-out guffaw. "God bless your innocence, lad. Tomas Quick is a smuggler certain sure. But he's an honest man for all that. You stay here long enough, you'll come to know what I mean."

Perry finished his pie, leaving the heads on the plate, and sucked the gritty remains of his coffee through his teeth. "I'm sure you have informers you could introduce me to," he said thoughtfully. "Other people who could tell me more. Come now, will you give me the tour of Porthkennack and teach me what I need to know to clean this town up?"

"I will do that." Jowan downed the rest of his beer. "Tomorrow. But I waren't joking. I've to be on the cliffs again tonight. I need to spend the afternoon asleep."

"Quick took his boat out on the rising tide," Perry insisted, standing to let Jowan edge his way from behind the table. "Suppose he's gone to drag up sunken casks—he knows you're sleeping. He'll be getting them in now before you're back up."

"That's as may be." Jowan passed his hand through his hair, setting it on end, and jammed his hat atop it. "But I'm sleeping nevertheless."

The lack of zeal could have been corruption, but giving Jowan the benefit of the doubt, Perry decided to think of it as mere laziness. He abandoned hopes of help from his partner and flashed to the next option. "The customs cutter—the *Vigilant*—where does it dock?"

"Just up from the warehouse. Lip of Long Cove. Captain Armstrong's in command—Harry Armstrong." Jowan smothered a yawn and raised his eyebrows at Perry, as if he found him humorous. "Good luck."

"We're just back from Newquay after creeping for rafts over the whole north shore." Captain Harry Armstrong stood with one foot on the gunwale of the *Vigilant* and one foot on the quay, his left hand casual on the stay, his eyes narrowed. "The lads want a rest."

The "lads" had the gnarled look of seasoned sailors for all that they were prissily uniformed in blue trousers and scarlet smocks. They gave Perry the same poisonous glare to a man, as he pressed the magistrate's letter into their captain's hand. "I insist."

Armstrong capitulated with sullen ill grace. "I'll go up the south shore while there's light. If we see 'im, we'll chase. If not, there's naught I can do."

So midafternoon saw Perry in the bows of the customs cutter as she slipped out into a brisk wind and a choppy sea, the spray coming up like grapeshot from her narrow prow, all the rowing boats she carried creaking in their ropes as she tacked against the wind and began to work her way toward Tintagel.

As if to register his protest, Armstrong shut himself in the cabin with a jug of rum. It was a younger officer who came and stood beside Perry with a telescope balanced on the hook that had replaced his left hand.

"Quick's probably gone over to France," this young man said. "And we shouldn't expect him back until next week. But there are shallows just off the coast at Boscastle. We'll look there just in ca— Oh!"

On their left, the coastline rose in a series of jagged grey monoliths. To their right and ahead, the surface of the sea seemed a paler green, and the pattern of the waves broke from its oceanic furrows into a confused scatter. In the midst of this strange water, another cutter was slowly slipping along with its sails clewed up and ropes hanging off the stern. Even to Perry, the green stripe and the ochre sails of the distant cutter were familiar. He straightened up like a pointer dog with a fallen pheasant in its sights.

It was a standard manoeuvre for incoming smugglers to attach weights to their contraband and leave it anchored to the ocean bed, ready to be fished up later while the authorities weren't watching. The smugglers could sell each barrel of liquor or lace for a huge profit. But if a customs crew found them instead, there was a salvage fee per barrel that would make the men very happy.

"Well, I'll be," said the young man with the telescope. "That *is* the *Swift*, and they do seem like they're creeping for casks. I see barrels on deck." He broke out in a grand grin. "We might have something here lads! Look lively! There's a share in the prize for every man if we get her."

Resentment vanished. Someone shouted into the cabin, and Armstrong clattered onto the deck. "Hoist the staysail!" he yelled to the helmsman. "Prepare to tack."

But his voice must have carried on the wind, because there was a sudden boiling of movement on the deck of the *Swift*. A man chopped through the stern ropes with an axe just as the main and jib sails were set. As the *Vigilant* got the wind behind her, the *Swift*—true to her name—filled her sheets and leaped ahead.

Someone pressed a speaking trumpet into Perry's hand. "*Swift*," he shouted. "This is his Majesty's Customs Vessel *Vigilant*. Reduce sail and prepare to be boarded!"

At the *Swift*'s helm, a man in a slouch hat raised his hand to his ear as if to say *I can't hear you!*

The wind blew the brim of the hat back enough to let a teasing hint of red-gold gleam out like a distant ember, and Perry let out a "Ha!" of exultation and determination. "Give them a gun."

It took three of the crew a whole minute to prime and load the small swivel gun, and in that time the *Swift* perceptibly drew ahead, her wake a jade-coloured path behind her.

"Fire!" Perry yelled, and saw the tongue of flame lance toward the *Swift* like his hopes, but even the ball fell short.

The man at the *Swift*'s helm—it must have been Quick himself, though his face couldn't be seen for the hat—made another pantomime of not understanding, and then with no warning put the helm right over. His crew flung the sails into a wrenching tack—the creak and moan of *Swift*'s timbers as she made an almost ninety-degree turn and shot downwind was a voice of portent.

"Oh shit, sir!"

And Perry knew. He knew it was going to happen before it did—managed to grab on to the forestay with arms and legs as *Vigilant* rammed herself into a sandbank concealed beneath barely a foot of rippling water and came to a sudden, yowling, catastrophic halt, the backstays snapping and the topmast breaking clean off.

Undeterred, the *Swift* sailed peacefully away, leaving them grounded on the sandbank that Perry had seen coming—the thing that had changed the colour of the water, made their quarry's wake seem like stone. The thing that in his excitement he hadn't recognized until it was too late.

"Fuck," said Captain Armstrong with feeling, once he had established that nobody was dead and that apart from a few sprung planks they did not seem to be taking on too much water. "Very well, then. Two of you get up and splice that stay. The rest into boats afore and by the sides. Let's see if we can drag or rock ourselves off."

They could, it turned out. But the exercise took another four hours. Long enough for *Swift* to sail triumphantly back to Porthkennack and land any cargo it wished.

"Not the best of first days," Captain Armstrong remarked. He had offered to take his crew to the pub when they finally reached harbour again, but did not extend the offer to Perry. "I hope you'll learn something from it."

"I will." Perry nodded and headed back to his hotel with a tremble of weariness in all his bones and fire in his heart. *I'll try harder next time.*

CHAPTER FIVE

THE BOUNTY OF THE SEA

Having taken his wig in to a small peruke-maker he spotted on the way back to his hotel, assured that he could collect it tomorrow afternoon with the dirt removed and the curls reset, Perry let himself into his sliver of a room and threw himself down to sleep. It being the summer, the light lingered seemingly forever, and the heat of the day rose from the ground and gathered in his tiny attic cell until he might have been in a sweat bath.

When he pulled his blanket over his face to block out the light, he could not breathe, but if he tossed the blanket off, he felt exposed, here in a town where no one knew him but everyone knew the man he had unmistakably declared his enemy. His heart beat strangely beneath his breastbone, its rhythm felt through his bones rather than heard. Downstairs the evening had only just got underway, and the roar of conversation and laughter through the floorboards drove out subtle sounds.

A bell in a distant clock tower gave ten rather strangled tolls, and Perry sighed, still fizzing with the need for action. Tomas Quick would be at his house right now, that oddly charming cottage that seemed too humble for a crime kingpin. Perry could go there and burst in, demand answers. But he had no evidence. He had seen nothing that could not be passed off as a fisherman trying to take up lobster pots. Even the fleeing might be cast as a free man's high-spirited refusal to allow the government to meddle in his perfectly honest toil.

It would achieve nothing, but the prospect of seeing that face with its spray of freckles turned up to him in lantern-light, like an angel spattered with mud, made it seem worthwhile nevertheless.

He groaned, at himself and at the heat, and rose to write another paragraph to his mother by the light of the lantern that lit the passage outside his door. A pitcher of water and a basin had been supplied by the inn, so he sponged himself down, then wedged the door shut, cutting out the light. It was still hot as Hell, but these steps had been soothing enough to bring him back from the edge of precipitate action, and this time when he cast himself down on the narrow bed, he slept.

A knocking woke him in time to hear the distant clock striking three. Taking his pistol from his trunk, he warily opened up, but it was only Jowan again, looking well rested and rosy—his cheeks reddened in the light of the lantern he held. "All right, my lover." He grinned, taking in the sight of Perry with nightgown and pistol with easy equanimity. "Time to show you our rounds. 'Tis a beautiful night, perfect for a ride."

"I thought . . ." Disappointment settled like an itchy woollen vest on Perry's shoulders, but he was already pulling on his breeches and stockings. "That I was seconded to Sir Quick to do what he asked."

Jowan chuckled. "True enough. But what the magistrate wants? That's by way of being extra, isn't it? Still got to do your job too, if you want to be paid for it."

"Of course." Perry flushed almost as hot as the inferno of his room at having assumed differently. How did Lazarus Quick expect him to bring down an archenemy if he barely had an hour in the day to devote to it? Was he trying to set him up for failure? Well, Perry would show him. He'd do it anyway, and he'd make it look easy.

He flung on shirt and jacket. Without the wig, his hat would not fit, but it was warm enough to go bareheaded, and surely anyone out at this time would not be too worried about decent standards of dress. "I'm ready."

Stepping out of the inn into the night brought little relief from the heat. The sky was blank above them—heavy cloud must have obliterated all the stars, and even a townsman like Perry could feel the weight of the air pressing on him like a hot stone wrapped in a wet blanket.

Jowan had brought him a mare, revealed by the lantern to be a dispirited, dun creature too apathetic even to sidle under him as he swung into the saddle. "You'll have to buy your own," Jowan commented, cheerfully, "for she's all we've got spare." She followed Jowan's equally enthusiastic animal nose to tail as they plodded out from the centre of town toward the cliffs.

Leaving the final building behind was like stepping into a mine. Perry, used to London, where every dwelling had a lantern hanging before its door to illumine the streets, was deeply unsettled by the absolute dark. Jowan's lantern light barely showed him the ground under his horse's hooves, and after a while of riding like this, it seemed as if they stood still, while a variety of rocks scrolled beneath them and the sound of the sea grew ever closer like the breath of an exasperated giant.

"How can they land anything in this without lights?" Perry whispered as though the dark itself was eavesdropping.

"Some of the best pilots can know where they are by touching the waves," Jowan murmured back. "Though sometimes even they need lights, and we spot 'em easy from that. Anyone who can'll be coming to harbour tonight, though. Can you feel that? Storm's on its way."

He had stopped. The circle of lantern light picked out rocks and grass below them as always. The trickle of breeze on Perry's face was hot. He wasn't sure what he was supposed to feel, but his hair seemed to strain at its roots. The tingle of rising gooseflesh swept across his skin just as—infinitely far away—a needle of intolerable light stabbed into the sky. In a flash, he saw the boiling black clouds above him and the sea below in waves as jagged as broken glass. He gasped, recoiling. They were on the very edge of the cliffs. Two paces forward off the path and he would have been falling to his death.

The grey blaze across the clouds snapped off, leaving him once more cushioned in darkness, yet shaken to the core. How easily Jowan could have thrown him off the cliff if he had wished. How easily a man might disappear in this country.

It was still and, save for the sea, utterly silent, and when the thunder came, what seemed hours later, it was almost too quiet to hear.

"I don't think we can expect the storm before tomorrow," Jowan murmured. "But if there's anyone out in it now, God save 'em."

The storm, as it happened, passed Porthkennack by. Only its edge brushed the town with a heavy rain early in the afternoon. Perry had been ready to return to bed by then, taking a noon meal that was for him his dinner in the Seven Stars with Jowan. He had just risen to bid his partner good night when a grubby boy with mud to his bare knees flung open the door and ran in beaming. "Wrack, masters! A great raft of it coming in now. Wrack on the shore!"

It was the first time Perry had seen Jowan really move. The big man rose as if jerked from his seat by a string and was halfway to the door before Perry thought to follow. By that time, he was part of a crush. The population of the room, who had been so peacefully falling asleep over their newspapers, had risen and there was a scrum for the door.

Outside, the whole town was aboil. Perry and Jowan dodged between tumbrels and barrows, women with baskets on their arms and hips, men with sacks, everyone pushing and jostling down the paths to the shore, heedless of the downpour.

The pilchard nets had been cleared, the barrels of fish already moved into storage or shipped away, but the beach was, if anything, more heaving with humanity than it had been yesterday.

A very different picture today. The swell of the waves rolled in like oncoming buffalo—as unstoppable and as dirty brown in colour. The beach was already strewn with splintered wood, and as soon as Perry sprinted into the surf, more wrack battered his shins.

"There's the boys!" Jowan shouted and began to shoulder his way to the inmost curve of the bay where Perry, following, recognized Mr. Gwynn, a pistol in either hand, standing guard over a wagon, while the other customs officers waded into the sea.

"Merchantman called the *Hyacinth*," Gwynn shouted. "According to what's come ashore. Must have foundered last night. Seize what you can. Mark where the rest of it goes."

Then it was every man for himself. Jowan bounded away after a barrel like a black fleck on the crest of a wave. Perry—looking for survivors on planks or swimming—searched the whole bay with a glance. He was struck briefly by the sight of a young man—thirteen or fourteen, perhaps—on a ledge of the cliffs, up where he could act as a look out, spotting the most valuable wreckage and shouting down to his minions below. It was only a brief glimpse and he didn't see the face, but the boy's long yellow hair stayed with him as something with which to identify a person whose house should be searched anon.

His gaze sweeping down from the boy, fell on another head of bright hair, this one more like flame. Tomas Quick was on the beach outside his house, waist-deep in the surf. He and three other men were hauling in a fat, foundering barrel. Perry ignored the desire to go storming off down the beach and accuse him then and there. There was nothing illegal about finding wrack. It was only if it was not turned over to the proper authorities that a case might be made, and—

A hump on a distant slab of curved hull caught Perry's eye. That slice of blue was a coat. The thing waving in the water was an arm. "A survivor!" he yelled, and as he threw himself against the power of the oncoming waves to try to haul the man to shore, three of the townsfolk turned from their salvage to join him. One of them even dropped a small cask and let it wash away in favour of going to the stranger's rescue.

His thighs aching from pushing against the swell, Perry managed to get in close to the driftwood, get a grip on its jagged edge. As he did, the tide sucked the sand out from beneath his feet, and he slipped face-first into the water, the current a mill race around him, pulling and battering at his arms and legs. His fingers burned and cramped and for a moment he was certain he would drown before he achieved anything at all in his life. But then the driftwood washed back into the shallows. He got a foot under him and pushed up, finding the black-bearded grinning face of the peruke maker meeting his streaming eyes. "Nearly lost both of you there! Hold fast!"

They are good people, after all, these Cornishmen. You could not blame them for delighting in gifts from the sea, when their hearts were in the right place.

"Will you carry this half-drownded lad up to the dunes?" the second of Perry's helpers said. Perry hadn't met this one before, but would know him again anywhere after this moment. "That's where the doctor'll be."

The castaway was cold to the touch, but fingers pressed to his throat discerned the push of a pulse, so Perry pulled him over his shoulders and staggered toward the dunes. The movement prompted his rescuee to throw up a considerable amount of seawater down Perry's left side, but the doctor, when he found him, assured him that was a good sign.

When he returned to the beach, there was already a stream of folk leaving, clutching bundles or rolling barrels between them. A group of young women went past with a bale of lace unwound between them, each one cocooned in hundreds of pounds worth of luxury that did not belong to them and crowing with laughter at their good luck. Nothing but thieves.

The woof and boom of a shot snapped his attention back to the customs wagon, where Gwynn had had to fire his pistol in a show of force to prevent their load of hogsheads from being overrun by looters who had now got a taste for the sport.

Perry plunged back into the crowd and the sea alike, trying to come to Gwynn's aid, but currents both of man and wave shoved him off to the left of the wagon. There, a group of burly sailors seemed to be helping a panicking castaway. Trying to . . . pull him up? But he was fighting them. Yelling. Yelling . . .

"I am a free man. My name is Barnabas Okesi. I am a freeborn Englishman and not a slave. I am not a slave."

Something both cold and hot at once swept over Perry from the crown of his head to his feet as he realized the men were not trying to help Barnabas at all.

Even in the capital, one of the risks any black person faced was that of being kidnapped off the streets and taken to a place where the protections of the law were a thousand miles away, had one been able to afford them at all.

As a healthy adult male slave, Barnabas was easily worth eighty pounds, and that was more than these men could earn in a year.

"Let that man go!" Perry yelled, pulling his own pistol from his waistband. The powder was now well and truly doused, but it would serve as a blunt instrument. As one of them clubbed Barnabas in the back of the head with a fish-priest, Perry ran heedless and bellowing into the knot of sailors.

Barnabas fell like a stone, just as something hit Perry in the back of the knees, lifting him as the waves swelled and pushed under him.

He toppled over backwards into the sea, getting one brief, bright glimpse of what had struck him. It was a slab-faced man with a cormorant feather in his hat and an oar in his hand. As Perry convulsed to get his feet back under him, the man brought the oar down, cracking it into Perry's temple. Again his weakened knees slid out from under him and, as everything went dark, the water closed over his face.

CHAPTER SIX

TOMAS IS QUICK TO ANGER

A wreck was a bounty Tomas could not ignore. But it was also a
day and night of toil. Having cleared as much of his trove off the
beach as he and his people could, it had taken all the hours of darkness
to dispose of it in places the customs men would not look.

Now dawn was just beginning to grey the eastern edge of the
sea. There was but one thing to do before he could lie his soaked and
aching bones down for a bare hour of sleep.

His eyes blurred and his head felt muffled and squeezed by the
hatband of his aged hat. He had emptied the seawater from his boots,
but his socks still squelched when he walked, and his sodden coat was
a drag on his shoulders. At the beginning of the night, he had walked
carelessly up from the beach in the dark, but now he was returning
through the twisted alleys that backed the fishermen's cottages on
Turk's Head Lane, and his step had shortened, quietened as he began
to stalk his prey.

He opened his mouth to breathe more silently even as his target
came in sight. A new gate in a newly built-up wall where once there
had been a pigsty and an outhouse at the end of Hedrek Negus's garden
was locked tight with two fist-sized padlocks. Negus's neighbour, old
Mrs. Trago, grew flowering vines over her wall, and in fifty years of
neglect they had sprawled over the brim and down into the alley in a
tangle of wooden ropes surrounded by the dipping white penumbras
of flower spikes.

Tomas pushed the vines apart and stepped into their shadow,
leaning his back against the spider-infested wall behind them, allowing
the cover to slide into place once more. He put his hand in his pocket

and ran his thumb along the back of his folded razor. His heart raced like a current, and his cold hands tingled, whether with nervousness or excitement, he didn't know. Didn't care.

A quiet moment passed, in which the cascading flowers blushed a little brighter in the first light. A cockerel crowed, and then he heard the *clink* of keys and the irregular steps of a one-legged man who had taken too much to drink.

He brought the razor from his pocket and unfolded it, leaned closer to the vines so he could peer through their tangle to watch Negus limp by, a cask of stolen brandy under his arm.

Tomas bit the inside of his lip, keeping himself steady and still in the dark. Negus passed him by, singing under his breath, and stumped to his padlocked door. He bent to place the barrel on the ground, and Tomas gently pushed the vines apart, slid his weight forward, quietly, quietly.

"Make these damn locks so small . . ." Negus muttered, padlock in one hand, absorbed in his attempts to stab the key into the hole. It was but child's play for Tomas to spring forward, grab the man's hair, pull his head back, and lay his razor affectionately against the hammering pulse in his throat. Negus flinched, struggled, and Tomas tightened the grip on his hair rather than move the blade an inch away.

"*Ren ow thas!*" Negus swore, his voice high-pitched from the press of the steel. "Who is that?"

Fury licked up through Tomas's bones, so hot it should have dried his coat. "As if you don't know! We had a deal, Negus. You said you would bring every slave to me. So where is he? I am owed him by your own word. Where are you hiding him?"

"Tomas Quick?" Another start of surprise, another wrench of the man's hair against Tomas's clutching hand. "I don't— What slave?"

The hair in Tomas's hand threatened to tear out. Liquid seeped against his fingers as the scalp bled. "Don't pretend you don't know. I saw him brought down. Who else in this town has the resources to keep prisoners?"

Belatedly, Negus stopped struggling, relaxed back against Tomas's soaked chest, obviously still trying to put distance between his skin and the razor. Tomas kept it pressed close, but in answer he eased his grip on his old rival's hair. "Did you get a good look at them?" Negus asked, sounding curious. From the abatement of his alarm, perhaps he was telling the truth. "Did you recognize them as my men? Because if so, they're acting without my knowledge and against my will."

Tomas had been all the way down the other end of the bay. Almost a mile away. He'd seen the capture only in glimpses while he wrestled with his own bounty. "I wasn't close enough to see faces," he conceded. "I didn't recognise the clothes."

Negus sagged further, his cheek now almost touching Tomas's, his back and arse pressed to him—the closest Tomas had come to a lover's embrace for years.

You sad bastard.

His hand moved the razor closer by itself, while his mind turned this over, and Negus squeaked as Tomas had rarely heard before from a fifty-year-old man with a voice roughened from a life at sea. "I swear to you, Tomas, I wouldn't cross you. And not just because you're a mad bastard with a knife. We had an agreement, and that agreement was good for us both. I don't want no strife between us."

It sounded genuine. A part of Tomas—a part that worried him betimes—insisted that he could cut a little, for a warning, and for fun—and that part was never to be let in charge. He brought the razor carefully away, folded and pocketed it as Negus eeled out of his arms and stumped round to face him.

The man's nose was still ruddy with drink, visible now the light was broadening, and his face was transforming to match it, the blood flaming back into it around wary eyes. "You want to manage that untrustful streak, my friend," he scolded, voice lower now, as if trying on his authority. "Might come back to bite you."

But Tomas was not in the mood to be obliquely threatened by a man whose life had been at his mercy a moment before. "If it's not you, who is it? Who has him?"

Negus's fingers traced his unmarked throat, scratching through the wiry hair that joined his beard to his chest hair. His composure was now fully back, solid and impenetrable. The very reason Tomas had needed to startle him and throw him off-balance to believe a word that he said.

"Son, you can't go round threatening your allies like this. Especially not if there's a new outfit in town, but—"

He had been so sure—so sure that the blade had felt like the sword of an avenging angel in his hand. But if he had been wrong...?

Tomas slumped, sighing. "No, you're right. I thought it was you, because who else could it be, but even so I should not have jumped you. Forgive me, I—" He shook his head and rubbed one sore and stinging eye. "This matter is personal to me, but I acted impetuously. Unjustly. I'm sorry."

Negus's laugh was three-quarters scoff and one-quarter indulgent. "Normally I'd ask you in for a brandy, but for some reason I've no taste for that at the moment. I will keep an eye out, though. See if I can find who *has* got him. There do certain seem to be a change in the air. Lot of strangers about, all of a sudden. Things being done that you and I wouldn't hold with. I don't want another rival in this town any more than you do. So I'll just forget this happened and we'll go on as before. Deal?"

Tomas sighed again, unhappy but with no excuse to take it out on someone he wished to retain as an associate. "It's a deal. Now if you'll excuse me, I must get to church."

"Is this not the fast that I have chosen:
To loose the bonds of wickedness,
To undo the heavy burdens,
To let the oppressed go free,
And that you break every yoke?
Is it not to share your bread with the hungry,
And that you bring to your house the poor who are cast out;
When you see the naked, that you cover him,
And not hide yourself from your own flesh?

"If you take away the yoke from your midst,
The pointing of the finger, and speaking wickedness,
If you extend your soul to the hungry, and satisfy the afflicted soul,
Then your light shall dawn in the darkness,
And your darkness shall *be* as the noonday."

The Methodist chapel's whitewashed wooden walls swung faintly around Tomas as he watched the door to see who was sober enough to come in. He did not give work—a chance to transport or store goods—to those who were only going to consume half themselves.

The day was already warm, and the chapel's reed roof smelled of drying sap and straw. His mother had pressed a hot toddy on him when he'd come in drenched, and insisted on making a fire and sitting him in front of it for half an hour. As a result of which he had not been able to get the sleep he had promised himself. Even as he'd shifted his wet clothes for his Sunday best, his mother had been worrying at the thought of their new riding officer. He had made quite an impression on her, simply by coming to the door.

"We had a eunuch that colour, when I was in my first household. Abdul ibn Yusuf. Such a clever man, economical, energetic, intelligent. Very fierce. I was quite terrified of him. Though that was because I was fifteen and terrified of everything."

"Yes, Mother," Tomas had said, struggling into the narrow shoulders of his good coat. He didn't like it when she reminisced about the harem, though she'd been there only as a lady's maid.

"My point is—" she must have seen his discomfort, giving a very unladylike snort before she leaned forward and pinned his hand with her own, seemingly both in tenderness and to emphasize her point "—that you must not underestimate Mr. Dean. Things are changing. All the women of my acquaintance are unsettled, and the more so because none of us can put a finger on why. If we were sailors, we would say there was a shift in the wind. And this riding officer has arrived like an omen in the midst of it. Be careful, son. I don't want to see you get hurt."

She had a point—she always did, brought up to intrigue and good at reading people as she was. Tomas had noticed it too. There were always new people making small smuggling ventures with a boat or two. Locals getting together a consortium to pool money and buy contraband in France, and so on. But always in the past he would be told of these ventures, he would know the people involved. Indeed, he would probably have been called in for advice.

The idea of a new outfit in which he knew *no one* set a weight in his belly. While ships passed through every day and to see a stranger in the town was no cause for remark, these wayfarers usually passed through the webs of Porthkennack like a mist, making no great change. Why would they begin interfering now? How could he even begin to pick out who was involved, if they were hidden among innocent passersby?

He pushed the heels of his hands into his gritty eyes. He was not presently alert enough to think this through.

While Zeb Trewithy, acting today as minister, set his threadbare elbows on the lectern and began to expound on the meanings of the passage, Tomas let his mind turn towards the other new factor instead.

Peregrine Dean. New men did not normally begin their career so vigorously. He had come after Tomas as though on a personal vendetta, but Tomas could not think how he might have wronged the man. Yet there had been a conviction in those dark eyes even Tomas could see, crouched on the deck of the *Swift* though he had been. What was the man? A zealot? A convert? Just a man eager to make himself so indispensable and successful that no one on seeing him would think of slavery—traitor and turncoat to his own people?

The plain glass window above the altar let in a bridge of white light that slowly advanced along the rag rugs of the floor. "What do this passage mean for us?" Zeb Trewithy thundered. The rest of the week, he was a tin miner, and when he gestured, his palms and nails still showed the stain of earth.

"Well, we've only got to look across at France. For year'n year a tiny few folk in France—the king, the courtiers—owned everything, had more money'n they knew what to do with. And did they use it justly, in the way as would please the Lord? They did not. They let the poor and the widows and the orphans to starve while they hoarded their riches in piles. Can any of us doubt that they made the rod that is now coming down on their backs? If they had obeyed the Lord and fed the hungry, let the working man work, left no babe unfed nor unclaimed, would they not have been secure in their place? I ask you—"

The barn door opened, letting in a gust of summer air that trembled the petals of the posies of wildflowers on the altar—a kitchen table beneath a chalice and paten of blue-glazed stoneware. Tomas was glad of the distraction. In ordinary circumstances, he was eager for news from France, subscribed to a newspaper club and a philosophical society to debate the ramifications of the hope for freedom that blew in from the continent, but the gist of Zeb's sermon was obvious and nothing he had not thought of for himself.

Instead he watched as Tom Gristel tiptoed in, sweating at the gazes turned to reprimand him for interrupting, and slid into place next to Tomas.

"St. Ia's is letting out early?" Tomas whispered as the sermon ended and the congregation rose for a song.

"No, I slipped out halfway. That new riding officer was in the congregation. So I thought 'Well, let's get the hearse out now while he's busy.' I packed 'er up tight with tea—that being less likely to slosh—and sent her off with our Allan and our Petre in full mourning, and my Molly in between them in widow's weeds to weep her heart out should anyone try to stop 'em."

Molly's weeping was an art form in itself. Tomas grinned at the memories. "Is that all the tea?"

"All but what we're sharing out."

"And the brandy?"

"I'll get to that next."

What it was to have an efficient network. "Good," Tomas said, watching the front rows of the congregation go up for communion. "You'd better slip back up again to be there when Dean leaves, but . . ." He debated not saying this, not revealing a weakness, but fairness won out. "Negus tells me he doesn't have the captive sailor. That means there's someone else operating here who doesn't care about my rules. That makes things dangerous. Be careful."

Tom was the perfect carrion crow of a man for his job on the hearse, skinny as the Grim Reaper and with a tuft of hair black as raven's feathers, but his smile was all sunshine. "I always am," he said. "You look after yourself too."

When church was out, Tomas made a point of mingling, if only to conceal the moment when a colleague from the customs office slipped him a piece of paper. He tucked it away and carried on until he had spoken to everyone, whether that was to give orders or sympathy, or just to exchange a moment's small talk about the weather. Afterward, Tomas stepped out into a noon where a buildup of grey cloud sweeping in from the sea suggested they hadn't yet cleared the edges of the storm. He turned for home hurriedly, reluctant to get wet again.

Droplets spattered on his eyelashes a moment later. He bent his head down to increase the meagre cover of his hat brim, and heard the distant rattle of iron-shod wheels and clip of hoofs behind him that suggested a carriage coming down from St. Ia's at a trot.

His thoughts were in his bed, soft and drowsy, when a voice he knew and hated called, "Stand aside there!"

Tomas made no decision. His body simply stiffened by itself, knees locking and a rush of cold going up his backbone, stirring the little hairs on his neck. His feet planted themselves, and though he turned to face the onrushing vehicle, he could have moved out of its path as easily as he could have walked through a wall.

The Quicks were on their way somewhere. Perhaps to the inn. Perhaps just driving in a lazy circle through the centre of town to show off their new carriage and their new clothes. The lace on Miss Constance's dazzling white parasol threw shadows like black swans on Lazarus Quick's steely face as he bellowed again. "You, fellow! Get out of the road!"

There was plenty of space. Even now, the liveried coachman was reining the team of four matched chestnuts to one side. They would go past and—

"No," Tomas heard Damaris instruct her driver, her voice like a bell. "If he will not move, let him be ridden down."

This time the anger told him he was tall as the lighthouse, immovable as the granite. It told him he was a magazine fire, and if they drove into him, it was they who would be burned. He felt his body reach down to the rock below and take hold. He lifted his chin, looked Lazarus in the eye, and smiled.

CHAPTER SEVEN

BUT HE HAS CAUSE

They were but a foot away. Tomas felt no fear, only a brightness. To him, the bits in the horses' mouths were like lightning and their coats like copper. The thud in his chest that lifted him off his feet and threw him into the nearby wall was accompanied by no pain, though the world around him seemed to quiver like a struck gong. A moment passed in which he no longer seemed to exist in the world at all, cleanly cut from the fabric of existence, and that, too, was a type of joy.

When he returned to himself, it was to find he had slumped onto all fours on the pavement with a bruising ache all the way through his torso from shoulder blades to sternum, and his hands and knees grazed from rebounding off the wall and falling forwards onto them. He had forgotten how to breathe, his lungs frozen into stillness by the great blow, and his eyes stung with unwanted tears.

Panic clawed up his throat as he struggled for air, but then the nearest onlooker reached him. Margaret Ede, who had been walking by with a baby in one arm, wearing a hat like a wagon wheel bedaubed with lettuce. She hooked a hand beneath his armpit, pulling for him to rise. At the touch, some unconscious process was knocked back into place, and he whooped in a great lungful of air, coughed it back out again, the water that had been pooling in his eyes spilling down his cheeks.

"I'm going to kill them!"

"No," Margaret shushed him, keeping her voice low and soothing, perhaps because her child's face had puckered up in a threat of wailing. Perhaps in an effort to soothe Tomas. "Don't say such a thing."

"They rode me down!" He shook off her helpful hand and struggled to his feet by himself, hurt. She was a good woman, Margaret Ede, kind to her neighbours, though a gossip and not by any means a good housekeeper. He had thought well of her before this, but . . .

"They was turning," she urged. "At the last moment. I saw it. They was turning to avoid you, but you was clipped by the shoulder of the lead horse. They were." She glared at the departing carriage, where the footman on his perch was visibly avoiding everyone's gaze. "They thought you would move, and then when you didn't, they left it too late. They didn't mean it, Tomas, I swear. You should have moved."

His legs trembled as he got them back beneath him, and shivers moved up and down his arms. He felt oddly unmade, as though an incautious move might cause him to fall apart. His breeches were ripped at the right knee, and as he brushed them down, he was aware of the whole crowd of folk who had now come out of the church. They seemed to be watching him, aghast and not sure what to believe.

"Why should I move?" he managed, dashing the wet streaks from his cheeks with the heel of his hand. "Why me and not them? Just because they're rich?"

Nodding answered him among the Methodist congregation. But Margaret got him by the elbow and muttered, "Talk like that'll get you in trouble. Go home, Tomas, and sit down. You've had a shock now, and you don't mean it."

His floating sense of invulnerability had left his body with that first gulp of air, and he did feel disinclined to argue in a public square with a customs officer's wife. Not that Jowan would make much of it, but he might repeat it to his new partner.

"Maybe I don't," he managed, the injustice of it bitter in his mouth. "But maybe if they didn't try to humiliate me as well as taking away my birthright, I wouldn't have to say these things."

The uncertainty of the crowd gave way to an exasperated, tolerant look he found equally unjust. As though they were saying *Tomas's off on his rant again. Normality is restored.*

He waved a grazed hand at the thought. "All right, all right, I'm going. I know better than to pick a fight on the Sabbath."

"D'you need someone to help you get home?" Margaret asked, while behind her, Tomas's friends and acquaintances stood poised in an attitude of eagerness to help. He would have welcomed their understanding, but he didn't need their pity.

"I'm fine."

The first step or two were tricky. He had to concentrate on bolstering his knees and ankles, which wanted to slide away from beneath him. Breathing naturally sent a hot, reverberating ache through his chest. But once he shortened his stride and wound both arms around himself to hold his rib cage together, he could get on well enough. Fixing his gaze on the pavement to avoid both concern and censure, he paced his careful way back home.

Someone must have got there before him, however. His mother was in the garden to meet him. Her hand beneath his elbow was less burdensome than Margaret's, and he allowed himself to lean on her support as he bent beneath the threshold and went in.

She left him in the same seat he had vacated this morning. The embers of the fire in the hearth were still live, and he was grateful for them, weary suddenly in a landslide of dark velvet that seemed to push his heavy head down and sew his eyelids shut.

"*Miyme qeremische*," she said, settling in the other side of the snug from him, gathering her petticoats in tight with swollen-knuckled hands. "Young Jim ran down here and told me the Quicks had tried to kill you."

Tomas dragged his eyes half-open and smiled. "Did he? I'm glad someone noticed. The rest are claiming it was a misunderstanding."

"I hope it was!" She raked through the ashes, tipping the embers into a bed-warmer one by one with the tongs. "But, sweetheart, imagine how I'd feel if they succeeded."

She rustled upstairs to put the warmer between his sheets, and he tried not to think about what she had said until she returned. "That's not the point," he insisted. "I don't care anymore that Father asked me to show them mercy. Told me it was Christian to forgive and be content. I don't care!" Something of his rage returned, like a live coal in his mouth. "He's not here anymore, and they tried to kill me! I'm going to find that birth certificate, wherever Father hid it, and I'm going to use it to fucking ruin them. They should be the ones who have to take in washing and boarders, and you should be the one parading about in jewels. You should have the servants, the carriages.

You should be sitting in that mansion on the cliffs, throwing parties, and I'm going to make that happen. I'm going to see them under my heel if it's the last thing—"

He staggered when she raised him to his feet again, pushing him up the stairs and supporting him when he swayed. "I don't want any of those things," she insisted, with a disappointed look that only infuriated him more. "We have plenty to live on. I need for nothing, except for the certainty that my son will be safe. Why will you keep provoking them—the Quicks, the law? You could be a tradesman, Tomas. Take my name, or your father's. Give up the smuggling and this feud, please God and your mother in the process, and be safe."

They had expanded the upstairs when his father began to earn money by his legal practice, during that short happy time when he had been both prosperous and alive. So Tomas had his own small room, with a sea chest, and a bed with a coverlet of blue and red knitted squares, even though they kept an additional room for guests and one for boarders—currently empty. He was grateful to have his privacy, but they should have had better.

The colours of the coverlet swam beneath his eyes as he sat and toed off his shoes with their Sunday Best buckles. He was barely conscious of leaning down and setting his cheek to the pillow, but suddenly his mother was upright and he was not.

"I don't want safety," he managed, the last of the anger slipping out of his grasp as sleep pulled him under. "I want justice."

"You are your father's son, after all," she said ruefully, and brushed his hair from his forehead as she left.

Tomas woke to voices downstairs, and knew that despite the light still flooding into the room, it must be the evening. His lieutenants had come to report.

His head ached worse than it had when he had lain down, but his breathing was easier, and his sinews seemed to have knitted themselves back together. *This collapse was due to shock, mostly.* He flexed his shoulders and felt the muscles pull without undue agony. *By tomorrow you should be fighting fit once more.*

Their front room was packed. His mother had thrown a shawl over her head and sat, slightly removed by the fire. In the seat he had occupied earlier, his pilot, Anne Lusmoore, was sitting and holding his mother's hand reassuringly, while the gentlemen were gathered around the table with their hats in their laps. Even after many years married to an Englishman, Zuliy was not entirely happy with unrelated men in her living quarters, and Tomas's associates had developed several ways of trying to seem inoffensive as a result.

"Tomas." Zeb stood to greet him. No longer a preacher, just a tin miner with an interest in ethical smuggling. "We heard what happened. Are you fit?"

"I'm fine." Tomas shrugged and eased himself into the only empty seat. "Or I will be by tomorrow. Bloody Quicks tried to run me down."

"Mm." Zeb glowered at him, brows as black as the ingrained dirt across his nose. "'Vengeance is mine, saith the Lord,' in case you was thinking of doing anything rash."

Tomas glanced at his mother and scoffed. "I've been told as much three times already today. I can only hope someone is lecturing *them* about their duty to the Lord too."

"They wouldn't listen to the likes of us even if we tried," Anne protested, sliding her bare feet through the soft, dead siftings of the fire. "But that don't mean—"

"I know. I know." Tomas sighed, and though he remained determined to bring the wrath of God down upon the Quicks as soon as he could find the necessary paperwork, he found himself mysteriously willing to be delayed. "I mean no more harm to them than their own deeds have wrought. That's not what I want to discuss tonight. Report."

"My lads've got all the barrels of porter dispersed through the mine," Zeb began, picking at the wax that overflowed his hat brim. "And the lace is being sewed into chemises by the miners' wives."

"Mrs. Hedges of the Widows and Orphans' is started on sewing the cotton inside pillowslips," Anne chimed in. "And we split the silverware with old Harry from the customs, 'cause he threatened to turn us in otherwise."

"Did he indeed?" Tomas writhed in place, his bruised spine protesting his straight-backed chair. "They get one zealot on board and suddenly they're all keen. We're going to have to teach them not to get cheeky. Any news of the captive?"

"No. None yet," Zeb replied. "I asked the congregation too. They either don't know or aren't telling. You think we've new competition in town?"

"I do," Tomas agreed. Defiance flared up in him like the sun tightly focused through a lens. "This is a dangerous time for us. Mr. Peregrine Dean from London, with his high connections and his ambition—he will have to be dealt with. And we have an undisclosed rival about whom we know nothing."

"So perhaps we could now be content to live an honest life," Tomas's mother chipped in, though the tone was of one who knew better than to hope she would be obeyed.

Zeb laughed. He picked a candle from his pocket and rolled it between his fingers, not meeting Tomas's gaze. "We don't need to go that far, but we maybe should go slower. Be a bit more careful."

"That's what they'll be expecting." Tomas bared his teeth. "This new riding officer and this new smuggler? If either of them thinks I will grow cautious at the mere threat of them, they know me not at all." He snapped out the piece of paper he'd been given at service.

"Since we have not yet identified our new competitor, we will first put our old adversaries back in their place. This is a listing of the contents of the customs warehouse; including the one hundred and ten barrels of best brandy they took from the wreck yesterday. Wrack that falls on Cornish shores belongs by right to Cornishmen. Not to the customs, no matter how emboldened they may be feeling with their new hunter on board, nor to the far away government in England. Why should they line their pockets while our neighbours go hungry?"

Zeb shook his head slightly, as if bracing himself for the rest, and Tomas carried on, a little less stridently. "At night, the warehouse is patrolled by four men, and two cannons defend it by sea. I propose that tomorrow night we storm the place and empty it. If young Mr. Dean is trying to give me a message, courtesy of old Harry, I will answer him."

CHAPTER EIGHT

A RAID ON THE WAREHOUSE

"We'm be shaving it," Anne Lusmoore whispered. Now with her long hair clubbed like a man's, her skirt exchanged for petticoat breeches, she lay in the bow netting of the *Swift*, so close to the sea that she could put her hand against its swell. Since every child in Porthkennack grew up around ships and larked about Cornwall's dangerous shoreline in tiny boats as soon as they could handle an oar, the town produced many fine pilots with an intimate knowledge of the rocks and shifting sands of the bay.

Typically, those girls who enjoyed the sport gave it up in favour of marriage by Anne's age, but she had yet to prefer a man to the sea, and Tomas was glad of it. She was the best, and if others refused to employ her because they thought she should be with child, it was their loss.

"There's barely a foot of water under the keel as it is, and it's running out as we speak."

"It doesn't matter if we ground outside the warehouse for half an hour at lowest ebb." Tomas whispered back. Before setting off, they had disguised the *Swift* by taking the jib down and re-rigging her as a sloop. With tarpaulined sacks hung over her green livery and the small cabin disassembled and stowed beneath, she should be impossible to recognize in the dark. "We'll need to be there awhile anyway to take the cargo on board."

"We'll be sitting ducks for the cannon." The white of Anne's eyes gleamed as she glanced at him over her shoulder. "The whole time. *Swift*'ll be shot to pieces. We should anchor in Long Cove, come in from the land side."

"That's what they'll expect," Tomas said again, mentally reviewing the measurements he had taken when the cannons were first installed, assuring himself again that this would work. "Trust me."

He straightened up as a gleam of moonlight poured out of the shifting clouds above and showed him the breakwater of the harbour within arm's reach off the starboard side. They coasted without lights ahead of a warm land breeze, strong enough to curve out the staysail and slip them forward at about two knots.

"I do," Anne huffed, taking stock of the oceanic waves. "Why else do you think I'm here? What time is it?"

He consulted his pocket watch, "Four thirty-three," and she smiled, committing herself.

"Get ready to throw 'er hard a-larboard on my mark, then clew 'er out at forty-five degrees."

"Aye aye." He moved away to relay the instructions to old Ben at the wheel and the men on the sails. As he did, the brief moonbeam waned and darkness rushed back in. All at once, the utter indifference of the ocean weighed on him. The sigh of it and the suck and gurgle against the breakwater were the only indications that anything existed outside the square of deck his feet rested on. He stood helpless in the hands of God, and the hands of Anne Lusmoore, and the thought gave him a momentary shudder.

Then Ben slid open the cover of his dark lantern, and the compass at the wheelhouse came into sight. Anne raised her voice. "On my mark. Three, two. Mark!" and Ben wrenched the wheel over while top and mainsail swung together to turn them on a course still invisible in the gloom.

Now the thrum against *Swift*'s keel was the pulse of the wild waves, outside the harbour, and Tomas could feel the current racing between the rocky teeth of the offshore islands. If they strayed into that, in the dark, this wind would not keep them from being swept to Land's End and beyond, but if they ventured too far from it, they would run aground on the sandbar at the entrance to Polventon Bay. Tomas, who was no poor sailor himself, did not know how Anne was threading her way between the two.

"Starboard two degrees!" she called, beginning to count beneath her breath, and then "Port your helm." The waves changed again as they came back under the shadow of the land. A lantern beneath the courthouse showed a square of cobbles. The loom of black beyond it was the warehouse they had come to rob.

It was so dark, the brass of the cannons gave no gleam, but two tiny red specks of light on either side of the building must be the glow of lighted slow-match. Which meant the cannons were armed and crewed.

Tomas strode to the binnacle and snapped Ben's lantern closed. The heave of the sea beneath had lessened, and the *Swift* felt as though she was all but scraping her way through mud, heavy and reluctant. He opened the arms chest and passed out pistols and cudgels, hoping the firearms would not need to be used.

A moment of foreboding moved through Tomas, sick and slow—a moment of anticipation before the storm. *My only King. Help us and forgive us, now and in the moment of our need.*

"Spill your wind!" Anne's voice pierced the darkness like a piccolo, and as the sail crew leaped to obey, *Swift's* keel ground noisily against the sand. Light dazzled into being above their heads where the cannon waited on the boundary of the warehouse, and someone shouted.

"Did you hear something?"

"Shit, Perry, you're right. They're coming."

Ben flung his own lantern wide and seized Tomas by the shoulder. "What are we doing? We just grounded! We're a sitting duck!" and Tomas bit his lip rather than laugh in the man's face.

"Unidentified vessel," someone shouted from the shore, "lay down your arms, surrender immediately, or we will fire."

"Fuck your surrender," Tomas shouted back, motioning for his armed crew to prepare to pile overboard, make their way to the steps on either side of the basin that would take them up to ground level. "Do your worst!

"They're going to be distracted and blinded by the blast," he continued in a lower voice. "Once they start, you pour up the stairs, get behind them, and take them while they're concentrating on the guns. Quickly—they're idiots, but we don't want to give them time to bounce back."

"Once they start?" Anne protested, but she pulled her neckerchief up over her nose and jammed her pistol in the back of her breeches, cudgel in the other hand. "We're going to wait for them to shoot us?"

"This is your last warning," came the voice from above.

Tomas flicked through his calculations again and resisted a wild urge to giggle. He covered his own face and jammed his hat further down over his revealing hair.

Dennis Percher and Alan Henry were crouching by the larboard gunwale with cutlasses between their teeth. Solid family men both of them, and not inclined to run wild, but he felt the need to remind them: "Try not to kill anyone, lads. We're gentlemen, remember?"

"Tell that to them up there," Dennis muttered through his thick beard, just as the bright points of the slow-match above floated, as if by themselves, over to the cannons and kindled the fuses.

"Eyes closed!" Tomas called. At the same time, the hiss of the fuse met the powder and both guns erupted in tongues of flame. "Go, go!"

The roar of the shot punched his ears, close enough to be almost instantaneous. Even confident of his maths, Tomas's eyes snapped open and his body froze for a heartbeat as it anticipated the smash of the cannonballs into the *Swift's* hull, the splinter of timbers and the spray of knife-sharp oak shrapnel.

None came, and he was alive again. "Go, go now!"

He leaped the starboard gunwale, with Anne and three men behind him, caught a rope halfway down to slow his fall, and landed upright on wet sand that was firm enough to run fast on. Above, on the pavement now out of sight at the top of the tall harbour wall, he could hear curses, the rumble of cannon wheels. Someone shouted "Get the wedges! Wedge them up!"

Another boom, another slap of blazing light, and still no sound of impact.

Sprinting now at his side, Anne Lusmoore let out a breathy laugh. "That's why you grounded us? Fucking cannons are too high. They're shooting right over the top of us."

"They expect to be firing on a ship with three foot of water under her keel," Tomas agreed. "But we need to disarm those guns before tide turns and lifts us on the way out."

By now they had reached the starboard steps. He coaxed more speed out of legs still offended by his fall—anger from the memory was a goad he used to overcome the ache. Anne was at his side, swarming up the damp stone with the confidence of one accustomed to clambering rigging. She was a sinewy whippet of a girl, and in men's jacket and breeches, indistinguishable from a thirteen-year-old boy. Hob Wright at Tomas's back was a carpenter in normal life, fond of big meals. His breath was thunderous as he forced himself to keep up, but his feet were light, and their approach was silent—the breath mingling with the sigh of the sea.

Tomas crouched to slip up the final few stairs. Expecting a pistol shot to the face, he emerged onto the pavement where the guns were chained. But when he straightened up, he could see that old Ben—who had remained on board as he was no longer spry enough for frontal assaults—had opened up his lantern again and was walking back and forth on the deck of the Swift as though he was passing orders from a hidden captain to an invisible crew. The customs men—and there were only four of them, two to each gun—alternated between speculating on what the old man was up to, and wrestling to load the cannon with more shot.

They had placed their own lantern between the two guns, to give light for the adjustment of the aim, and with their night vision thus destroyed, they didn't see Tomas's crew ease into the darkness behind them.

Tomas slunk within reach of the first, still silent enough not to cause alarm. He drew his arm back, calculating the angle, and struck cleanly, his oak-and-leather truncheon smacking into the side of the customs man's neck. The man choked out a cry as he fell, and his partner turned, met Tomas's eyes for a brief, vivid moment before Hob lurched out of the darkness behind him and took him down with a lead-weighted fish-priest.

On the second gun, Dennis and Alan had done the same, dropping the warehouse's defenders cleanly, not a blow landed on them.

"Milksops!" Anne crowed. "That was easy!"

It was, but it was also the end of surprise. The whole town would have heard the cannon fire; reinforcements would already be on their way. "Anne!" Tomas called. "Tie them up. Hob and Harry, Dennis and Alan, start loading everything you can onto the Swift. I'm going up front to be sure there's no one else on guard. Fast as you please, we need to be ready to sail as soon as she lifts."

The back doors of the warehouse stood open, a powder barrel and two small pyramids of shot being kept dry inside. A tallow candle burned dim orange in a distant window where the warehousemen must have their office. Tomas would be stepping into its light as soon as he passed the threshold, and though there were shadowed corners aplenty in the aisles full of bales and barrels, that would be the moment when he was likely to be shot.

He went in first anyway. An instinct of the building's largeness and his smallness rolled over him strangely, and almost distracted him from the metallic *click* in the aisle of damp spices. He dived, and the plume of fire roared out over his head as he rolled back to his feet and dashed straight towards the gunman.

It was a narrow thing. The man had finished tamping down his next shot and was ready to lift the rifle to his shoulder again, when Tomas rammed into the man as if he were trying to break down a door.

They both went flying. Tomas, on top, grappled for his opponent's throat, squeezing the man's heaving chest with his knees—like riding an unbroken horse. Dark hands closed around his wrists with a grip that threatened to splinter them, and he looked down into the furious face of Peregrine Dean. None the worse for wear for apparently having been half drowned by overeager treasure hunters on the beach, he wrestled Tomas's hold with terrifying strength.

"I know who you are," he spat, eyes trying to pierce the shade of Tomas's hat. "I'm going to take you apart, one way or another. Your time is done!"

Tomas's blood was up, and the thrum of the man's breathing, felt through Tomas's thighs, was warming. The defiance on that broad face, mahogany brown in the ruddy light of the candle, was magnificently self-confident considering that—

"Put your hands by your head. I don't want to shoot you, but I will." Anne had arrived. Tomas disentangled himself, so she could better train her pistol on Dean's face.

Dean's rifle had spun out of his grip on Tomas's impact with him. It lay further away than he could easily reach without being shot, and as he visibly contemplated his odds, Tomas took his own gun from his belt and cocked it.

Dean slumped and allowed himself to be tied up, hands behind his back, a noose of rope securing him to the nearest pillar.

"I will see you hang," he insisted, as Tomas's crew rolled as many barrels out and down the harbour stairs as they could. "I promise you that."

It itched Tomas more than it should have done not to be able to reply. But he had been careful with his clothes, and the only thing about him that might be recognizable was his voice. So he could not give back the verbal blistering that pressed behind his teeth.

He had to be content with taking two score hogsheads of brandy and leaving just as Dean's reinforcements began to pry at the bolted door.

CHAPTER NINE

AN UNCOMFORTABLE INTIMACY

By morning, the postbattle euphoria of Tomas's spirits was long gone. Sailing out of the bay with the keel a bare inch from the sea bed and renewed cannon fire behind them, he'd had such an unquenchable grin that his cheeks still ached with it. But since then, they'd had to work hard to rerig the *Swift* back to her normal sail plan, hide the disguising canvas down a mine ventilation shaft, and decant the hogsheads of brandy into smaller vessels that could more easily be hidden.

Most had gone to the mines, where Zeb had a small army of friends and colleagues willing to conceal them in worked-out corners that no one in their right minds would ever visit. But Mary Castille of the Angel and Eagle had hinted to him recently that she was having trouble making ends meet, so he had slung two of the small kegs on a pony and taken them up there as his final task of the night.

Mary employed several of the town's orphans as potboys, giving them houseroom and refuge in the attics. Arriving just before dawn, Tomas had found himself wading through them as they scrubbed up for school at the pump in the yard. Already, they knew better than to watch him arrive with two kegs, but a chorus of good mornings reached him once he was safely relieved of the horse.

By that time he was weary again, and his buzz of action had turned into the dragging dread that inevitably came after. He had certainly sent his message to the forces arraigned against him: *I am not afraid of you.* But had he overreached? Had he been too arrogant? Disaster must surely be coming—it was only a matter of time.

"You look worn to unravelling," Mary said, once she had hidden the spirits among her own casks. The household was barely astir, and Mary herself still wore nightcap and gown over her stays. Though her youngest son was clattering in the snug as he raked out and reset the fire, the old inn had a thick aura of sleepiness and frowsty comfort about it at this time in the morning—an unwashed intimacy that few but the owners saw. "Sit down and I'll make you breakfast before you go home."

Sardines with mustard sauce and a small beer had put the heart back into him, and he stayed to watch the arrival of the first coach out of Porthkennack and exchange a meaningful glance with the driver, who'd had several packets of the best Brussels lace sewn into his seat cushions last night.

It was full day by the time Tomas finished his meal and walked back down to his own house. Both dread and excitement had settled, and he was ready to sleep again, and to contemplate a voyage to France sometime later in the week.

The day was fine and fresh, the sun bright. So a horrified shudder went through him to see his front garden occupied with nothing but flowers. Marigolds were vivid to the eye, but the blue front door was closed, and in this drying weather not a stitch of laundry fluttered.

Tomas ducked into the shadow of his next-door neighbours' pigsty. Its inhabitant snorted at him and raised itself to its hairless legs, snout upraised and twitching for a treat. He passed it the heel of bread he had brought in his pocket, and pretended the trembling in his hand was due to the stench.

What to do? If the laundry was not out, it meant his mother was either lying unwell indoors *or* someone dangerous to him was indoors with her and she was warning him to stay away. The devil was that he could not tell which.

With the pig distracted, Tomas climbed over his neighbours' wall, let himself through the house—all doors were open in Porthkennack at all times—and out onto the small path that picked its way between the cliff edge and the backs of the terrace. Flattening himself against the house wall, in case someone was looking out of an upstairs window, he slid crabwise sideways to where he could peek through the kitchen window.

His mother sat at her kitchen table demurely paring carrots with hands that did not waver a jot. But her hair was covered with her shawl, her mouth was pressed tight, and across the table from her, Peregrine Dean sat with a pistol trained on her face.

A hot icicle seemed to crash through the crown of Tomas's head and freeze-burn his innards. There were innumerable things he could do. Go away. Send a neighbour to ask for Zuliy's help. Set a fire in one of the derelicts on the beach. Sail past the window and thumb his nose as he went. But even as he thought of them, he was raising the latch, thrusting the door open. Too hard! Too hard—he must not startle the man who held a gun on his mother.

The man was holding a gun on his mother!

Tomas strode straight in, slapped his hands down on the table. The pistol swung to point at him. His mother winced, rose as if to come to him, the paring knife a glint of sullied silver in her fist.

Tomas didn't try to dissuade her. Didn't look at her, his gaze fixed on Dean. The man was smiling—damn him—the smile a plush curve on broad lips. Smug as hell.

"What the fuck do you think you're doing?" Tomas demanded, some semblance of wit beginning to return to him now his mother was out of the line of fire. "By what right do you come in here and threaten a respectable woman? How dare you!"

Dean's elbows were on Tomas's kitchen table; his arse was in one of Tomas's chairs. It didn't matter that the mouth of his pistol pointed unwaveringly between Tomas's eyes. He was in the wrong, and he would learn it.

Dean's brow furrowed. "I know it was you," he said eventually, the rumble of his voice oddly intimate in the heart of Tomas's house.

"You know *what* was me?" Tomas leaned forward, precisely as invulnerable as he had been ahead of the charging horse, and pressed Dean's pistol down onto the tabletop. "And don't wave that thing around. Someone could get hurt."

"I saw you!" Dean's eyebrows climbed into his hairline, and his eyes widened until the sunlight brought out a glint of bronze in their darkness. "We were this close. You can't possibly—"

Idiot. Does he think I'm some kind of amateur to be terrified by weightless threats? It rankled, if so. "You saw me where?" Tomas insisted. "Doing what? What could possibly justify this kind of outrage?"

"You're going to pretend you don't know?" Dean seemed surprised by the fact, as though London smugglers routinely rolled over to him and showed their throats. And yes, he was a big man with a belligerent presence, but Tomas had grown up in a world where most men were larger than himself. It had ceased to threaten him a long time ago.

His mother wiped her hands on her apron and—disregarded now—left the room. At the sound of the front door closing behind her, Tomas cooled a little, pulling out a chair and sinking into it, relieved.

"I *don't* know," he insisted. "I . . ." He shook his head, like an honest man trying to be civil. A part of him still wanted to break Peregrine Dean's back for giving his mother a moment's fear, but that impulse was waning in light of the fact that she was unharmed and out of danger. "I am conscious that you are only doing your job. And that you're new here and you don't know what you've run your neck into. On my own accord, I am willing to forgive you for mistaking me for whatever criminal you are in pursuit of today. But insult my mother again and there will be consequences. Are we clear?"

Dean stood, monumental and solid, slightly too tall for their kitchen, frowning. Tomas's heart beat loud in his ears as he watched Dean's fingers tighten on the pistol—a bullet in the stomach would be worse than one between the ears. But then the fingers relaxed and Dean gave a rueful smile. "I'd like to see you try." He paused, but Tomas refused to rise to the bait, just watched him, silent now and assured.

Dean uncocked the pistol and tucked it back into the waistband of his sober breeches. His whole outfit said *well-to-do professional, probably a lawyer*, which was jarring in several ways. This was a man who took himself seriously. Tomas could respect that, and he reminded himself not to get cocky.

"Well, if you're going to play innocent," Dean said, "then yes. I have received intelligence that you were involved with the robbery of the customs warehouse last night. I must insist on searching your house for contraband."

Tomas smiled—tried not to make it too smug. *Received intelligence* meant that Dean did not have evidence against him sufficient to convince a jury. He knew Tomas had been there. But "a tall, slight man in a large hat, with a mask over his face," might be anyone as far as the court was concerned.

"By all means look around, since you are here." Tomas shrugged. He had nothing to hide—literally, since everything was already off the premises, and his accounts and deals were done by word of mouth and memory, leaving no incriminating documents.

Over the next half an hour, he followed Dean as he searched the house, digging through the ashes in the range, feeling up the chimneys, pacing out the rooms from both within and without to check for lost space, hidden cupboards. He was thorough and imaginative—even Tomas had not thought of boring holes in the roof beams to hide coins or jewels, though he would do in future. Knowing himself to be unassailable, it was a pleasure to watch the man work, and to learn from him.

They ended the search in Tomas's bedroom. He stood by the window and contemplated the way Dean's back and biceps flexed as he manhandled the bed, stripping it to get at the mattress, checking the floorboards beneath for anything loose. To protect them from soot, Dean had taken off his coat and waistcoat downstairs, and in the summer heat, with his exertion, his linen clung to his powerful frame. Tomas was absolutely not going to touch, but he relished the opportunity to look.

"I hope you're going to remake that," he said, enjoying himself now, as Dean completed the ruination of his bed by shaking his pillow until the tiny down feathers flew.

Dean turned toward his mockery with a flush and a snarl, and in a flash of imagination, Tomas saw himself being pinned to the wall with an arm across his throat. He tilted his chin up in challenge, as the very sunlight through the window seemed to thicken and pulse.

Then a boy's voice shouted from downstairs. "Mr. Quick? I just come from the summersea lode. You been asking how much for the slave? They say they'll take fifty pound."

All the heat in the room plunged abruptly to ice. Whatever else had been behind Dean's fine brown eyes—the beginnings of a reciprocal enjoyment for a game well played, perhaps—it drained away and contempt replaced it.

Dean turned to look as Ruan Nancarrow hobbled up the last step and froze, his young face caught in a picture of guilt.

"Here is proof at least that you've been in contact with the wreckers. That you are intent on purchasing . . ." Dean's voice fell off, and in a flash of empathy, Tomas knew he could not force himself to call a captive man *stolen goods*.

Tomas's honour revolted from what he was about to say, but his life and freedom were at stake, and he needed those. "The boy is talking about a deal I'm making with the captain of a slave ship in Liverpool to buy a man to train on a vessel stationed in Barbados. It is a perfectly legal deal, for which I will be happy to provide you with the papers when I return. But if the agent is waiting for me this instant, I must go at once."

Dean's mouth was set in a harsh line, his eyes flat. He moved as if to block the door, and Tomas pushed him, angry himself and disgusted to be playing this part. By his knee, Ruan was so apologetic he was clearly trying not to cry.

"Do you have any legal reason to stop me?" Tomas insisted, pushing again.

Dean begrudgingly moved aside. "Not yet," he said. "But I promise you, I will find one."

CHAPTER TEN

NO HONOUR AMONG THIEVES

Speed was of the essence, for if the word had gone out that the shipwrecked sailor was available for purchase, Tomas did not wish to turn up at the summersea lode and find out he had already been sold. He regretted leaving Dean in possession of his house, but there was nothing there to condemn him except for Ruan. Doubtless the man would question young Ruan, but the boy was sharp and silent enough when he knew himself to be under suspicion. He would not say anything more.

It would have been better to know which miner in particular he should speak to, but any further questions would only have destroyed his cover story, so Tomas withdrew fifty pounds from his bank, picked up his pony from the stables, and headed out onto the high moor, prepared to speak to whoever would speak to him.

The pony had a fixed idea of what could be demanded of it. It would walk, doggedly along any path, scramble up piles of unmarked rocks. But if it was asked to trot, it would do so only for five minutes out of every fifteen, and spend the rest cropping the tough heather and thistles that swept in russet and purple patches over the moorland's rough grass and mossy rocks. It would have been a pleasant ride, inland with the cool of the sea yielding to a great warm smell of sap and flower and soil. But Tomas paid no attention to the seagulls wheeling above like flecks of light cast from a diamond, nor to the skylarks, their voices like running water and bells mingled.

He did not like to be looked at the way Peregrine Dean had looked at him when they parted, but it rankled more than it should. He told himself it was only that he liked his enemies to respect him, but felt a churning certainty that the truth was nothing so simple.

It was a relief when the drying house came in sight—a small stone hut with a mossy roof nestled beneath a sloping face of granite, where bent trees clung with determined roots among the nests of plover. Summersea's diggings were so old they had begun on the surface, and the entrance to the mine required no wheelhouse. One walked into it on a slowly descending path cut into the cliff, beside which a clay sled-track had been laid to make it easier for the ponies to drag out their loads of ore.

Tomas had brought no lantern nor change of clothes, and he did not know the layout of the mine. Rather than venture alone into the dark, he put his head into the drying house in the hope of finding someone to help.

Water trickled into the mines at all times. Sometimes braver or more foolish souls would follow a line of ore out beneath the sea, only to have those diggings collapse and flood lower levels. Whether or not it rained above, water seeped through the soil and ran down every wall, so the miners could as often be digging mud as solid rock. Down there in the dark, it was warm enough to keep body and soul together, particularly when the miners were working hard and sweating. But coming out, exhausted, in wet clothes, to a cold, clear Cornish sea breeze? It had been known to kill.

So each mine had a drying house by its entrance, where the miners could strip off their soaked clothes and leave them to dry, wash the worst of the caked earth off their skin and hair in the warmth of a decent fire, and put on clean garments before going home to their wives and children. This one, Tomas was relieved to see, contained not only a hot water copper and basins, wooden drying racks spread out with an array of steaming rags, but also a miner in a blue neckerchief, sitting at his ease by the fire, blowing smoke rings from a long-stemmed pipe.

Tomas didn't recognize him—he was not a Porthkennack man— but that was natural in the mines, where any man hale enough to dig might seek his fortune. Despite the rakish touch of a single pierced ear, where a small black feather with a green sheen hung from a twist of silver wire, this elder had an honest face. The earring said he too had been a sailor at some point, but now he was dressed as a countryman, his flannel shirtsleeves folded back over forearms as ropy and strong as the tree roots above.

"You're the one I should talk to about buying the slave?"

The man took a long, considering pull at his pipe and let the smoke out through his nose after in two plumes. He seemed to be weighing Tomas up. "I am."

"I want to buy him," Tomas said, as though this was not obvious. "Bring him out to me, please."

Another cloud of smoke—the entire room seemed to hum with the peaty smell of tobacco, even though the door stood wide open to the scented summer air.

"I'll need to see your money."

Used to Zeb and the above-board way he and his associates did business, Tomas was surprised at the distrust. He had always been on the best of terms with the miners—terms of honour and acceptance. To be asked to prove himself after the years he had spent diverting wealth into the mouths of these hard-working, hungry people? It was—

But this man didn't know him either. He was newly arrived from somewhere, perhaps, where well-dressed merchants who turned up wanting to buy illicit merchandise could not be taken at face value.

Tomas swallowed against a feeling that everything was shifting under his feet. New people. New rules. A reputation to earn again. He didn't like it, but he would deal with it. Taking the bundle of notes from his pocket, he unfolded twenty-five of them. "Half now and half when you bring him to me."

"Deal." The miner shook his hand, folded the notes away, and tucked them inside a waxed leather pouch that hung from his neck. Then he quickly stripped off trousers and jacket and replaced them with a below-ground set. "They got 'un a fair trek in," he said, attaching a candle to the brim of a hat so permeated in stone dust it was more of a helmet. "Give me a half hour if not more. He may be a trouble on the way out."

Tomas imagined it—the choice between walking into the grasp of a "master," giving up one's freedom, or tearing oneself out of the hands of one's captives only to be lost in the absolute dark, perhaps never to be found again. He shuddered. "I'll be here."

On this fine day, the hut was too hot for him. He occupied himself peaceably enough sitting on a hummock of turf outside, spotting wildflowers among the heather. A litter of foxes came out to chew the grass and play on a shelf of the cliff above his head, and their antics kept him amused and smiling for a further fifteen minutes. But when they ran back beneath the holly bush from which they'd come and he checked his pocket watch again, an ache of dissatisfaction began at his tailbone—uncomfortable on the dry-baked earth—and rose to pulse behind his eyes.

When he had waited an hour, he got up and paced to the mine entrance, peering in. Nothing stirred in the sloping tunnel, though a faint tapping slithered up the walls and made him think of goblins. After he had gone to and fro a dozen times, another hour had passed, and a ball of seething darkness, heavy with resentment, was gathering in his chest.

"Where are they?" he snapped at the pony at last. It raised its head from the grass and bit his coat pocket, perhaps hoping for an apple. The grinding teeth grazed his hip bone as they closed, and he sprang back with a sense of fucking betrayal that began with the bruise but increased in mass and momentum as every other new misery added itself to his thoughts. "God's bollocks. He's not coming back, is he?"

Tomas put his face into his hands and dug his fingernails into his hairline, trying to use the pain to offset another inferno of anger. Fuck-shit—the fire gave him power, courage when it was directed at someone else, but at himself? It went from glory to burnt, black desolation far too fast. "Fuck it!" He raked his nails deeper in, giving himself a crown of thorns. "I just handed an unknown man twenty-five pounds and let him walk away. How could I be so stupid?"

Undeterred, its stringy black tail swishing flies from its back, the pony went for the other pocket. It was the trigger Tomas needed to stop clawing his face and turn his anger outwards. He clenched his fists and spun toward the drying hut. This new man thought he could just run off with Tomas's money? Shimmy up one of the air shafts or stroll out of one of the less-used exits? Abuse Tomas's trust and steal from him? No.

Dashing into the drying house to raid the stock of candles, he put two in his pocket and lit the third. Gluing it to his hat brim with the spilled wax, he stormed into the mine shaft, heedless of the mud ankle-deep over his shoes. Heedless of the fact that he had no idea where to go.

The entry tunnel ran downward shallow, then suddenly steep. Ropes had been rigged along its length, tied to metal rings hammered into the wall. An air from the depths guttered his candle, sent the shadows flapping around his head like bats. The tapping continued, growing louder as he descended, slipping on the viscous mud. Then the very earth shook beneath him, vibrations shaking his bones as dirt rained from the rock above him, and a gust of hot smoke, reeking of sulphur, engulfed his clammy face. In a distant gallery, someone was blasting through rock. Tomas could not help but wonder whether this would be the final jolt that brought the whole riddle of tunnels down.

As the tremors rolled on beneath Tomas's feet, he braced himself against the wall, mopped disgraceful sweat from his brow and tried to catch a breath gone tight in his chest. Deprived of air, his anger seemed to waver like the candle, and his resolution with it.

Galleries had already opened off the main tunnel on either side—some large enough for a pony, some that had to be crawled through, or would admit only a thin boy turned sideways. Tomas was fairly familiar with the workings beneath the Hope & Anchor, but the Summersea mine was new to him. He knew better than to turn into a shaft at random, so he continued down the wide main shaft, hoping to find at least a boy at the bottom, left in charge of the horses, whom he might send to fetch the foreman.

But when he emerged into the cavern at the foot of the shaft, he found only the ponies, idling in their traces, sleds half laden. As far as his light could reach, the gentle arch of the stone chamber was pierced with tiny passages, where the lack of light fooled the eye into thinking them flat. Haphazard scaffolding of mud-covered wet wood gave access to the upper lodes, and rope ladders trailed down into the holes in the floor.

At this central point, it was impossible to say where the tapping was coming from, so he could not follow it to find aid. Worse—when the next explosion blew, it shook down flakes of stone from the cavern roof and made the rickety spiderweb of wooden structures groan aloud. Smoke puffed through a dozen small passages, and the flame of Tomas's candle swooped and went out.

He was familiar with the sea on a cloudy night—the sense of its vast power and his own fragility before it—but that was an abyss he knew how to navigate. This was not, and he couldn't find it in himself to sit in the crushing dark and wait for someone to come. Not when his trust had been so badly bruised. Had even the summons here been a lie? Ruan was a good, honest boy, but like most children, he was easily deceived. Particularly by a man whose appearance of candour had fooled Tomas himself. No—he would have to find another way. Sore at heart and defeated, he set his hand on the handrail and followed it back out.

CHAPTER ELEVEN

THE EXAMPLE OF FRANCE

My dear mama,

I recall that you warned me I would be bored in such a small backwater as this after the bustle of the capital, but in truth there has already been so much excitement I fear to tell you of it in case it worries you. In the course of a free-for-all incited by the arrival of a wrecked cargo on the beach, I was clubbed about the head and would surely have drowned if my partner had not hauled me to shore and revived me. I was also held at the point of a pistol by the man Sir Lazarus Quick has trusted me to investigate. All this in the first week!

I ask you not to fear, for this action suits my temperament, and I have felt no pull toward the vices of gambling or drinking since I arrived. Life is too absorbing to need augmentation.

I wonder betimes why my quarry did not simply shoot me. He was in disguise; I was alone. There was nothing to stop him at the time or convict him afterwards. I find it in myself to wish I could think well of him. He should have done, for I will certainly see him hang.

Perry had let Quick go, knowing there was no following the man in broad daylight. Instead, his gaze had fallen on the boy trying not to weep by the door. An ugly little creature with a harelip that showed the gleam of one front tooth even when his mouth was closed. The boy's legs were bowed out with rickets, and one foot turned sharply inward, so he must always be falling over it. His trousers were whole enough, but his coat was more darn than fabric, a washed-out moon-colour that might once have been indigo blue.

"I ain't done nothing wrong." The boy sniffed until his hazel eyes were dry, then wrapped the overlarge jacket almost twice around himself. "Can I go now?"

"What's your name?" Perry asked, as gently as he could—it would not do to blame a child for the sins of his elders.

"Ruan." The boy wiped the sniffles from beneath his nose with a grubby fist. "I don't have to tell you anything, my mum says."

This time Perry's smile was more genuine. Ruan's attitude reminded Perry of the mudlarks of the Thames, who scraped a living by combing the river's silty banks for lost coins and rags they could sell to the paper mills for a penny a bundle. He remembered when he had been that defiant himself, and that convinced that he was very grown-up.

"Well, she's wrong." Perry smiled, softly but implacably. "I can in fact have you brought in front of the magistrate, and he can force you to give a statement."

Ruan's eyes widened, but the glow of self-importance on his small face suggested he was imagining what a heroic figure he would cut. How the other boys would envy him. "Would they flog me? Would they have *thumbscrews*?"

Since this speculation didn't seem to be producing the effect he had intended, Perry took a step forward, tensing himself for the moment the boy turned to run. "Let's not get ahead of ourselves. Where do you live, Ruan? I'd like to talk to your mother."

That certainly seemed to put the fear of God into the boy. He turned, and as he did, Perry reached out a long arm and lifted him off his feet by the back of his collar.

"Let me go! Put me down!"

"I don't mean her any harm. I just want to have a sit-down with her and a chat."

Ruan's legs thrashed in an attempt to kick or to run. "But I got a baby. Baby sister. Cadan says you people eat babies."

"Cadan is enormously ill-informed and ignorant," Perry shot back, refusing to lose his temper with a child. "But if I promise not to eat anyone, will you take me to your house? I can stand here with you dangling from my fist all afternoon."

The leg windmill flailed to a halt, leaving Ruan dangling as limply as if he had been melted. "All right, I will. But only 'cause I know you'd find it anyway."

"That's the spirit." Perry smiled.

Ruan's "house" was a lean-to of driftwood and tarpaulin in the shelter of a middle-class family's outbuildings. It was one such hut among several similar shambles, assembled around what had once been a formal knot garden, but was now a square of packed earth with an open fire pit in the centre. Perry had to step over three insensible adults—one lying in a pool of gin-scented vomit—to reach the greasy upright that Ruan indicated, and scratch on the tentlike wall for anyone inside to come out.

"Shh, shh, shh!" An older woman with a dandelion head of frizzled white hair clambered through the low door and straightened up with a groan at the sight of him, one hand on the small of her back, the other holding the tent flap closed. The gesture was reminiscent of Zuliy holding Quick's door closed while he made a run for the sea, but this time the dwelling was so tiny, Perry could see all around it, could see that no one was escaping.

"Don't wake the baby!" Ruan's mother whispered, pushing Perry backwards toward the fire. "Poor mite. I give her a nip of gin to take the pain away, but this'll be the first time she's slept going on two days. What can I do for you now lad? You in trouble?"

"He *is* trouble, mam," Ruan piped up. "This is that new customs man as was almost drownded the other day trying to help that slave. He says he don't eat people, but—"

"Of course he doesn't." Ruan's mother had the same deformity of the foot, and she limped forward like one whose every joint is sore, but the hand she laid on Ruan's head was proud. Reassuring. "Come by the fire," she said to Perry, indicating a couple of sawn-through barrels evidently meant to serve as seats. "And I'll make you a cup of tea."

She took down a piece of brown-stained linen from a line stretched above the ashes, and shook what were evidently twice used tea-leaves into a pot. A cauldron of water was already simmering, hung from a tripod of driftwood, so a ladle or two later she was able to pour the tea straight into a hand-gouged wooden bowl.

"Tastes like piss water," she commiserated when he winced, and stretched out her bare feet toward the fire. "I buys the leaves already used from Matthews the grocer in town. He gets 'em from the Quicks, and they charge a pretty penny for 'em, though I reckons they use them three times themselves and add nettles to bulk it out."

If she could afford tea of any kind, she had aspirations and resources above the very lowest of the low, but the poverty still made Perry itch with shame. It was worse, somehow, to see the squalor of human desperation amid the clear floating light of the Cornish coast. In London, it at least harmonized with the fog and the dirt.

"Speaking of Quicks," he began in a gentle voice, "I was visiting with Tomas Quick when young Ruan here ran in to say he knew where the sailor captured during the storm was being held. Do you know anything about that?"

"Could've asked me that," Ruan interrupted, scooting up tight to Perry's side and reaching out a filthy hand toward Perry's embroidered waistcoat. For some reason, it had taken Perry's fancy to wear his best clothes to arrest Quick, and the waistcoat was heavily stitched with golden flowers. According to Perry's mother, it made him look dashing, but Ruan was not the person he had hoped to impress. He twitched his coat shut and buttoned it.

"Barnabas, his name is, and the miners at the Summersea lode are keeping him. That's all I know." Ruan offered the information, and his mother nodded.

"That's as much as I know too."

"But Mr. Quick was looking to buy a slave?" Perry's gut wrenched at the thought—another combination of anger and shame—the wish that he never had to be put into this manner of situation ever again. Even his waistcoat rebuked him. Ruan's hands, after all, might be cleaner than Quick's.

"Tomas Quick be dealing in slaves?" Ruan's mother frowned at him over her flavourless tea. "No, you don't know the man. He don't hold with that."

Perry snorted a humourless laugh. "He told me himself he had a deal with a slave trader in Liverpool. This is a very flimsy tissue of lies, madam, with each of you contradicting the other. You had better just tell me. If the unfortunate Mr. Barnabas is found and liberated, then no crime has taken place, and you, madam, will have been the agent responsible for restoring the boon of liberty to a suffering soul."

Ruan's mother tucked a limp strand of iron-grey hair into her bonnet—an item that was exactly the same colour as the tea-cloth. She laughed. "You should write poetry in your spare time, Mr. Customs Man. I'd be moved if you han't called me a liar first. But I ain't lying." Her gaze slid off him and wandered to the end of the street, where the skeleton of an old, burnt-out house was being crawled over by a gang of builders. A rumble and cloud of dust spoke of an untrustworthy wall being taken down.

"I were up at the Angel," she offered, "this morning. That's where I heard about the miners being the ones who had Barnabas. Tomas Quick, he'd already put the word out he was to be tole if anyone knew. But not so he could buy 'im. So he could free 'im. He's a gentleman, is Tomas. Which is more'n I can say for the others of that name."

"To free him?" Perry repeated, refusing to acknowledge the stir of relief in his breast. This was nonsense of course—the sort of thing any criminal might say of their accomplice. "Then why would he tell me otherwise?"

"I don't know." She laughed and, digging deep in her skirt pocket, brought out a penny, which she passed to her son. "Go buy us a loaf of bread and a fish for dinner, Ruan. Your brother gets paid tomorrow."

They ate well enough, then; Perry revised his estimate of the family's wealth upwards. Money to stretch until the next payday was luxury on par with money to splash out on tea. Though, doubtless, not having to pay rent was a factor.

Ruan's mother watched him limp cheerfully away, and turned back to Perry with a convincing expression of candour. "Tomas Quick's proud, ain't he?" she said. "Or humble—with him the two ain't that far apart. Didn't want to boast, is what I'm thinking. Or didn't want you to blab to folks in the excise who might not be trustworthy. But he's probably organizing with some friends to go rescue the poor man right now."

This was plainly ridiculous, if only because Perry wanted to believe it so much. He imagined the subterranean darkness being riven by a lantern held by a tall figure who moved through the gloom with the cutting certainty and speed with which his ship leaped though the waves. Imagined being rescued—chains falling away, and the blissful climb into cleansing sunlight. A pleasing fairy tale. That never was how it really went.

"And that absolves him of being a smuggler, does it?" Perry asked, catching his jaw before it could clamp tight.

Ruan's mother laughed again. "If he was a smuggler—and I don't say as he is—you'd do better to come to some arrangement with him. Folks around here would thank you for it. When my husband drownded last winter, I thought we'd all be dead come spring, but Tomas Quick give my eldest a job, and so we eat, and soon we'll have money enough to move into a proper room. You take him away, there's a lot of poor people'll be after your neck. Can't say the same for any of the other Quicks. Met any of them?"

"I have the honour to have been personally chosen by Sir Lazarus to clean up this town and restore the rule of law," Perry said. It didn't sound as impressive, heard aloud, as it had when cherished in his heart, and Ruan's mother scoffed at it, rolling her eyes.

"That whited sepulchre? His time is coming, and the time of all like him. Their heads will roll and their blood will water the ground. Just look at France."

Chapter Twelve

PERRY IS UNWELCOME

*P*erry was not certain if an unfettered revolutionary populace would be kinder to the men of his race than the status quo, and as he seemed to have got as much help from Ruan's mother as she was willing to give, he made his excuses and let her be. She had let something slip for all her partisanship; "*I were up at the Angel. That's where I heard about the miners being the ones who had Barnabas.*"

So someone at the Angel & Eagle public house could tell him more. He set out at once for the pub's commanding position on the lip of Big Guns Cove.

His quick pace brought the blood into his injuries, made the rope galls around his wrists sting and ache from where he had struggled against his bindings in the warehouse. Though he had dashed off a flippant line about the experience to his mother, he had barely had time to think about the incident at the warehouse since Jowan had rolled up late at the head of equally reluctant "reinforcements" and laughed at him for being outplayed.

The customs men stationed on the cannons had been coming round by then, commiserating with each other over the bad design of the cannon platforms and the strength of their headaches. But even they had been curiously phlegmatic about the incident. There had been no outrage or anger, only ruefulness as though this kind of thing was only to be expected.

"Don't you care?" Perry had asked, as soon as he'd been cut free. Jowan's continual smile, in the centre of all that open space where once there had been salvage, had irked him more than usual. "They made a fool of us." *He made a fool of me.* "They may as well have announced in the town square that they have no respect for us, and that criminals may do what they please. It needs to be stopped!"

Jowan had given an easy shrug. "Wrack from the sea," he'd said. "It don't belong to customs, nor fine folk in London. We lost our bonuses for recovering it, but the wealth will come back to Porthkennack one way or another. It's naught to lose your life or temper over."

As Perry turned onto the narrow coastal path that would take him up the cliffs, he wondered if he should report the entire town to Lord Petersfield. The riding officers were apathetic to the point of collusion, and everyone he spoke to seemed to be implicated or at the very least supportive of the smuggling. It was hard being the only honest man in the service. Little surprise that Lazarus Quick was so sour, with even his own house servants against him.

Did he know the poor people of Porthkennack were wishing murder on him? Should Perry tell him?

He rubbed at the hinges of his jaw, where the inevitable ache was building, trying to forestall the blossoming of full cranial pain. If wishes were horses, everyone would ride, and he had no desire to bring trouble to a homeless woman and her child. Mere jealousy was probably at the bottom of her words, and who could blame her for that?

The Angel and Eagle was a fine, whitewashed building, Tudor in style. The exposed beams were black with protective tar, and the times of the stagecoach were written over the arch into the stable courtyard.

A pump in the centre of the cobbled yard had a narrow bed of feverfew around it, the pungent lemon scent doing nothing to disguise the reek of horses. The stables themselves seemed clean—the tack hanging from the walls supple with oil, the mangers full and the piles of hay in each cell brown only at the edges.

There were a hundred hiding spots for small kegs and bales in the ground floor alone, and above it a hay loft beneath a thatched roof that might conceal a thousand more.

The path had been dry, but he scraped his boots off at the scraper by the side door anyway and went in.

Two steps down and along a short, twisty corridor, he found the door for the main room. The din of voices within faltered and fell silent as he stepped inside, but he had expected as much and stared back coolly at the other guests. Sailors, for the most part, undoubtedly drinking down their wages on their shore leave, faces florid and pockets overflowing. A knot of miners sat by the fire, where a pot of something savoury bubbled—a kind of fish stew by the smell. A woman with a ladle and a choker of Belgian lace was the first to stir out of that forbidding silence and acknowledge him.

She rustled over—a comfortably plump woman in a rusty-red petticoat and embroidered yellow day dress of a fabric that must have cost a pretty penny when new, but had been worn thin. It might have been bought secondhand, or saved up for and worn continually. It was right on the border of suspicious luxury, as was that flash of swan-embroidered lace at her throat.

"I'm the landlady here; Mary Castille. What can I do for you, Officer?" she beamed. Her voice seemed overloud, but perhaps that was her nature. "You are that new riding officer, started here this last week? I was sorry to hear about the warehouse being emptied. You must be shook."

Someone hidden behind her fichu-wrapped shoulder sniggered. Perry marvelled again at the speed with which local gossip ran around this town, and wondered what swan-lace reminded him of.

"Perhaps we could speak somewhere more privately?" he asked. "Your husband, yourself, and I, that is."

"You'll have a job speaking to my husband. He's been dead these ten years." She shrugged. "But come help me change a barrel in the taproom and you can have a word there."

From the brief glimpse he saw of them, before he had to concentrate on rolling a hogshead of ale up the stairs, the pub's cellars were extensive, and doors opening on every wall suggested they ramified beyond his sight. The barrel he had been asked to move was marked with the red star of a local brewery, but without examining all the others, there was no knowing what contraband might be stacked among the lawful purchases. He should be making a search even now, and would be, if he had not been hard on the scent of the kidnapped sailor. But a human life was of more consequence than a few smuggled barrels, and—

And so I find my own reasons to neglect my duty, he chided himself. But his reasons were at least good ones.

"All right, then." Mrs. Castille cocked her head at the sight of him rolling the barrel laboriously up the steps. The regular grunt of Perry's effort and thud of the wood rolling onto the next stair brought the volume of her voice down to a level that approached private. "What was it you wanted to say?"

"There was a man taken up alive from the wreckage that came ashore last week," Perry started without accusation or pressure. "A sailor, like so many other men of this town. But because of his complexion, this man is being held captive and sold to the highest bidder like a pile of crockery. A freeborn man, risking his life on the sea in the service of this country. Tell me your heart does not go out to him."

Mrs. Castille's hands dropped to her beer-stained apron and twisted it. Probably from a trade spent working indoors, she had a nigh-aristocratic pallor, against which her green eyes stood out like plaques of sacred jade. There was some emotion in them, but Perry couldn't tell if it was guilt, regret, or fear.

"It does," she agreed, opening the door at the head of the stairs so he could bump the barrel over into the corridor. "I do have a heart for any sailor on the sea. But I also have a responsibility to my own children, don't I? Both my sons of the body and my little foundlings who'd have no one to care for them without me."

"You think Barnabas's captors would harm you if you spoke to me?" Perry halted the roll of the barrel and straightened up for a moment, trying to impress her with his sincerity and willingness to protect her. "If you are afraid of someone, tell me and I'll deal with them. Or call on me when you need me—"

Mrs. Castille laughed, like a woman trying to be encouraging about a child's slate of wobbly first words. "They don't make appointments, these people," she said, in a genuine whisper now, hard even for him to hear. "They're not going to give me time to send a boy running to you and wait for you both to arrive."

The front of the inn looked out on farmland golden with barley, but the back overhung a cave-riddled cliff beneath which the long breakers of the Atlantic beat. The shore-path there was more suitable for goats than humans, passing by a dozen sheer drops where a loose-lipped woman might disappear forever, weighed down by the money in her pocket.

"I could ask Sir Quick to furnish a guard for you. If you were willing to testify in court to information that allowed us to put some or all of these villains in jail, I'm sure he would consider it."

"Bless you, love." Her regretful expression transformed into something worldly, even patronizing. "You do want to talk to that Sir Lazarus. You do, right enough. But not about giving me guards."

"What then?"

She set a red boot to the barrel and gave it a shove, sending it rolling once again. A series of practiced kicks took it over the threshold to the tap room, with her following close behind. "And that's all I'm saying about it."

When Perry went to follow, the door closed in his face.

He rocked back and set his shoulders to the wall opposite, while he overcame his instinct to shove back in just because he could. Cultivating informants who knew they could trust him was important, and was not achieved by being overbearing.

A heaviness settled in his stomach as he let her words sink in. While the whole town seemed to cheerfully agree that Tomas Quick was a smuggler and a good man with it, these hints of accusation towards the magistrate and his family also recurred. Perry found them almost more suspicious because they were so wary, so tentative. No one, he realised, was afraid of Tomas, nor reluctant to admit a connection to him, but Lazarus was a different matter.

It had been like sitting in a silver box, in Lazarus's study. Surrounded by opulence, beauty, culture. Perry's desire to be part of that world was so intense it almost tasted like salt in his mouth. He would not believe that a man with such power and such position would use it badly—What could he possibly gain that he did not already have in plenty? No. It was jealousy, simple as that. Jealousy and an attempt to throw Perry off the true scent.

Tomas's vivid face was bright and contemptuous in his memory, unimpressed by the pistol trained between his eyes. Looking at him was like looking into the flame of an oil lantern, where the fire was blue hot and a kind of raging magic was almost tangible. As a child, Perry would have poked at the flame, trying to touch and know it.

So now he decided to go back and talk to the man again. Something would give if he did—he could almost feel it now, realigning in his own chest.

He left the inn by the back door and walked with his right hand swinging out over the sail-flecked sea. Another cloudy morning had cleared into sunlight, and a sky like an indigo dome sealed over the land. He was watching his feet amid the tan dust of the narrow path, clambering over inset rocks and trying not to crush the yellow samphire flowers, and at first the faint sound of voices didn't strike him as threatening. It was the laugh, maybe, that made him stop and look back, piercing him with a fear sudden as a marlin-spike through the eye.

Three young men were on the path behind him, cockades of black feathers in their hats. That should not have been suspicious in itself, but for the way they met his eyes—a cold gaze, a malicious smile, and a challenge.

To Perry's right, a foot of grass sloped at a forty-five-degree angle before giving way to an almost sheer drop over needles of rock in a basin of spume. To his left, a wall of rock rose higher than his head—nowhere in sight to hide. He sped his pace, aiming for a bend in the path where an ancient blackthorn tree made a tangled thicket of thorny boughs. Maybe there he would find a cut-through, where he could get out, up onto the tussocky moor that swept up to the barley. Anything to get off this narrow ribbon of a foothold over a deadly drop.

His pursuers sped up behind him. And when he rounded the faithless tree, two men straightened up, truncheons tapping against the palms of their hands, and smiled as though they had been lying in wait specifically for him.

CHAPTER THIRTEEN

A GOOD USE FOR A PRESS GANG

Perry drew his pistol, flattening himself against the rock wall on the land side of the path. Fleetingly, he wished for his partner. Would even ambush wipe the smile from Jowan's face? Probably not, considering he might easily be complicit. There was no friendship in this town for Perry—no one who would come to his aid now.

"The first one that moves toward me gets a bullet in the head," he threatened. At least if he had to kill the locals, he knew the magistrate would be on his side. "And the next goes over the cliff."

Something smacked into the wall just beside his gun hand, peppering his skin with sharp flakes of rock. A stone. One of the men on the high ground, on the inn-side of the track, had a slingshot. Already another pebble was in its pouch and the man was whirling it above his head. He might have pockets full of stones, and he could pick more straight off the ground. Perry swung the pistol in his direction but hesitated. For now, they were holding back—none of them eager to be the person who took his bullet. But once that single shot had been taken, they would all be eager to rush and overwhelm him before he could load the pistol with another.

"You talk like we ha'nt done this before," said the taller of the two men downhill from him. Perry almost turned to look—was almost distracted enough to miss the silent flight of the next shot. But he caught the movement as one end of the sling was released to fly out like a black whip against the blue sky. He jerked violently to the side, and the wind of the projectile swept his cheek as a rock the size of his fist passed his face and shattered on the wall. Splinters of granite drove toward his eye.

Instinctively, he shut both eyes and flinched further away, his aim faltering. That was when they charged.

Bodies slammed into him from both directions, hurling him hard against the wall. He managed to get his arms up to protect his head from the truncheons, but the long bones of his forearms threatened to break as the heavy wood came down on them like hammers. Pain seared through him. His hands shook, and though he could not see where he was pointing the pistol, he fired it anyway.

The boom and blaze of gunpowder bought him a brief space while his assailants froze. In that pause, Perry braced himself on the wall, got both legs up between himself and the man directly in front of him—the one who had spoken—and kicked him away with all his strength.

The man reeled backward, across the narrow width of the path. He doubled up, his hands clutching at the air as he tried to slow his momentum. But then his foot was over the drop, his toe slipped on a patch of moss, and he went over, hands scrabbling for purchase all the way.

Fuck me, thought Perry, who had never killed a man before. *Oh shit, this is real.*

Until now, a part of him had believed he was only facing a beating—that he would surely end up unconscious and trussed up for Jowan to find on his rounds. Tomas's robbery of the warehouse had given him expectations of being treated gently. But those expectations dissipated now, as the man with the slingshot drew a long knife whose glitter pulsed like lightning in Perry's already spinning head. A part of himself was shrieking, thin and shrill, but another part had come up out of the darkness like a bubble of lava, and his chest was full of power and fire.

Getting his feet back under him, he launched himself at the man with the knife, grabbed his wrist, and pulled with all his weight, forcing the man's hand into the wall behind him. The *crack* of knuckles meeting rock was like the *pop* of distant shotguns. The knife jangled as it hit the ground, and its wielder yelled bloody murder, punching Perry in the throat with his left hand.

Knife-guy reeled away, clutching his bleeding fist to his chest, but Perry's throat seized up too—something seemed to have broken in there. He couldn't get air past the obstruction.

He fought to breathe, as silver spots snowed before his eyes. The hunched posture opened his back to his attackers, and a cudgel cracked down on his spine. Another lunged in to his ribs, horizontally, and the shattering pain of both forced him to whoop out a sob and proved to him that he could still breathe.

His discharged pistol was in his hand. Bent over, he brought its hard wood and steel pommel down on an attacker's knee, hoping to force another man to withdraw.

Instead, the man fell heavily, straight onto Perry's back. The unexpected burden made him tip forward too. He had barely caught himself on his hands and knees when knife-guy kicked his elbows out from beneath him, and the third man flopped his weight on top of the pile, flattening Perry against the ground.

Breathing felt like raising the world with one hand. His bruised ribs shrieked, and his eyes watered at the pain. His heart stopped dead as knife-guy picked up his blade with his off hand and tossed it a couple of times flamboyantly.

"I'm going to cut your throat now, you tuss! You're going over that cliff, and to hell with it."

Panic roaring through him like a leaping fire, Perry heaved against the weight pinning him, and felt the body-pile rock to starboard. He was aching and exhausted. Everything hurt, but with a harder heave and a sideways shuffle, he might be able to wriggle out again, get past them, and sprint away down the track to safety.

As he prepared himself, bracing for a second all-or-nothing shove, a snatch of the tune of "Rodney's Glory" gusted to him on the wind, hummed by a gravelly voice. Was someone coming? Were they rescuers or another threat?

"We shouldn't kill him, Eli," the fourth man, who had hung back on the edges of the fight, intervened. Only his ankles were in Perry's range of sight, and they were thin and bare. His voice was diffident and young, shaking slightly. "We should put him with the other one. Sell 'em both, that's a whole hundred pounds between us."

A guilt Perry had been scarcely conscious of feeling lifted off his back like the weight of a third man. These were the slavers—the ones who had taken Barnabas. If anyone deserved to be kicked over a cliff edge, it was them.

"Billy, you leave the plotting to us," said knife-guy, aka Eli, "He knows who we are, and he's got fancy patrons here and in London. They'd listen to this one if he got out and he lived."

The humming was definitely coming closer—coming from further down the path. A voice spoke, and another laughed in answer. A group of people must be walking up the coast road toward the inn.

"Help me!" Perry yelled with all his might. "Help! Murder!"

The bodies draped over his back jolted with surprise. He seized his chance to buck them upwards, and then rolled out from beneath them, spilling them onto their backs. They scrabbled to their feet, but he was already running at a crabbed trot before he'd managed to straighten up. Outrage and fear gave him a speed and sureness of foot like a spooked deer.

The path turned in a sharp bend outwards, to the right, and another weathered tree, clenched into the cliff edge, had masked the approach of strangers. He had run into the middle of them before he registered their clothes—pea jackets worn open over trousers of white duck, the seams of which were embroidered with ribbons. Little round hats with a black ribbon around the crown on which, in gold, was embroidered the name HMS *Harbinger*.

At the back of the party, a naval lieutenant, shiny in blue and gold, caught Perry's eye and held it with interest. "Murder?"

Perry thought fast. The sailors, too, were all carrying cudgels. A press-gang then, going up to the inn to recruit every admissible man to his majesty's navy.

He blessed his habit of always carrying his papers. "I'm Riding Officer Dean of this county." He offered them to the lieutenant. "I was just set upon by four smugglers. Good seamen all, I'm sure. Once you've pressed them, I would value a chance to question them—a man's life is in danger."

The lieutenant ran a snappy dark eye down Perry's identification and recommendation and raised his eyebrows in momentary surprise. But then he nodded, and six of his eight tars broke into a rolling bulldog run, inelegant but very fast, up the path toward Perry's assailants.

Perry followed—he wanted to see the tables turned, see how *they* enjoyed being outnumbered and overwhelmed.

The initial shock of the encounter was all he could hope for, as Eli was knocked off his feet by the first two seamen and pinned to the dusty ground himself, cudgel down hard on the nape of his neck as the second tar bound his wrists behind him. As he was passed back, writhing and kicking, into the hands of the lieutenant's two guards, he took the chance to spit in Perry's face.

Perry wiped it off with a smile. It was not quite slavery to which the man was going, but he'd be confined to a warship for however long it took to break him in, to ensure he would not run if he was let loose. Not perfect, but Perry would wring whatever irony he could from it.

It was hard to see what was happening with the other three men, mobbed as they were. A moment passed in which the knot of elbows and shoving clubs could not be parsed. And then one of the smugglers tripped, taking his attackers down with him. There was a brief gap in the scrum, and the thin boy, Billy, used it to scrabble out of reach.

He gave a great grasshopper leap, long arms outstretched. His fingers latched on to tiny gaps in the sheer rock wall of the landside of the path. His toes, in his soft seaboots, seemed to grab on too, and spiderlike he swarmed to the top and threw himself over onto the moor.

If he got away, he would tell Barnabas's captors that Perry was following. They would move their captive, or lie in wait for Perry and shoot him this time.

Without finishing the thought, he threw himself forward, shouldered his way through the brawl and faced the wall himself. He would not have believed a man could scale it if he had not seen it with his own eyes, but perhaps if he put his right hand in that hollow, he could reach up with the left and cling where the tiny outcropping of speedwell was already bruised by Billy's weight.

Fighting the urge to close his eyes, the narrowness of the path behind him and the knowledge of the long drop on its other side pressing on his mind, he splayed himself flat against the rock wall and followed.

CHAPTER FOURTEEN

INTO THE DARK

By the time he reached the top of the wall and rolled over onto a patch of long-leafed grass and moss in the moor beyond, Perry's legs were trembling and the palms of his hands were scraped raw. Muscles in his fingers, that he hadn't known he possessed, ached and shook. Behind him the sound of the brawl rumbled on, but as he raised his head, he forgot it all in a wave of incredulity and thankfulness that he had not been a little later.

From where he lay, the moor undulated gently up to the farmland. The grey greens and ambers of the heather, blotched with emerald mosses, were bisected by a ruler-straight line of golden crops. No trees or boulders marred the view which seemed to stretch on unimpeded from one side of the Porthkennack promontory to the other. He would have sworn there was nowhere to hide, if he had not been watching with his own eyes as the torso of Billy seemed to slowly descend into the earth itself.

The boy's back was to him, so Perry was free to gape as the narrow shoulders in their scruffy yellow coat, the long plait of chestnut hair, and finally the head with its unfortunate woollen hat disappeared into the ground with a sliding, swaying motion like one going down a ladder at sea.

Afraid of being seen, Perry crawled forward on hands and knees, never taking his gaze from the spot where he had had his last glimpse of felted mushroom hat. If he looked away, he could search for days without finding the place again.

Even when he came close enough to see it, it was hard to believe. A square of utter darkness had opened in the land. Its lip was two inches of soil threaded with white roots, giving way to nothing with terrifying abruptness. There was a hole in the country, just lying there uncovered for anyone to fall down, and from two feet away it was as invisible as a ha-ha from a mansion window.

When he had overcome his horror at the unnatural nature of the thing, Perry straightened up and paced carefully around it. Once he was on the opposite side, he could see that sunlight did in fact slant into the hole and light the side that Billy had been facing. Below the thin scrim of turf on the surface, the ground became solid rock. A hand's breadth from the top, two ring bolts had been hammered into the stone. A rope ladder hung from them, its cord and its round slats covered in mud and moss.

This must be a way into the mines young Ruan had mentioned—an escape route or an air shaft. Perry flexed his grazed hands, willed his legs to firm up, and sitting on the edge of the shaft, he felt for the first rung.

He was in to his waist when a wind stirred the darkness below him and an unearthly groaning hummed up into his face. The shock almost loosened his grip, made his hard leather soles slip on the treacherous rungs. But he clung tight and thought of organ pipes; they were close to the sea. Perhaps the water was moving down there, displacing the air. Such a phenomenon might cause a moan of impeccable philosophic provenance. If it moaned like a wounded monster, that was surely only Perry's poetic imagination.

Still, continuing down the shaft as the light failed, with no way to guess the depth of the drop, his arms and legs cramping and shuddering, was one of the bravest things he had ever done. When his questing foot met a rough stone floor instead of another rung, he put his face to the wall and clung there a moment, breathing steadily, half in thanks and half in an attempt to piece his nerves back together.

It was not, he saw when he turned his face to the passage, pitch-dark down here after all. A brown glow lit the walls to his right, though even as he watched it seemed to grow dimmer, and the darkness rushed forward from Perry's left to fill the rough-hewn places it had vacated.

Billy must have lit a lantern, be walking away, carrying it. Quietly as he could, Perry followed, arse aching as he fought to move silently over the rough ground.

The passageway, which had been large enough for him to stand up in, drew down until he was crouched with his hands braced on his knees. He passed the black mouths of two other tunnels, and one that shone faintly. Only when he had gone past it and lost the ability to see his own hands did he realize that the light he was following had turned off the straight path. The tunnel was now so tight that he couldn't turn around. He could only shuffle backwards until he could find a side passage that seemed to be slightly more illuminated than the others, turn into it to try to catch up, pressure and panic nagging at him, as though his whole existence depended on keeping close to the tail end of the light.

Two further turns and then a ladder, even more rickety and thickly coated in slime than the one at the entrance. He lost all confidence that he was still following the right man. What if Billy knew these tunnels well enough to navigate without a light? Perry might then simply be following the closest miner. What if Billy had known he was being followed, extinguished his light while Perry had gone on into that blind corner, and Perry, coming out again, had followed someone else entirely? Then all this would be for nothing.

Perry had nightmares like this sometimes, dreams in which he began by mislaying something important, only to search for it endlessly down ever ramifying corridors, until he would gladly have given it up if he could only stop. If he could only get out.

At the top of the ladder, his will-o'-the-wisp guided him down another crabbed tunnel. And then, as if there was not horror enough in being totally lost and buried under the earth, the tunnel floor fell away into an abyss. He stopped in time to see a pebble, dislodged by his foot, fall into nothingness, and felt as though he had plummeted with it.

Across the abyss, which was a little over ten feet wide, two unsecured planks had been dropped. In the waning light, he could still see the muddy footprints over their surface where someone had scampered as confidently across them as though they were unending stone.

The drop seemed to suck at his feet. His tongue felt hot and coppery as his mouth dried, all the water in him seeming to concentrate in his legs. Every place that had so recently been injured seemed to wail in his bones in protest at the thought of carrying on. His feet would slither out from under him if he stepped forward. He would overbalance. He would fall, and no one would ever know where he'd gone.

His mother's letter lay unfinished in his room. It would be packed up and sent to her with his small chest of belongings if he disappeared here, and the thought of her mourning was like a blow to the chest.

But every moment he hesitated, the light he was following drew away. And if he did not cross, he would be as lost down here as if he had fallen.

"CARELESSLY over the plain away, Where by the boldest man no path Cut before thee thou canst discern, Make for thyself a path! Silence, loved one, my heart! Cracking, let it not break! Breaking, break not with thee!" he thought, consoling himself with poetry. Then, holding his breath, he plunged forward.

The planks bounded under him like the deck of a ship, forcing him into a stumbling run. Panic hit him like lightning—he was going to fall—but he managed to get another foot under him and to push himself to fall onto the platform of stone on the other side, the bruising impact of stone on his knees a benediction.

As he paused to gather his breath and nerves, the sound of distant voices caught his ear. From this position, the glow at the end of the passage was stronger rather than fainter. He could see where the tunnel kinked to the right, and could smell gunpowder and tobacco and the sweet-sour reek that was human sweat dried into unwashed clothes.

Enemies or no, the presence of other people gave him strength. As silently as he could, he edged up to the bend in the tunnel and peeked round.

Two steps beyond the turn, the tunnel opened out into an underground gallery the size of a small cathedral. A pile of barrels at the entrance blocked most of Perry's view, but was also a good place to hide and observe. He crept up behind them, noting that while most were marked as containing blasting powder, at least two had the broad arrow of government supplies, and one, barely in sight even in the improved light, bore the *Hyacinth*'s name and the symbol for brandy.

He wedged himself in between two of the lowest tier of barrels and watched through the crack. Now he could see into the large cavern, which was well-lit with candle lanterns. White stalactites like canine teeth lanced down from the ceiling and gave the place an unpleasantly organic air. It was clammy enough to be the inside of a giant's mouth, certainly.

The men who had gathered in the cavern seemed too deep in conversation to be made uneasy by their surroundings. And perhaps as miners it was homelike enough to them. They sat on tumbled boulders and unladen sleds with their pipes lit as if they were in their own living rooms.

Billy was not among them. Nor could Perry see feather cockades in any of the hats. Every one of his attackers had borne one, and it had come to him since that perhaps the feathers were a badge—an emblem of some organization or crew. So perhaps . . . Perry loosed a deep sigh that made his ribs throb. Perhaps he had lost his quarry after all, and this was an innocent meeting of working men.

"Maybe the doctors should charge less. When the revolution comes—"

"You young pipsqueak! It won't come, not here, and even if it does, 'twill be too late for Amos's daughter. We got to do this, for her."

The first speaker was beardless and rangy, his face a red mask of mud, and his hair sticking stiffly around the brim of his hat as though he had clutched it with clay-covered hands. The second, if his position in the middle of the circle of men was an indicator, seemed to be an authority of sorts. He was twisting a cloth in his hands, then stroking it over his face, leaving his skin and grey beard damp and cleaner. His hands seemed to tremble, and there was a tic in his left eye that was probably due to nerves.

"We could have a whip round," the boy insisted. "Between the lot of us, surely we can raise—"

That drew a clamour of voices: "I can barely feed my own childer."

"If I don't make the rent this month—"

"My Mary needs a doctor too. Are you going to pay for her?"

"Look, none of us likes this," said the elder, still wiping himself down—*like Pontius Pilate*, Perry thought, *that's not going to make you clean*. This might not be Billy's crew, but something untoward was afoot here nevertheless. "But we got to make ends meet. And none of us wants to make enemies like young Mr. C." He raised a hand to forestall another protest. "Plus, it's the life he knows. Probably doing a kindness to him. Not as though he's got big prospects outside, is it?"

Perry frowned. Was he wrong about Billy's black-feathered crew being a different organization than this? It did sound like they were discussing doing something inimical to a person, and selling a man into slavery would fit. Who was this "Mr. C."? And what did they mean by "it's the life he knows"? Barnabas was a free man and a sailor.

Perry edged forward a little, in the hope that an obvious cell door would be visible. But it wasn't—the cavern only opened on more passages, disorganized and dirty and likely impossible to navigate without a guide.

A guide I must have, then, he thought, conscious, now that he had stopped moving, of the draught of clean air blowing in from the passage down which he had come. It hit his back and ruffled the small hairs at the nape of his neck, carrying the rhythmic sounds of distant knocking from where miners were at work in other galleries. If Barnabas was a prisoner here, it would be necessary to wait until someone was sent to feed him. Then he would follow them. He would have to have some method, afterward, of inducing them to guide Barnabas and himself back out into the light, and at that thought he began to try the lids of the closest gunpowder barrels. If he could just get powder enough to recharge his pistol . . .

His fingers were around a lid, rough and stinking with sulphur, when the air grew suddenly warmer at his back. He barely had time to realize that *Those were footsteps I heard. Footsteps, not chisel blows!* when the man who had come up the passageway behind him brought something down hard on Perry's head and all the lights went out.

CHAPTER FIFTEEN

FACE-TO-FACE WITH THE UNDERWORLD

Perry's knees throbbed with a sharp red pain that he was aware of a long time before he realized that his head was also splitting. The head pain had been so ubiquitous that at first he had thought it was only some texture of the darkness—that the world itself naturally cycled through tides of squeezing and nausea, rather than the pain being something inside himself.

It was a little like the night terrors he had suffered as a boy—his mind had wakened, but his body lay as if pinned under a demonic weight—and for a long time he could not move or even groan.

Knowing what he would see if he opened his eyes before he was truly awake, he concentrated on flexing his toes, clenching his fingers. Nothing seemed broken. When he did risk cracking an eyelid open, the faintest bloom of brown spilled in through an iron-barred gate and showed him the roughly hewn walls of a tiny storeroom.

"Ugh. Not again," he moaned, trying to push himself up onto an elbow. The movement made his nausea crest and a wave of inner dark explode behind his eyes. He clamped his watering mouth shut and swallowed down the reflex to vomit.

Slim hands tucked themselves under his armpits and tugged him until he was sitting. He tried to keep his eyes open during this manhandling but had to pinch them closed when his vision clouded with milky lights. There didn't seem any ill intention in the hands— once his torso was upright, they guided him to lean back until he was reclining on a slender chest, this support interposed between him and the wall like a living cushion.

"Barnabas?" he managed, when everything had stopped swaying.

The narrow chest behind him took in a shaky breath, but when his cellmate spoke, Perry understood neither the words nor the voice itself. A woman's voice? Or the voice of a child—but the chest was flat, and the hands that still cradled him were long and knob-knuckled like those of a man.

Perry wished for water and then for a greater light, feeling out of his depth and stupid. So stupid. Whatever was going on here, he had not comprehended it at all.

He levered himself away from the person's grasp. They clung to him as though they were taking more comfort from him than they were giving. As soon as he turned it became clear why: this was a black teenager, acne scarred, in water-stained silk trousers and a little waistcoat embroidered with gold thread. Even peering closer, Perry wasn't sure if they were male or female—beardless, with a soft layer of fat on their oval face, and their long hair—despite the sea—still weighed down with oil.

"Well, you're certainly not who I came to save," Perry muttered, mostly to himself. "But I'm going to save you anyway."

He turned to the bars and examined them. They were, unfortunately, the matt black of newly forged iron, not a bloom of red rust anywhere. The upper ends fitted firmly into sockets chiselled out of stone, the lower into two slabs mortared together. He tried rattling them, but they were firm on both ends and did not move.

Into this grille of bars, a narrow door had been set—he heaved on it—on simple ring-and-pin hinges. Under his straining effort, the door rose a finger's breadth on its pins before the upper edge clanged into the bar that had been soldered over the top to prevent an inmate from lifting the door off its pins. That bar, too, was soldered and solid.

The pin of the padlock was almost as thick as his finger. In the absence of a crowbar, he would not be forcing it. But with his face jammed between the widest bars, he could just make out the distant archway that was the source of the minimal light. The stalactite that hung like Damocles's sword over its jamb was the one he had seen when he was hiding behind the barrels, and that meant the door was an entrance to the large cavern. Perhaps if the clay-haired boy was there, he could talk his way out.

"Hey!" he shouted. "Hey, you in there! You're detaining an officer of His Majesty's Customs. I won't disappear as easily as a few barrels of brandy. This is a road you don't want to travel."

He thought of Jowan and his indolent smile. Jowan was not perhaps the greatest of threats to hold over these men, but he was what Perry had got.

"Let me out, or you'll have cause to regret it. You may think you have the customs in your pockets, but that will change in an instant if you kill one of their own."

He hoped so, at least. In the London station, even the most hated of colleagues—even Ellis Mobray who drowned puppies for a giggle—could count on the aid of every officer in a pinch, if only because next time it might be them. There, Perry would have known his friends were on their way. Here—walking on this knowledge was like walking on quicksand; he might still be regarded as expendable. But the miners didn't need to know that.

"You'll end up swinging from the noose," he yelled, "and who will look after your daughters and wives then?"

The distant doorway flickered and seemed to elongate into a strange shape with a darkness in the centre. When the shape seemed to snap, he saw it was the older man—the authority—carrying a lantern in his hand, its sphere of radiance separating from the light of the room as a bubble separates from the glass bottom of a tankard.

Perry's cellmate said something alarmed. Maybe a warning? Then they shrank to the back wall, jamming themself into a corner with their arms around their knees. They tucked their face into the cage of limbs—protecting themself. The little winks of gold from the embroidery on their clothes trembled like stars seen through flying cloud, and Perry's headache boiled away as anger filled him right up.

"You!" he snapped at the approaching miner, getting a guilty, peevish look in return. "What's your name?"

He had affected his most respectable accent, the one Lord Petersfield had instructed him to use when addressing nobility, and it seemed to shock a response out of the miner almost against his will.

"Jack, sir. Old Jack, on account of my brother's son is Young Jack."

Perry turned the silver spoon in his mouth into steel. "Well, Jack, my people will come after you. They will *come after you* and they will see you hang. I am a personal friend of Lord Petersfield of Marylebone. I cannot just be swept under the rug like insignificant dust.

"And this young man." He felt bad immediately at calling attention to the youth who was so carefully making himself into an invisible ball. But it had to be done. "He may have once been a slave, I don't know. But the moment his foot touched English soil, he became free. That is the law. There are no slaves in this country, and you are imprisoning an innocent . . . *person*. Let us both go now and I'll say no more about it, but—"

"I can't. I *can't*, master." The man's kerchief was now so soiled that when he wiped his forehead again, it left a red stripe. His eyes were wide, almost pleading, as if for Perry to have pity on him. "I'm a poor man, and if I don't do as my betters tell me, I'll end up on the street. Me and my family. I dursn't."

"What betters are these?" Perry asked, hoping and yet also dreading to hear the name of Tomas Quick. "If there is corruption afoot, I can help you. We could work together to free you from these noxious obligations."

"I . . ." Jack swallowed, his eyes following the bars of the cage until they came to rest on the ground in front of Perry's feet. His sigh was so disconsolate Perry wanted to scream—*If you don't want to do this, then don't do it! Have some heart, some backbone. Be a fucking man!*

"I dursn't go against the Quicks."

Perry's anger faltered in the face of something colder. So Tomas was responsible for this after all? It hurt to think of that beautiful vivid face harbouring so monstrous a spirit, but if his more righteous cousins wanted nothing to do with him because of it, that was remarkably progressive, laudable in them. No wonder they had been so quick to accept Perry—to give him their confidence and their trust.

"You are backing the wrong half of the family," he insisted. "Soon Tomas and his mother will be unable to harm you. I work for Sir Lazarus—he is intent on bringing the man down."

Old Jack's mouth fell open and he pressed his red rag to it to stifle some outcry. Perry thought it was protest but the ground shifted under him when he saw the shaking shoulders. It was laughter. "Bless you," Jack choked, his eyes shining with mirth. "For a moment there I thought you knew what you were talking about. It's Lazarus who'll buy you. Him or one of the Roscarrocks. Got plantations in the Indies, haven't they, and always an eye out for a bargain."

"Wait!" Perry exclaimed, because Jack had already begun to turn away, chuckling. "What do you mean?"

"Nearly the end of our shift." Jack turned fractionally back, to make a performance of checking his pocket watch. "So I'll say farewell now. Someone'll be by soon enough to put you aboard a ship for the colonies. Don't show off so much for them—they won't like it, and it won't do you no good." He paused, guilt washing strongly over his features again, and for a wild moment of hope, Perry believed Jack was having second thoughts. He allowed himself to wish for rescue.

"Maybe you can escape when you get there," Jack said, as though this was a consolation more for himself than for Perry. He walked away.

His light went with him. For a short time Perry and his cellmate were left in the dim gloom to which Perry had awoken, but gradually, insensibly, that began to dwindle too. The dark crept closer like a wolf at the edge of a failing fire, and the weight of the stone above his head leaned directly on his chest until he could barely breathe.

Another miner must have gone, taking his lamp with him. It had become almost too dark to see, and the sense of being trapped, suffocated, turned into an object that could be placed in its locked box until it was needed, became unbearable alone. Understanding the youth's greeting now, he lurched across the room by the last of the light and folded himself around the other person there, as if to confirm by touch that they both still lived, still breathed, still mattered.

Keeping thoughts of chains, of slavery out of his head—he would fight, he would kill them or himself—he took the youth's hand and patted his own head with it. "Perry."

"Perry?" the youth repeated, in that voice, strong as a man's, sweet as a woman's—an angelic voice, like that of a castrato singer. He was a eunuch then, Perry realized suddenly, one small mystery solved. He brought Perry's hand to his own head. Perry uncurled it and rested it there, on ringlets strangely textured by oil and dried salt water.

"Iskander."

This poor child. How long had he been down here, dressed for the harem in his flimsy silk pantaloons, at the mercy of these ghost-faced foreigners? Had the miners fed him since the shipwreck? Had he lost friends, lovers, on the ship that had gone down?

"I'll get us out of here, Iskander," Perry promised. His pistol had been taken from him, but his belt remained. He slipped it off and knotted the holed end around his hand. The buckle would make for a weighted whip that clawed its victim even as it bruised. These stupid miners could only get through the door one at a time. "I'll knock them down and we can run—I will remember the right way out when I particularly need to. It will be fine. I promise."

CHAPTER SIXTEEN

TOMAS DOES NOT FIND THE MAN HE SEEKS

The dark sat on Perry like a mountain, and by insensible degrees robbed him of thought and courage. He tried to hold on to his sense of time at least by counting his breaths, by counting the rise and fall of Iskander's ribs in the circle of his arm. But the numbers seemed to scuttle away from him, leaving only a sense of tides ebbing and flowing endlessly. The small warmth that gathered between them was just enough to lull him to sleep, and then sleep robbed him of his count entirely.

In his dream, a tawny monster with blazing eyes rattled the immovable bars outside the cage. He startled awake to find it was the light—the light had returned. A key was rasping in the lock.

Perry edged his feet under him, his weight on his left hand as he prepared to spring, his belt still wrapped loosely around his right.

The gate swung open, and a figure moved through it, silhouetted by the lantern Old Jack held behind it. The beam of light caught Jack's beard and his floral buttons, and lanced out to make the figure's white hands on the bars shine like new snow. They wore a boat cloak, its hood pulled low over their face. The hands were the only identifiable mark, and they were empty.

Perry had expected weapons, cuffs, and chains, but he wasn't going to pause now to think about their absence. As soon as the cloaked person stepped out of the shelter of the door, he threw himself upwards, whipped out the belt, and as they flinched away from the snakelike punch of the buckle, Perry barrelled into them and got an arm around their neck in a deadly chokehold. He squeezed.

"Ayi!" Iskander yelled from the corner.

Almost at the same time, Old Jack croaked out "Let him go, you heathen. Let him go. He's trying to help you!" and Perry realized that his victim was not trying to pry his arm away—he was simply tapping it, as if to indicate that he yielded.

All this and they expected mercy from him? Perry growled and shook his captive until the hood flopped down from his head and revealed red-gold hair, shining like his hands in the beam of Jack's lantern.

A strange revolution twisted all the fibres of Perry's body. He became breathlessly aware of the long, sinewy body against his not as a threat but an intensified level of reality, as though his mind had thrown on spectacles and everything about the experience had sharpened. His arm slackened, and he felt Tomas Quick take in a deep gasp of air as the ribs of his back flexed against Perry's chest.

Perry struggled to make sense of any of this. Was this not the party that was to put him aboard a ship and sail him into life-long captivity? Was that why neither of them had so much as a walking stick for a weapon?

"What?" he managed.

"The gentleman done pay for you both," Old Jack mumbled, mouth drawn down and eyes dissatisfied.

"I'm not being *your* possession!" Perry let go. Tomas turned, folding the cloak back over his right shoulder and exposing a green worsted waistcoat. The way it nipped in his slender torso, drew the eye to the line of white shirt exposed where it had not been fully buttoned up . . . Those things should not be occupying Perry's thoughts at this time. He wrenched his gaze away and up to the hot shock that was those luminous eyes.

"It was a *bribe*, you idiot. This is a rescue," Tomas said, clearly angry, but perhaps not with Perry—for Jack shuffled from foot to foot at the tone, looking hard done by. "You should not have been in this position at all. I apologize on Jack's behalf. He has been sadly misled."

"I still have them cousins of yours to get around," Jack wheedled. Despite his stained grey beard, he stood like a scolded child next to Tomas Quick, who commanded respect as a drawn dagger commands it. "God knows what they'll say to me when I tell them the bird's flown."

"You'll blame me." Tomas shrugged.

"I will!"

Accepting this change of circumstances, albeit with scepticism, Perry backed towards Iskander, who was still flattened to the far wall, watching with wide eyes. "It's all right," he said, his voice as gentle and coaxing as he could make it, his hands beckoning. "Come with me. He says they're going to let us out."

"*Algebagnim.*" Iskander shook his head, pressing himself further into the rock. "*Betam asnalew.*"

Tomas's gaze snapped to the youth—the first time he had looked away from Perry during this whole encounter. He narrowed his eyes. "*Türkçe biliyor musunuz?*"

Iskander's face lit up. "*Evet yaparım,*"

"*Benimle gel.*" Tomas nodded toward the cell door, which remained open behind him. "*Her şey yolunda.*"

Perry remembered his earlier musings on what it must be like to have some bright saviour come down into the dark and throw open every door. He had thought it would be sublime, but as it turned out, it itched. Until a moment ago, he had been Iskander's hero. A moment ago, he had been master of his own fate, his own rescuer, and while being rescued was excellent, he wasn't sure he liked the sense of obligation it brought. Tomas Quick was a criminal, after all, and what he wanted in recompense for this act of charity was probably going to be more than Perry's conscience would allow him to pay.

The man's pale gaze was on him again. He felt it like a tether between them, and that was not a good thought in these circumstances.

"Do you speak any Turkish, Mr. Dean?"

"No." Perry gave up waiting for anyone else to move, and pushed past Old Jack, out through the cell door. Watching this, Iskander took a tentative step away from the wall. "Why should I?"

"Mine is poor." Tomas took Jack by the arm and pulled him out of the cage too, clearing the space. "But my mother's is better. She will be able to talk to him, if you help me bring him to my house."

Why should I trust you? Perry's faith in human nature had been all but destroyed by the hours he'd spent in the dark. Why should he trust anyone in this place anymore? But that was shock talking, and moral injury, not his rational self.

"What about this?" Perry jerked his chin at Old Jack, who had resumed his endless hand-wiping as soon as Perry got within attacking distance. "This peddler of human misery? Am I to be content with the fact that he has made money by holding myself and this poor foreigner captive? That he was about to *sell us*?"

Tomas's cupid-bow mouth twisted in some combination of amusement and frustration. "I suggest that contemplating your revenge should wait until *we get out of here*, Dean." His face softened abruptly, as though he had noticed the shivers that were still working their way up and down Perry's spine, and he nodded towards Iskander, who had finally stepped across the cage threshold and now stood with his thin arms hugging his inadequate waistcoat closed across his bare chest.

"The child is distressed, and I believe you are too, though I know you'd rather cut off your nose than admit it. Come to my house. Have tea. We'll talk this all through there."

"It is not an uncommon occurrence," Tomas said later, when they were sitting around the kitchen table where Perry had held him at gunpoint earlier. "For the 'property' that washes ashore after a shipwreck to include slaves. Although legally they become free men the minute they set foot ashore, in practice their fate depends very much on who they have the fortune to fall in with."

The sun shone through the many-paned windows and the door was propped open to the sea breeze. Light gleamed from the glass-green water in the bay outside, and from the bright scoured copper pans that hung above the range. In Zuliy's bread oven, something was crisping with a smell of toasted cinnamon, and Zuliy herself, in a dress and a turban of turquoise linen, was chatting in Turkish with Iskander, whose back was almost pressed to the heat radiating from the stove. He was wrapped in a blanket and hunched over a bowl of oatmeal rich with butter.

The dark, however, lingered in Perry's heart—he found this scene impossible to believe in. He was waiting, he realized, as he watched

Tomas Quick's long hands fiddle with his teacup, to wake up, to discover that this was a dream and reality was bars and indifference.

"The Methodist congregation here has a fund put aside for the ransom of sailors and other travellers who find themselves in such a situation. And though to my shame I wasted half of it on a con man, I was not without means to make up the difference myself."

"Why did you tell me you were going to buy a man from Liverpool?" Perry asked. He was certainly tired enough to still be asleep. Tired with a bone-deep weariness that was more in the spirit than the body.

Tomas gave a huff of laughter and turned his rope-calloused palms down against the tabletop. The backs of his hands were not the fresh snow that Perry had thought them—they were scattered all over with freckles like flecks of copper, a lighter colour than the constellations that had been splashed over his cheeks. Tomas studied them with his head lowered almost bashfully. "I did not want to show away in front of you," he said, smiling with a rueful warmth that struck Perry to the core. "As though I were boasting about doing that which any decent man would do."

He did have the most beautiful smile. That rosy-pink mouth was all but obscene, and his unexpected shyness made Perry want to ruffle him further—make him laugh, or moan. Those lips would look even better around his cock.

"And it seemed to me that you would not believe it, since you already supposed me to be such a villain."

Oh. Well there was a bucket of water thrown over that train of thought. For yes, he *was* a villain. Or if not a villain, a criminal, and were not those two things the same?

"What will you do with the . . . Is he a boy? What will you do with Iskander now?"

"He's a eunuch, I think. Mother?" Tomas called over to the pair at the range just as his mother slid a wooden paddle into the bread oven and brought out a plaited loaf. She transferred it onto a board, and brought it to the table, saying something that made Iskander come too, carrying a pat of butter and a small pot of honey.

"What is it dear?"

"Did you find out who our guest is?"

She pulled the bread into quarters and pottered away, returning with plates for everyone. The reddish crust was sticky under Perry's fingers as he tore off a piece to butter, sweet as sugar and spicy with nutmeg and cloves. Soaked with butter, dipped into honey, it satisfied a deep need for comfort in him that he had barely been aware he had. She watched them eat for a moment, Perry and Iskander both, and smiled as they sighed with relief.

"He's originally from Gondar in Ethiopia." She touched Iskander's hand reassuringly when he looked up, as if recognizing the names. "He was travelling to visit his grandmother when he was captured by slave traders and castrated." Her eyes were knowing and sad as she caught Perry's gaze. "That's a terrible ordeal, poor boy. Most of them die, but the ones who survive are more valuable for it. The traders thought they could sell him to the Sultan, but he developed the . . ." she gestured to her face, perhaps indicating the boy's acne, "the spots. So instead he was sold to a silk merchant as a companion for his wife. That's where he learned his Turkish—in the harem— just as that's where I once learned mine."

She huffed, the same small laugh her son had inherited. "*Biz ikimiz ayniyiz, sen ve ben*," she said, and Iskander forgot himself enough to grin.

"*Hamd Allah'a mahsustur.*"

"He and his mistress were sailing up the coast on their way to their summerhouse when their ship must have caught the tail edge of the same storm that wrecked the *Hyacinth*. He says that the lightning inspired him with a kind of madness. When the crew were distracted fighting the waves, and his mistress prostrate, he threw himself overboard, hoping at least to die free."

CHAPTER SEVENTEEN

A PRETTY PASS

Hearing of Iskander's ordeal and bravery, Tomas settled a hand on his mother's arm. It didn't even tremble, and he was again proud of her rocklike composure. Though *rocklike* wasn't quite right; she was as enduring as a ship that flexed to meet the waves, one that could conform itself to the shape required, but retain everything inside itself untouched.

"You are not Ethiopian," Peregrine Dean offered, his frown tentative as though he knew it was rude to question Zuliy's word, but couldn't quite help noticing...

"I am Circassian, originally." Zuliy smiled at the customs officer in a way that was friendlier than he deserved. "My people are prized as slaves among the Turks, for our complexion and our hair colour. I, too, was shipwrecked off a xebec, and when I washed up here, my owner was among the survivors and insisted on having me back. Tomas's father, Peder, was the lawyer who argued for my freedom." She leaned over to pour Dean more tea, catching his eye. "Whatever else you think of us, you will not think that we are involved with this business of that poor sailor. My son has been working tirelessly to find him and save him—something of which I think you have cause to be grateful."

Tomas winced, glad that she still occasionally gave in to the motherly urge to defend him, but embarrassed that he might be thought of as in need of defence.

He was embarrassed too on Dean's behalf. The man still seemed a little dazed, his responses a moment or two late, and his colour ashy. He had been, so Tomas's friends told him, all over the town searching for evidence with which to hang Tomas. He had been vocally in support of Tomas's usurping cousins, the bastards who had stolen Tomas's father's inheritance and good name, and who now swanned around town flaunting the wealth that should have been his. But it was hard to maintain the pure flame of his anger toward the man, when Dean was so shaken, and had been subjected to such an indignity.

Dean fidgeted in his chair as though his thoughts were biting ants. "I am grateful," he said, reluctantly. "I am—some things that I took as certainties are shaken up in me. Old Jack said I might be sold to the Quicks, that they have plantations to which Iskander and I both might have been sent. Is that true?"

Tomas wished for brandy or rum rather than the slop of twice-brewed tea he was currently drinking. They had a box of good gunpowder tea in the thatch over the outhouse, but of course that could not be offered to a riding officer. "It is. Sir Lazarus has slave-worked estates in Barbados and in Boston, and always an eye out for a bargain. If we cannot find Barnabas anywhere else, it would be a good idea to raid the Quicks' storehouses, to be sure he isn't being held there."

Some of Dean's warmth flamed back into his face as he jerked his head up to meet Tomas's gaze. "No. No, I will believe he might buy a slave himself, but not that he might kidnap a free man off the shore and deprive him of his liberty, knowing—"

"You think he's such a saint!" Tomas's ever-present grievance spat itself out of his mouth without his permission or consent. He heard himself sounding bitter, jealous, irrational, and hated that he couldn't deny he was any of that. But why should Lazarus have Dean's good opinion, when he didn't deserve it? Why shouldn't that approval belong to Tomas instead? Why shouldn't Dean be his and not the magistrate's?

"He treated me with respect!" Dean flamed up in return, half rising from his seat and pushing his face close to Tomas's. His breath fanned across Tomas's eyelashes, smelling of honey and spices, and although Tomas knew it was a threat display, he could not help dropping his gaze to Dean's mouth. Even curled in challenge, it looked soft, tempting to kiss.

Tomas collected himself with a hiss, and his anger with himself came out in another attack. "How much respect do you think he has for you, really, when he keeps men of your race in chains?"

Dean flung himself back into his seat as though he too realized he had come close to a gesture that could never be made in public. *He wants me*, Tomas thought, glee turning his annoyed arousal into a heady, spiky thing it both hurt and gave pleasure to rub up on. They shouldn't. He mustn't. But how nice to know that they both desired it.

"I don't need you to point out that slavery is their first thought when they see me," Dean choked out in a mixture of disappointment and anger. "But it will not always be so. I, in my own person, will make it better. They will look at me and they will see that I am a man of intelligence and action, in every part as good as them. They will *have to* acknowledge that—"

His chin compressed, and he put his face in his hands. In the uncomfortable pause that followed, Iskander rose from his chair and draped himself over Dean's shoulders, hugging him from behind.

Tomas frowned and turned to Zuliy to explain this development, because it was Iskander who had suffered longest. It was Iskander who should be needing comfort, flying off the handle and weeping, surely?

"The shock is greatest at the start," Zuliy said, giving him a sad smile. "The first time you realize how very unimportant you are—how vulnerable you are, and how little anyone else cares. Iskander would have been through that when he was first captured, and by now I dare say he has grown some defences. He has become at the least a little numb. Mr. Dean has not, and is newly devastated."

She rose and drifted over to the pantry, giving Tomas a conspiratorial smile as she went. "Perhaps a picnic in the fresh air will restore his spirits, and you two can begin this acquaintanceship again, coming to a better friendship this time."

"And what should I do with Iskander? I can always use sail hands. Or he can stay here a short time while I put together a trading cartel to fund an expedition to Ethiopia."

His mother laughed and put a mixing bowl down on the table. "You forget that he and I were trained for the peace that comes when all the men are gone. Leave us in our own quarters. We'll have a nice afternoon baking and chatting while he has time to think. He doesn't need you breathing down his neck for decisions on the spot. Go on." She put a satchel of linen-wrapped ham and cheese into his hands, and a small jug of milk, then made sweeping motions toward the door. "Out."

A moment later found Tomas and the customs man on the edge of the back garden, looking out to sea. Tomas suppressed a worry that his mother knew him too well, and struggled with the ruthless part of himself that told him to make friends with Dean in order to corrupt him—to have some hold on him that could be used to calm his zeal against smuggling. Just now, with his clothes covered in red mud as though he had bled out of every inch of his skin and with the colour barely coming back into his cheeks, Dean was too vulnerable for Tomas either to attack or to seduce.

"A picnic with me is probably the last thing you want," he offered. "I will not tell her if you choose to go back to your lodgings instead."

Dean took off his wig. It was a sodden and bloodstained object, and he looked better without it, his short-shorn natural hair a thick cap of curls above eyes so dark they reminded Tomas of the night sky. "No," he sighed, wide shoulders slumping, but the voice giving a gentleness to his surrender, as of a proud man who finally accepts a comfort. "I think we should talk."

"If it's a day out, then we should go to the castle." Tomas smiled. The walk would do the man good, and the talk of ghosts up there made it an excellent place for privacy. "Follow me."

"A lot of people do, it seems." Dean watched him out of the corner of his eye as they made a leisurely way onto the high land and down to the very end of the peninsula, where the Black Knight's castle was a jumble of fallen rock walls, the bleached tan of sandstone laced over with bright-blue patches of cornflowers. There the grasshoppers were shirring away with their sawed legs, and the day's heat rose in spirals from stones where slow-worms drowsed. "A lot of people follow you—speak well of you. I can't get a word of condemnation out of them."

Praise went to Tomas's head as it always did, swoony as good wine. "I'm glad to hear it," he said. "I work hard for that reputation. I take my Methodism seriously. 'What doth the Lord require of thee, but to do justly, and to love mercy, and to walk humbly with thy God?'" His mother would have laughed at the idea that he was humble, but . . .

"And yet you are a smuggler." Dean's stride had opened out over the short journey. When he saw the two stories of round tower standing up from the ruins, he hurdled the walls between himself and the entrance with his old easy confidence, and smiled at Tomas as he ducked inside.

Tomas's unusual glee returned in a rush of giddiness, as though a bubble of joy were curving all around him, and through it every landmark acquired a new beauty, a gilded touch. He laughed. "You can't prove that."

"I know it was you in that warehouse."

"I don't see how you can." Tomas grinned back. "I wasn't there."

His voice echoed in the damp passageway between the keep's outer and inner doors as they passed through the wall, and then they were inside. Ancient timbers overhead made half of a roof—the other half had been blown apart by a cannonball two hundred years ago. But what was left cast the circular room in cool shade, and ferns grew out of the gaps in the walls. A tree nestled in the guardroom fireplace, covered in the yellow-pink buttons of unripe apples.

"But consider this—a lot of the people of Porthkennack are living hand to mouth. The miners do well enough when they strike a lode, but they can have months of digging out dirt, and unless they strike ore, they are paid nothing—they must depend on their neighbours' charity even to eat. To afford new clothes for a whole family? Who can manage it? So their children are in rags, starving."

Tomas's indignation had not worn out with time. On the contrary, his fervour had only increased. It didn't hurt, either, that Dean was watching him with a captivated look, as though he was seeing and understanding something wondrous for the first time.

"Meanwhile obscenely rich people in the government are spending a fortune on luxuries like brandy and lace. Why shouldn't some of those unnecessary cargoes be used to feed the people of this fine country? Why should the fat pigs get everything, and those who work their fingers to the bone still not be able to afford to live? That is injustice, and it would not be an un-Christian thing to attempt to put it right—to feed the starving. All too often around here smugglers make the difference between life and death. Of course the poor people account them righteous! What man of feeling wouldn't?"

"And you are very much a man of feeling," Dean wetted his lips. Without meaning to, Tomas had backed him into the wall, stalking forward to emphasise his points. Now they stood so close their thighs were interleaved. They were closer than they had been at the table when Tomas had almost forgot himself and kissed Dean because he'd looked so sad.

Dean's eyes were shining now, and his mouth was soft, half smiling. Waiting.

Unwisely, perhaps ruinously, Tomas leaned in and kissed him anyway.

CHAPTER EIGHTEEN

LEADS TO A WRECK

For one soaring moment, Dean responded, his mouth softening and opening beneath Tomas's with a delighted gasp. For one moment, Tomas allowed himself to feel buoyed up, raised like a cork on an ocean of praise, triumph, defiance—a mixture as heady as black powder dissolved in brandy. Out here in public where anyone might see, no less, playing with the man the Quicks intended for his nemesis.

He made a *mmm* of approval, assent, in the hollow of his throat. The next thing he knew, Dean had clamped both hands around his upper arms, physically lifted him from his feet, and thrown him away. To make the humiliation worse, Tomas caught his foot on an apple tree root, and staggered like a fool before he could right himself.

He glared at Dean, feeling the blood come furiously to his cheeks. "What the fuck was that for?"

Dean was scrubbing at his mouth with the back of his hand, glaring, like he hadn't known it was coming, as if he couldn't have stopped it if he'd tried. "This is a ruse, isn't it?" he accused. "You have me feeling vulnerable, and then you make an attempt on my virtue? Is this a literal seduction to your cause or is it merely some half-baked plan to compromise me—because if that's the case, you must know you can't use it without implicating yourself."

Tomas's humiliation turned into a coat of spikes. He bristled up like a steel hedgehog. "Oh, you know everything don't you, Mr. My-friend's-a-lord. I don't know why I keep giving you the time of day. Should have bloody left you in the mines."

"I don't owe you anything for acting like any decent man should—"

"I didn't say you did." Tomas bared his teeth, now so outraged that his fingers were calling for a knife. It was time to end this for all their sakes. "But I had hoped you would at least consider me a decent man, afterward."

He rolled his shoulders, shook down his spine, as though he was snapping the parts of a sextant together, making it ready for use. "Evidently nothing I can do outweighs the lure of the rank and money you can gain by attaching yourself to my cousins. Good day to you, then."

Dean took in a deep breath as though he was about to protest this accusation, but Tomas was already walking away, stinging at the thought that he had brought the man to one of his favourite places, and that now its tranquillity would forever remind him of offense and . . . and loss.

Beneath the fury, disappointment rolled like a layer of oil, black, clinging. For a moment there, he'd glimpsed such dreams. What could he not do, with an energetic, intelligent customs man on his side?

His long, angry stride brought him quickly down to the bay again. In this shifting mood of sorrow and frustration, he was not fit to go home. His mother would not thank him for bringing such a tornado of ill will into her refuge, not while she was trying to make young Iskander feel safe.

No one deserved to deal with him when he was like this, so he hauled on the rope attached to the ring at the end of his garden, reeling in his jolly-boat, and hopped into it with a sense of thankfulness at the bounce and sway beneath his feet. He unhitched it from its blown-glass buoy, lifted the stick of a mast from its trees, and shipped it into its socket. The sound of the rope rattling through the pulley as he hoisted the single sail was soothing, and when he had picked his way through the various craft moored around the shore and was out among the glassy roll of blue-green breakers, the huge regular heartbeat of the cold ocean comforted him.

The sea didn't care if he lived or died. Didn't pay attention to his humiliations or his triumphs, and that was a cleansing observation— how much did it really matter after all, if the sea didn't care?

Sunset was the colour of a flame—deep-orange sky across which a dozen banners of piled golden cloud seemed to glow more brightly saffron as darkness swept in from the east. The sight of it made him think of heaven, and heaven brought him by degrees around to the thought of forgiveness.

It's not as though I wasn't *hoping to corrupt him to my purposes,* he acknowledged to himself, a prickle of damp cold sweeping up his back and teasing the hairs on the nape of his neck. *He was right to assume I was. A man like him on my side would make everything easier, not least because no one would expect it.*

Tomas had friends and sympathizers among the local riding officers. Friendships he cultivated by sending them a spare barrel of liquor every now and then, or allowing them to rake up an occasional net full of wax-wrapped lace for their wives. But they were a poor lot—lazy, mostly, complacent. Making a living like most people and not inclined to go on crusades or to bestir themselves in the cause of feeding the hungry or giving solace to the widows.

On the one hand, this was ideal for Tomas's business, but on the other, a man who sympathized with Tomas's mission to turn this windfall of useless luxuries into lifesaving resources for the town? A man who was capable of turning his own strength and drive into that harness with Tomas, and helping him pull? Well, a man like that would be a prize, and Tomas did not think there was anything wrong with him because he found Dean's usefulness as attractive as his person.

We're both more ambitious men than our circumstances can contain. His anger simmered down as the amber faded from the sky. *We would do better together.*

Behind him, he could feel the oncoming rush of a cold front, and when he turned, it was to see the pellucid sky snuffed out by heavy black cloud around a jet-black epicentre. The wind was picking up. It was miles still to the dark heart of the oncoming storm, but already his cheek was spackled with flying water.

He had been too preoccupied by his own moods and taken those of the sea for granted. That way lay death. He turned and flew for the shore.

As he struggled to tack upwind toward the harbour, an arm of the storm slid over the descending sun, and it was as though it had been extinguished. One moment the visibility was on the greyish side of a bright evening, the next it was a starless night, with only a sullen red underglow in the east where the ashes of the quenched sun were still smouldering.

About a league to starboard Tomas caught a glimpse of something white, pointed like an arrowhead toward the heavens. He narrowed his eyes, trying to make it out, wishing he had brought a spyglass. That was a sail, surely? It must be the very tip of a sail catching the light before the shadow rolled over it.

Darkness curdled inside Tomas, weighing him down. If that was a ship . . .

As he watched, the sail, now a dim blur, came into view entirely. Another white blur behind it was a twin of the first. She was hull up, growing larger by the minute, and he saw she was a snow, running, running before the storm as though she had no idea she was windward of a shore that was a thousand grinding teeth.

Tomas had sailed these waters since he was a toddler, and even he did not want to chance his luck in this weather. Contradictory winds blew water into his face with such force that the droplets smarted. He fought with the sail and tiller, trying to keep her on course though the storm was gusting in all directions. A particularly hard shove from north northwest had him bracing his back against the tiller to keep it over as the jolly-boat heeled until she was almost standing on her side.

When the blast eased, and she righted herself, the mysterious snow was closer still. Tomas was tacking into the wind, but the snow was flying before it and the distance between them had narrowed so much that even in the dark he could make out the horizontal stripes of the American flag snapping forward over her deck from the flagstaff in the stern.

She would drive herself onto the Needles if she didn't alter course. Cursing the need for a third hand, Tomas lashed tiller and sail to the larboard gunwale and scrambled through the small lake that was accumulating in the bilges until he reached the canvas-wrapped bundle lashed in the bows where he kept a candle-lantern and a dry tinderbox.

The canvas was soaked and unwieldy, and with no one to compensate for the wind, it battered the jolly-boat like a racquet batting a tennis ball. Tomas was now so sodden that water ran off his fingertips as he tried to make a spark catch for long enough to let him light the lantern, though he kept his eye on the dim bulk of the coastline—the familiar shapes just about discernible against the sky—to be sure *he* wasn't being blown onto the rocks himself.

It was because of this vigilance that he saw something gleam across the heaving sea. He thought he'd imagined it at first—one of those grey pinpricks that comes when one rubs one's eyes—and it faltered out almost at once. But no sooner had he told himself it was an illusion than it shone out again, a vibrant yellow star, the only coloured, the only steady thing in this grey and howling world.

But what was it? The lights of the town were grouped along the inner edges of the harbours and could not be seen when one had passed their sheltering walls. The lighthouse was further along the coast, visible to ships coming from the north east, but invisible from this southern approach.

Not for all his abhorrence for the Quicks did he think that they would have the inhumanity to kindle a light in a seaward window, and anyway, this was not coming from the Quicks' house on the very top of the land. This was lower, on a . . .

His nausea returned as though someone were twisting his bowels. This was on a cliff edge. Someone out there was deliberately standing still on the cliff path with a light.

The American snow slid past Tomas's jolly-boat at eight knots or more, jostling him with its wake. Above its name—USS *Kittywake*— he caught a brief glimpse of a boy in the stern windows. A youngster, someone's nephew or son or little brother, brought aboard to learn navigation and the ropes. Then the snow club hauled and turned toward the light.

Something unconscious must have been calculating positions and speeds all along, because the moment they turned, Tomas was shouting "No! No! You'll drive onto the Needles. No! Listen!"

His hands were chilled and wet, fingers swollen. He tried twice more to strike a good spark, but now the tinder was soaked from the rain. Hopeless.

Tearing his jacket off, he pulled his white shirt over his head. His jolly-boat's sail was, by design, tea coloured so that it should be invisible by night, but a lookout might see a pristine white shirt if he waved it hard enough. He did, and hollered until his voice gave out. But the gale blew his words away, and the snow sailed primly on, thankful perhaps for that glimpse of salvation in a howling world.

Tomas threw himself back to the tiller. Could he catch them? Could he reach them before—

Even in the wind's shriek, he heard it when she struck the rocks. The masts moaned like enormous bassoons. The rigging snapped with whip-crack staccato notes. In the belly of the ship something crashed—it must have been the galley, the lit galley. Smoke poured out from her hull from holes it shouldn't have. He thought, hoped, that was the worst of it— She'd crashed but she'd retained her shape. If the sailors could anchor her to the rocks and ride it out then—

An enormous swell picked her up, drew back and then dashed her a second time on the anvil of the rock. Her spine broke with a roaring *crack* like that of lightning. Then a moment later the fire must have reached her gunpowder magazine. She exploded from within.

CHAPTER NINETEEN

WE DRAW THE LINE AT MURDER

When the debris had stopped falling and Tomas had straightened up from his defensive crouch, the surface of the sea was covered in wreckage—some of it yet alight. The storm still raged, and his jolly-boat's rigging was hard as iron with the strain. If he wanted not to join the snow in drowned and wrecked pieces, he should really resume his course for the shore, but . . .

How would he live with himself if he sailed away and left the sailors here to drown?

He wrestled his sail down and shipped oars—the jolly-boat was as buoyant as a cork and slid over the crests of the great waves and down the hollows in between with an almost exhilarating motion. Carried by tide and wind, the wreckage moved with him. He rowed among the shattered timbers, searching for the ship's crew by the light of her own destruction.

There was a head, a shoulder, their rounded shape distinctive in the slowly ebbing flames. He leaned over and grabbed at the soaked material of the man's jacket, pulling him until his head left the water. It lolled back as he tried to haul the man closer, and he saw the splinter of iron-hard wood that had been driven through the man's neck. No hope for him.

Tomas let him slip back into the ocean, the burial chamber for so many sailors. He would be in good company wherever he fared to now.

Almost absently, while he continued to pick his way through the wreckage, a part of Tomas was aware of the weather. He felt the wind slacken as though his whole world had sighed in relief. But then the rain came down in earnest—a drenching so thorough he had to turn his face into the shelter of his elbow in order to breathe air rather than water.

With a great hissing and the scents of burned tar and saltpetre, all the various fires began to go out. He didn't see the plank that rammed into his stern, only felt the jolly-boat leap and groan under the impact. He almost let go of an oar, flung sharply against the pillar of the tiller, its rod jabbing him in the armpit. Freezing, on high alert, he hushed and listened for the sound of planks separating, of the jolly-boat pulling herself apart.

It didn't come, but as he waited, the water rose an inch in the bilges, slipping above his shoes, creeping up his ankles. She was sprung somewhere.

He brought the oars back on board and secured them. Then, going to his hands and knees in the rapidly deepening bilgewater, he felt over the hull for the breach. If it was bad, there was still time to lash oars and mast together and cling to them as a makeshift raft, but . . .

Ah! An incoming current pushed against his sweeping left hand. Examining it with his fingers in the dark told him the snow's debris had staved in one of the jolly-boat's planks. It was bent inward, letting water through the gaps at either side. Like a surgeon setting a bone, he nudged the plank back into shape, and pushed strips of his conveniently removed shirt into the gaps between the deformed strake and its neighbours.

As he worked, the rate at which the jolly-boat filled began to slow. When he had done the best job he could, he sat back on his heels and reached for the baling pail. The scoop and splash of dumping the water out of his little vessel was soothing to the nerves and kept him warm, but when he had her almost dry and felt around the edges of the patch, he found that the sea was coming in still. It was welling through the cracks, seeping through the tightly woven fabric faster by the moment.

He sighed and rubbed a freezing hand across his hot forehead. Another blow like that and she *might* crack in half. Another body's weight in here and she might sink. It was questionable enough whether he would make it all the way to the shore himself or whether he might have to swim. There was nothing more he could do.

By now, he and the wreckage had all been swept within view of the lighthouse. Praying that the comforting pulse was not also a lure to disaster, Tomas raised his sail again and steered south southeast of it, to where he believed he would find the mouth of the bay.

The wind behind him clamoured with imagined voices, cursing him for leaving them, screaming, pleading, and although this was an artefact of his own imagination, it still wasn't far from the truth. He was leaving them to drown. He was turning his back. His cheeks were so cold that the warmth of his tears burned like acid as they fell.

Or perhaps that was an outward sign of his inner fury.

Wreckers!

Tomas was a smuggler himself. For the reasons he had tried to impress on Peregrine Dean, he was not uneasy in that respect. He saw it as no worse a way of gleaning a living from the sea than fishing. Nor did he condemn the practice of making off with shipwrecked goods that had been brought to one's shores by the hand of God himself. The sea brought its goodness to Cornwall's beaches, and it was her people's right to harvest that.

In the process, they should—and usually did—help those voyagers who were washed ashore with the produce. Many a shipwrecked sailor had found himself being nursed back to health by a Porthkennack fisher family, sometimes to be returned to their people, sometimes to fall in love and stay forever.

That was how it should be—established in time immemorial. A blend of cupidity towards the goods and mercy towards the unfortunate people of which surely even God approved.

But wreckers were something different. To deliberately engineer a shipwreck so one could profit from the massive loss of life? To know that those at sea, gripped in the greatest terror of their lives, would see the light as salvation, would rejoice that some human habitation was nearby, would turn towards it as if to their lover's embrace, and to thus be ruined?

It sickened him. And it filled him with the fear that he was losing his grip. For ten years he'd thought he knew the character of the people of Porthkennack, and that it was good. Yes, there had been occasional run-ins with ambitious men like Hedrek Negus—one interesting occasion where Negus had suspended Tomas from a yardarm by his feet to try to wring a concession out of him. Those things were in the manner of business, and no real harm had been done. And yes, there were desperate hungry men like Old Jack Baily, who sometimes allowed themselves to be led too far. But Tomas had not imagined anyone in his town would dream of wrecking a living ship and thereby murdering its crew.

Slavery and wrecking.

The storm continued to fade, and he heard the crash of breakers against the land. Hard to be sure in the pitch darkness, but it sounded like the approach to Mackerel Cove. The strong winds had turned fitful, gusting and veering, so he lowered sail again and rowed around a headland he could not see, counting the strokes of the oars and measuring off the distance travelled on a mental chart of where he believed he was.

His back was cramping and his arms and thighs were sore when he passed the final bulk of rock and saw the house lights around the harbour, barely stronger at this distance than a string of stars, but so very welcome.

Slavery and wrecking. And both had begun with the arrival of this new crew in the town of whom no one could tell him anything. All his normal sources of information would say was that the newcomers were strangers. That a man rarely saw the same one twice, and they seemed to not even know each other, as though each was taken on for a single job and then let go before he could become recognizable. And uniformly Tomas had been told that the new crew did not talk to the locals, and the locals dared not press.

Frustrated, Tomas grounded his jolly-boat on the beach, coupling her to the nearest buoy. Stepping out proved that he'd overdone it—liquefied his bones with overwork. He staggered up the cliff stairway, infiltrated his house through the back door. The place was quiet, though a mummy-wrapped lump on the chaise, visible by the light of their porch lantern filtering through the window, must be Iskander asleep. His mother would be in her room, perhaps listening out for him.

He made sure to step on the squeaky floorboard as he passed, to open and shut his door with an audible *click*. Then he stripped off his wet clothes before the ashes of his fire, dried with a linen towel, and forced himself into a nightshirt before falling into bed.

He had imagined he might have nightmares of drowning, but it was not the wreck that came to his mind as he drowsed, it was the shove of Peregrine Dean's big hands in the centre of his chest. Increasingly as he contemplated it, it knocked the wind out of him. Perhaps he wasn't a good man—perhaps he was mistaken in his self-belief—but he would do a lot to gain Dean's trust, to make it so that next time the man drew him in and did not reject him.

The man is an idealist. Tomas turned on his side and pulled his pillow toward him so he could hug it. *And he is known to be honest— insensitive, quick to anger, but incorruptible.* A man of honour, and one with no smuggling business to enlarge, no particular iron in this fire. With such a man working with him, Tomas would not need to fear betrayal or double-crossing.

As he slipped toward sleep, his thoughts softened, growing golden, returning not to the rejection but to the kiss before it, the flare of heat and brightness and victory. Drowning voices clamoured at the back of his mind, but he shoved them down, promising them revenge.

Wreckers changed the game. He would go to Dean with the news tomorrow, make him . . . an accomplice? No, a partner in the business of stamping them out. If they freed Barnabas together and brought the wreckers to justice, that would forge a bond between them. And if Tomas were to kiss him again then, in the rush of victory, surely he would respond, he would yield. They both wanted it after all, and to that noose, Tomas was positive Dean would not betray him—equal in desire and in guilt.

And in joy too, if Tomas had his way. He would give the man joy, if he was allowed.

Chapter Twenty

A SUITOR IN A CRIMSON SUIT

The next day was one of mizzle—grey clouds above a grey sullen sea, and the air filled with a thin mist that did not so much veil the world as drench it. A solid pot of porridge had been left to keep warm on the fire, and Tomas cut himself a piece and ate it from his hand, ducking into the front room to make sure all was still well.

His mother and Iskander seemed to have decided to retrim all her hats. They had shoved the seats to the edges of the room and were sitting cross-legged on cushions, ribbons and silk flowers and hat pins scattered all over the floor around them.

Zuliy seemed tired but calm. She smiled at his inquiring look. "Iskander did my Sunday bonnet yesterday while you were out, and it's so much more stylish, I thought we could do them all."

"It does not distress you, Mother?" Tomas asked. She was brave and good, but she might not want this continual reminder of a life when she had not been free. "And how is he?"

Iskander's shoulders and back had stiffened at the sound of Tomas's voice, but after a moment, he raised his head and met Tomas's gaze with an expression of somewhat forced confidence. Already, dressed in clothes Tomas had outgrown in his teens and having had a good night's sleep and a meal, he appeared stronger, cleaner. His ringlets had been teased out and re-dressed with—if the smell was an indication—the linseed oil Tomas kept in the woodshed for finishing treen.

"How are you?" Tomas asked Iskander, keen to support the boy's efforts to re-engage with the outer world but not quite sure what to say.

Zuliy repeated the question in Turkish, and translated the answer. "He says he's very well, and he heaps a thousand blessings on us." She rolled her eyes. "But I think you make him nervous. Would you mind spending another day outside?"

"He will have to decide what to do with himself eventually," Tomas muttered. Watching the protectiveness with which his mother treated the boy gave him an uncomfortable mixture of pride and jealousy. "Try not to get too attached—you know what the town will say if we keep him."

"If he decides to stay with us," Zuliy corrected, skewering a bow onto a flat straw hat with a hatpin almost as long as her arm, "Then they will say that he's your brother, because that's what I'll tell them to say."

The absurdity of it—of her baring her teeth at him like a mother cat protecting her kittens—made him laugh. "If I'd known you were so apt to adopt lost things, I would have bought you a puppy."

She threw a pink paper rose at him, and he ducked away with a smile. "Don't be rude."

Iskander had dropped his eyes again and was teasing ribbons of five different shades of red into an intricate chrysanthemum that would perfectly complement the shade of Zuliy's hair.

"Well." Tomas sighed. "Don't overinfluence him. I don't want you breaking your heart if he decides to return to his home."

"It is my heart to break," she said.

Recognising a lost cause, he returned to the kitchen, where he made himself a pot of the good tea, gnawed his porridge, and considered his next move. The snow's wreckage would even now be washing up on shore. He was not needed to supervise the retrieval of goods from the sea, or advise on their hiding places, but he liked to be present anyway so that none of his contacts forgot who was in charge.

He still had no fresh information on where Barnabas might be being held—the thought of which was another guilt, because the longer his ignorance lasted, the more chance there was of the man being moved out of Tomas's reach, beyond his help. But he could not attack a problem without any idea of where to start.

He contemplated asking the *Swift*'s crew to help him to break into Sir Lazarus's boathouse to search for the man, but no matter how he hated his cousins, he couldn't honestly see Lazarus being involved in something that might be proved to be overtly illegal. Damaris would have his hide—the old lady was one of those iron matrons, who ruled her family with a tight rein, and though there was little human warmth in her, she would not abide the possibility of disgrace inherent in doing anything against the law.

No, there was nothing to be done there until he knew more.

In which case, he would do as he had decided to do last night. He would approach Peregrine Dean and hope... His mental voice ran on with *hope to forge some connection*, but a giddy thing in his chest told him not to be so pragmatic, not to lie to himself—he was hoping not just for an ally but for a lover, and it had been so long. So long since he and Hector Jones had been apprentices together on the river wherries Hector's father had run, sharing a bunk because there was so little space in the cabin, lapped in a darkness so absolute they had no fear of discovery and scarcely any sense that the sweetness they discovered between them might be the same thing as the degeneracy so loudly condemned in the papers.

Those two years had been among the best of his life, before the business went bankrupt, Hector had decided to become a tar, and Tomas had returned home feeling very much a man and ready to make Porthkennack bend to his will as willingly as Hector had.

He caught himself humming "Love Will Find Out the Way" as he made his way down to the beach. What were the words?

"You may train the eagle
To stoop to your fist.
Or you may inveigle
The Phoenix of the East.
The lioness, you may move her
To give o'er her prey;
But you'll ne'er stop a lover;
He will find out his way."

Perhaps it was not just his mother who needed to guard her heart.

His morning was spent on the beach amongst the wreckage. He exchanged pleasantries with the usual suspects, working his way slowly from the west to the east side of the beach and keeping an eye out for Dean. Around midday, Jowan Ede told him that he might find

Dean up on the cliff above, sheltering in the huer's hut and shouting down to alert his colleagues on the shore when anything notable was swept in.

"Didn't want a repeat of last time, did we?" Jowan shrugged, though there was an unusual hardness in his easygoing eyes. "I don't know what would've befallen him if I han't seen him go down and dragged him away from them kidnappers."

"Do you know who they were?" Tomas asked. "There's a new player in town, and I don't like his style. If we could capture his men, an enquiry could be made."

"I don't know." Jowan gave him a twisted smile. "I were bent over young Perry, giving him a bit of a slap to wake him up. By the time I straightened, they were gone."

The Edes had five relatives in total serving aboard Tomas's ships. Good people, though inclined to indolence, and Jowan had always been a most obliging opponent. So Tomas believed him. He smiled back. "Well, I am glad to hear Mr. Dean has at least one friend in his office."

"Not two?" Jowan raised dusty eyebrows. "I can't tell the lads you vouch for him? They'd feel better about him if you did."

Tomas huffed, somewhat touched. "I can't go that far yet," he admitted, "but I'm working on it. It is my hope that Mr. Dean will fit in here comfortably once he has shaken off some bad influences."

Jowan nodded. "Them in the big house."

"Exactly." Tomas turned toward the path that would take him up to the small white hut on the cliff, and paused. "Your Margaret is fond of hats, is she not?"

"She'd put a flat iron on her head and call it macaroni," Jowan scoffed with fond amusement. "Why?"

"Tell her to call on my mother. We have a guest who is a talented milliner, and who also needs friends in the town."

"Got your finger in everything, you have."

"That's how I like it," Tomas agreed and, walking away, thought, *I will be a big man in this town one way or other, fucking Quicks be damned.*

The mizzle seemed to be turning into yet more rain. Tomas was glad to be able to duck under the roof of the huer hut. Here, watchmen usually stood gazing out for shoals of pilchard, so they could call down to the bay and alert the boats. But today Dean was here, in a crimson suit that might be conservative in London, but here was peacock fine. He looked magnificent in it, the colour rich and opulent against the umber of his skin.

Perhaps hearing his footfall, Dean had turned from the window, was watching Tomas slap the raindrops from his hat by clapping it against his leg. There was a consciousness about the man's gaze now that Tomas found delightful. Dean might have disowned the kiss, but it was there in every visible doubt.

"I like a man in a suit." Tomas grinned, dragging his eyes from Dean's shoe buckles to his eyes, lingering a little on the sturdy calves in their silk stockings. "Going somewhere special?"

Dean blushed a deep plum colour, very becoming with his jacket, but his mouth twitched, as if amused. "My other set of clothes are being laundered and repaired. I had not conceived how hard this posting would be on my linen."

There were several salacious responses Tomas could make to a sentence like that, but perhaps they would be unwise. It was hard to tell how appropriate he was being, when Dean's presence seemed to hit him like wine, leaving him drunk and happy.

"I'm not here to renew my attentions," he began bluntly. "Have no fear. I'm here as a concerned citizen to report an incident of wrecking. After we had our talk, I went out in my jolly-boat to cool off. You recall the light went suddenly and the wind blew up? The snow that is currently washing up in pieces on the beach passed me in the dark and turned towards a light on the cliff, sailing directly into the Needles as a result."

Dean's awkward intimacy faded. The very shape of his face seemed to sharpen. "You think it was deliberate?"

"I'm sure of it."

"Do you know who it was?"

Tomas huffed out his frustration. "I don't. I've spoken with a lot of people, and their feeling is that it's someone new to our town." It was his turn to blush, this time in genuine shame for the sake of his home. "You are not seeing us at our best, Mr. Dean. This slaving and wrecking? I've never known either here before. I hoped we could work together to prevent it happening again." A vivid memory of the ruined ship—fire on the water—flashed behind his eyes, and he was hotter, angrier about this than even he had thought. "There are things which are crimes because the law is an ass and the rich have all the power. And then there are things which are abhorrent because of their terrible ruin to human lives and happiness. Those things I am utterly against, and if you will help me, I will— Mph!"

Dean's mouth had silenced him, sealing against his own. The unexpected kiss was like touching a match to a fuse—a startled snap followed by a growing fire. He melted into the strong embrace with some of the relief of an addict, as though their first interrupted intimacy had already established a habit, and when Dean's mouth moved to his jaw, he laughed from sheer delight.

It was a bad move. Dean turned to stone against him, and then— again—he stepped away. "I'm sorry. I still can't."

"Because you insist on being the unpaid lackey to my evil cousins," Tomas mocked, unhurt—that had been a much gentler rejection. One that promised to turn into an acceptance in time. "Mr. Dean, I—"

Dean laughed too now, ducking his head as though that could hide his somewhat bashful smile. "I think by now you can probably call me Perry."

"Perry? No wonder I've been drunk on you since you arrived."

This second laugh was louder and more astonished, as though no one had ever flirted with the man before and he didn't know how to take it. His eyes were still sparkling when he looked Tomas straight in the face and said, "We cannot get involved because if I find evidence that you are the rogue I have been told you are, I will still see you hang."

Tomas didn't know what it said about himself that he found that breathlessly exciting. He had to swallow hard before he could speak. "I'm willing to take that risk if you are."

CHAPTER TWENTY-ONE

A WEIGHTY DISCOVERY

At that kiss, Perry's mouth had dried as a great wave of heat pulsed out from the core of him, passing through every fibre before it reached and darkened his skin. He had dropped his eyes to Tomas's perfect mouth, still flushed and damp from kissing, and desire seemed to pull him forward like a harpoon through the chest. He wanted, needed to take that risk, but—

He had not overcome every obstacle in his life by weakness of will. The very yearning itself frightened him, as a force he had never had to contend with to this degree before. He'd had illicit encounters, of course, reading the condemnations in the papers and using them as guidelines to parts of London where others like himself congregated. But the excitement had always been admixed with a queasy dread, lest he be found out, lest he let his patron and his family down. He was recognizable, after all, and after the first few fumbling times—scarcely worth their while—he had resigned himself to fantasy and his own hand.

One day, he had told himself, he would be wealthy enough, respected enough, to have love on his own terms. To find someone he could do more with than fumble in a shop doorway on a rainy night. Someone he could fuck, and yet also sleep with, rise with and come home to.

Until that day, he would not settle for less.

As though he was tearing his own skin off with the motion, he stepped back, heart labouring at the effort, and a pain like a belly full of icy water in his stomach. "You. You are . . ."

He wasn't sure what he wanted to say. He was appalled at the way Tomas's eyes shone at the thought of Perry killing him. Perhaps the word he was looking for to describe his tempter was *merciless*? Did Tomas have no softer feelings? No human warmth that should revolt at the idea of a love affair that ended in murder? Perry was romantic, and he could appreciate the idea of a doomed love in art, but in his own life, no. He could not risk being drawn further in because his heart once set was set forever. It would have to be torn asunder if Tomas truly was guilty, and . . .

And maybe that was the point. The ice water in his stomach was joined by a chill in his spine as he remembered that Tomas *was* guilty. Briefly there, the man had made him forget the warehouse robbery. Just because he couldn't prove it, didn't mean it hadn't happened. And now he was being seduced into forgetting that along with his duty.

"They were right. You are a dangerous man. A menace to public safety. You need to be taken down."

Tomas winced, and it looked real. It looked so convincing that Perry knew, for a moment, that he was being unjust—that whatever Tomas was, he was not cold enough to be unaffected himself by this pull between them. But it made no difference. Perry clenched his hands in his pockets and backed away. One day, Perry would have to stand in a courtroom and condemn this man to death. On that day, it would be better if Tomas did not have a crime of equal weight to accuse him of in return.

Kisses would get Perry ruin enough. He could not go further without risking his integrity in its entirety.

"And you continue to be a tool of those who would enslave us all." Tomas wiped his hand over his mouth, as though erasing the kiss. The movement bared the milky skin beneath his jaw, where the sun rarely touched, and his galaxy of freckles had not ventured. Perry's teeth ached with how much he wanted to bite there, to leave his claim in arcs of red and purple.

He turned his back and walked away.

Fortunately for Perry's nerves, by that time the beach had been mostly cleared, so his coming down from the huer's hut to help the rest of the customs men to haul their bounty of salvage up to the warehouse was not remarked upon.

An hour shifting barrels and writing up and signing off lists was a comfortable thing, giving him no time to think about his predicament. The snow was unknown to the local area, so he wrote to the registries in London, to inform them of her fate and allow them to trace any local shareholders to whom the cargo might be returned, and when that was done, he found Jowan Ede, standing by his desk with a red cap wrung between his hands and an obliging smile.

"Time to go and visit the usual suspects."

By this point, Perry's honour and duty, his sense that he was in the right, and that his integrity demanded nothing less than the abandonment of all his earthly wants, had begun to wane. He followed Jowan out to the stables with legs heavy with uncertainty and a mind to which work was far down its list of priorities.

"What happened to the spring in your step?" Jowan observed as they led their horses to the mounting block. "You all right? All this being hit in the head can't be good for you, I reckon."

"Who told you I'd been knocked out again?" Perry asked, sharp at the revelation that his misadventure with the miners was known to anyone but himself and Tomas. "Has Tomas Quick been bragging?"

"I don't know what Tomas Quick has to do with it," Jowan said in a placating tone. "'Cept as he has a hand in everything around here. I heard it from Zeb, who heard it from Old Jack, by way of repenting of his sins. Zeb told me not to spread it around, but thought I ought to know, since I'm supposed to be your partner." He looked askance at Perry as they turned onto the high street, aiming to go up and check the cellars of the Angel before swinging round to search the houses off Big Guns bay.

"No one would know I was your partner, mind. Next time you go into something like that, you take me with you, all right? That's why there is two of us, so no one of us has to take this on alone."

Touched, Perry smiled at his partner. "I'm beginning to see why you and everyone else suggested that I was not appreciating the complexity of the situation. I'm sorry I haven't . . ." It would be hard to say *I haven't trusted you* and have it not be taken as an insult, and it was still impossible to say *I trust you completely now*. But something middling was necessary. He had a vast need for a friend right now. Someone who—unlike his letters to his mother—would answer him as soon as he spoke.

"I'm sorry I haven't paid better attention to your wisdom. I should have listened more attentively to what you were trying to tell me."

Jowan smiled back, but his eyes were sceptical. "Fine words," he said. "I'll wait and see if you can back 'em up."

Mary Castille must either have been watching out for them, or have been warned by someone who was, because she met them at the front door of the Angel and fussed about their horses in a way that made Perry suspect that she was delaying them deliberately so that someone inside could hide the barrels. He pushed past her, hearing her snort and Jowan's apology behind him as he went straight for the cellar.

Jowan caught up with him, whistling as he swung a bundle of keys from one finger. "If you'd have listened to me then, I'd have told you she'd hand these over if you asked. I don't want you to sweet-talk me. I want you to act like you think I know what I'm doing."

"Do you?" Perry asked, annoyed with himself and needled still with the deep disappointment of having rejected something he wanted as much as Tomas. He was right to have done it. He was. But it had left him holed beneath the surface. He felt like he was sinking. "Oh damn. I'm sorry. My head is in such a spin, and my heart is . . . I don't know what to believe."

Slowly and deliberately, Jowan unlocked the padlocks of all the doors in the cellar one by one, never seeming to get the right key at the first try. Perry was convinced that above him the innkeeper and her little army of foundlings were hastily shoving barrels into the thatch. But if he stormed up there and found them red-handed, he would have to arrest Mrs. Castille on charges of receiving stolen goods, and what would become of the children then? It would be as though he had turned them out on the streets himself, to starve or thieve.

Heavyhearted and undecided, he turned toward the stairs, to do his duty anyway.

"D'you think you can believe me when I say you're backing the wrong Quicks?" Jowan flung out, sharply, and Perry knew he was being managed, but he allowed it, because this was a question that pressed on him so hard he could scarcely breathe.

"Do you have any evidence against Lazarus and his family other than hearsay?"

Jowan drew in a hissing breath through his teeth and steadied his lantern on a perfectly legitimate barrel of beer. "You mean, apart from the way that they bought out all the grocers so anyone wants something they can't gather themselves they got to buy it from the Quicks at a hefty profit? Other'n the way, when the miners tried to get a living wage, they brought in strike breakers from England who all but killed some folks?" He gave a humourless chuff of laughter. "No, I'm not saying there's anything illegal about any of it. Lazarus don't have to be illegal, do he? He already is the law. But he's not . . ."

Jowan spread his hands, as though he despaired of his own eloquence. "He's not the side of the angels, Perry. You got to ask yourself in the end, what side are you on? Are you on the side that feeds the hungry and gets doctors for the sick, or are you on the side that raises the rent on every property in the town till the poor have to sleep on the streets?"

"It is not my business to make moral choices. My business is the law," Perry exclaimed, hot with shame and panic. And then he heard himself. That was what he believed, was it? Dear God.

When he forced himself upstairs anyway, it was with doubt clawing back his feet on every tread. Was he on the side of the angels, or was he on the side of the magistrate? If forced to choose between his own advancement and the lives of the common poor, what would he choose? Why could they not both be the same thing? Who was the truly honest man here—Lazarus or Tomas Quick? His whole frame seemed to clench with terrified desire at the thought there even was a choice, but he reached the top step without growing any clearer as to what he should do.

A scuffling in the saloon interrupted his sense of having run over a precipice, waiting to fall. With Jowan's feet heavy on the cellar stairs behind him, he strode into the room. Found it empty.

And yet there it came again, a shuffling scratch somewhere within the walls. Jowan burst through the doorway behind him, Mary Castille on his heels, but neither were fast enough to stop him from bending beneath the fireplace and twisting until he could peer up the sooty length of the chimney.

Above him, the toes of a pair of shoes poked over an almost invisible ledge. He got his arm up, soiling his crimson sleeve exceedingly, and clamped a hand around a bony little ankle. A child's voice squeaked with fear, and when Perry tugged, it all came down together—a boy of about seven, carrying a box that clanged as he fell.

The boy landed on his back in the ashes of the fire like an enormous dislodged bird's nest. He tried to scramble up, grab for the box, but Perry put a foot on his chest and held him still.

Both Jowan and Mary made an abortive dart forward, as though they meant to stop him. But it was too late; he had opened the box and seen inside six plates and six dishes of solid silver, with a decorative rope edging, and the accusing words *USS Kittywake* stamped in unforgiving letters around the rim.

CHAPTER TWENTY-TWO

A MORAL QUANDRY

Perry's first thought was *I should have let Jowan catch me. I should have stayed in the cellar. If only I hadn't known for sure, I could have gone years without bringing ruin on this good woman and her children.*

The thought made him pause, made him lift his restraining foot. The boy scrambled out from under it and flew to Mary's side, cuddling into her apron as though he were still a babe in arms.

She put a possessive arm around his back and pressed him closer in, her face gone curd-white, but her eyes very fierce. "You can't blame the boy. He were only doing what I said. He's not grown enough to understand—"

He was a homely child with large ears and a red, puckered birthmark, or burn, across one cheek that swept up his forehead into a patch of lost hair. When he craned his head around to snarl at Perry, it was a little like being menaced by a gargoyle. "That's not true," he gasped. "I done it. It was me on my own. She didn't know it was there."

He was a gargoyle with a noble heart, though, trying to take all the blame so his stepmother and his family would not suffer. Perry's insides tried to strangle him at the thought.

In London he had searched ships for hidden compartments, and when he found them, he had faced only grown men who knew they were guilty, who faced the courts as an occupational hazard. It had not been within his knowledge or concern what the money raised from smuggling had been used to achieve. He had supposed it was done out of greed and shiftlessness—the unwillingness to get an honest job.

But here, in this town where so many folk were barely scraping by, it all looked very different. If he threw the boy in jail, he would be a monster. If he took Mary in, a dozen orphans would be left starving, and he would be a monster.

"They'll buy this place from under me." Mary spoke coaxingly, as if she could see Perry wavering. One hand gently stroked her boy's head. "The Quicks've been after this pub for years. I can't expect no mercy in court—he'll use it as a way to get rid of me. My childer'll be packed off back to the poorhouse, or to America. I can't . . ." Tears came to her eyes. "I can't abide the thought of—"

So this was what they meant, the people of the town, when they said that Tomas was an honest man, even though they all knew he was a smuggler. As Jowan had said, here was the choice stark before Perry now, between the law and the dictates of his conscience. Anger struck at his spine like a snake. The law should protect people. It should not be the thing they needed protection from.

"I . . ."

To some extent the decision was made for him. He could not turn either of them in. Faced with that possibility, he simply could not. But what to do instead? He shut the accusing box, surprised by how small it was, when it felt like a fulcrum on which his entire world balanced. "I . . . found the box in . . ." Where? Where could he have found this that would not incriminate anyone in particular? "A mine shaft?"

A hand landed on his back as if in congratulations and made him all but start out of his skin, though it was only Jowan, grinning like a new moon. "There's a whole load of them little caves down along Big Guns Cove where you might find something and not know who'd put it there. I'll show you 'em."

He patted Perry again, which was reassuring now Perry knew it was coming. "Don't fret, lad. You done right. Knew you had a heart in you somewhere."

Mary let go of her child, shooed him out of the room as though to get him away before Perry could change his mind. She had been weeping for some time, silently, her face quite still, but the tears welling and descending in ruler-straight lines to drip from her chin. Now she raised her apron to her face and wiped them dry, sniffing. There was still a hint of mistrust in her gaze as she fixed it on Perry, as if trying to work out whether he would ask more for his silence than she was willing to pay. "I can't thank you—"

"Don't," he interrupted. "Just . . . obey the law in future. Don't put me in this position again."

She gave a watery laugh, making him conscious of how desperate he had sounded, both of them raw in this moment where society's expectations had failed them both. "I won't," she said, almost certainly agreeing only to greater caution in future. "But I were going to say that I heard you wanted news of the wreckers. By way of thanks, I had one of them new bully boys in last night—the ones that wear the cormorant feathers. I dursn't tell you who it was, on pain of my life, but I will tell you this: go up to the Merope Rocks. Look between the one known as the Lizard Stone and the one known as Bloody Mary on a night of storms, and you'll see for yourself."

Infuriatingly, after this hint, the weather set in so fine that the ships in the harbour were becalmed, and it was not worth rowing them out to the open sea for there was no breeze to be caught there either. Since this at least meant that Barnabas would not be shuffled on board and sailed out of Perry's jurisdiction, he managed to be patient as day after day passed with no action.

During this time, he made his rounds with Jowan and finally paid attention to what the man said, learning the unwritten rules of the town—who should be let alone because their lives were hard enough anyway, and who were fair game. They were not all sob stories. One cartel and two independent entrepreneurs were as professional and as avaricious as Perry's adversaries in London, and he took great pleasure in finding and emptying their stores and thwarting the beatings he attracted in return.

It gave him great pleasure too to find that Jowan's good opinion of him spread by degrees to the other customs men, until he could go into the office and be sure to receive a chorus of *morning*s rather than a murder of glares.

None of this completely drowned out the voice that accused him of having been corrupted, of having lost his honour and his honesty, but it let him walk the town mostly unaccosted, and grow familiar with its oily, fishy streets, growing protective of it as though it were his own possession.

He was still unsettled in his inner self, aware that he was now avoiding investigating Tomas Quick's enterprises for fear of having to precipitately make a decision about Tomas that he would have to live with for the rest of his life, when a little black page boy stopped him in the doorway of the Seven Stars.

The boy was about nine-ish, an extravagant figure with madeup eyes, dressed in a brazen-orange silk suit. A white turban on his head was secured by a carnelian brooch from which the eyes of three peacock feathers protruded. Under the astonished gazes of the passersby, the boy seemed very solemn and uncomfortable, and his eyes went wide and perhaps wistful when he saw Perry. "You're Mr. Dean? Mrs. Quick sent me to tell you that you must come and wait upon her at once. It's urgent, and I am to say that you are not to delay a moment, or she will be displeased."

"And what will she do if she is?" Perry asked, wishing there was time for him to return to his lodgings to smarten up—he had got into the habit of wearing a kerchief over his hair instead of his wig, saving his full formality for Sundays. But he was aware that his reluctance ran deeper than clothes. A summons to his esteemed colleague's house should be an honour, if not a delight, but instead it came with a dirty flood of guilt and dread.

"She will not feed me, sir. And she will not allow the girls in the kitchen to go home after dinner. And we will all be very sad and uncomfortable."

"What's your name, young man?"

"Elijah, sir."

The child's perfect diction and adult manner of speaking was charming. "Well then, Elijah, lead on." Perry began with a smile, following the small figure onto the path to the Quicks' mansion. But over the course of the walk, his face fell. Damaris kept the boy as a page? He had seen this in London; ladies kept "exotic" children as some combination of fashion accessory and lapdog. In that light, Damaris's sending him to fetch Perry began to feel like an insult.

See, I do not regard you as a colleague at all, but as an ornament and a possession. Now come at my call like a good dog.

In mental turmoil as he had been for two weeks now, he feared he was being unjust, seeing slights that were not meant, but returning to the salmon-pink room was like walking into a dock. Once more, the whole family was there, this time with the addition of a fair-haired young man in a mint-green suit, who was, by his strong personal resemblance to Constance, probably her brother, Clement. The young people sat by the window, Clement reading, Constance stitching a sampler. Damaris was rigid as whalebone on her throne-like chaise, and Lazarus greeted Perry standing, and as his mother spoke he began to pace.

"We shouldn't have had to call you here, Mr. Dean," Damaris began. She was today wearing a sack dress of gold silk that toned decoratively with Elijah's suit when he came and sat on a stool by her feet. "It has been almost a month. I should have hoped you would have results by now. What are you doing to get rid of this pirate we asked you to hang?"

Treacherously, Perry's lips chose that moment to tingle with the memory of Tomas's kiss. In this stuffy room, the thought of Tomas was a bracing chill, a sense of light and sharpness, like the lemon in the icing of a lemon cake that prevented it from cloying.

This was not an appropriate answer, but he licked his lips anyway. "I am having some difficulty in finding any evidence against him, ma'am. The townsfolk speak well of him. He is a benefactor of his church, a philanthropist, and as far as I've seen, a very public-spirited gentleman."

"'Gentleman'!" Lazarus scoffed. "As if. He is the son of a common tar and an ex-concubine. You have a strange idea of what constitutes a gentleman. Though perhaps I should not be surprised about that."

Perry's wish to stay on good terms with the rich and powerful of the county took a hammer blow at this, but he told himself that a certain amount of restraint, of humility, was always going to be necessary if he was to succeed in becoming rich and powerful himself. "You are correct, of course," *technically*. "The man's birth is nothing to boast of. But his efforts on behalf of the town seem sincere. Only the other day he approached me himself—though he knew I was investigating him—to let me know there were wreckers abroad. I turned my attention to investigating the wreckers because—"

"It is not your job to stop wreckers." Lazarus's tight voice made whispers of guilt race along Perry's backbone. Why exactly *was* he here defending Tomas when he, too, believed—no, knew—that Tomas was as guilty as Lazarus said? "It is your job to stop smugglers, and this one in particular. The man's suborned you! I might have known."

It was true, but also unjust, inhuman. "Any man of sensibility would recoil from the idea of wreckers, sir. Are you not appalled at the great loss of life? It is murder on a grand scale, and surely far more heinous than—"

"Keep your voice down, goddamn it!" Lazarus bellowed, making little Elijah flinch. "My daughter is delicate. I will not have you discussing such matters in her presence. You will distress her."

Automatically, Perry turned to regard the young lady. Her gold ringlets, gleaming in the light of the window, were almost the same colour as the polished telescope that lay beside her. She wore green today to match her brother, and its tint gave her a sickly look, bruising the bags under her eyes.

He was quite ready to pity her, but then she raised her head and fixed him with a glare so cold it was like being speared by an icicle. He'd rarely encountered such venom in a gaze, and wondered what he could have done to merit it. Did the loss of life distress her so much she hated Perry for mentioning it? Or was he just getting in the way of her small concerns and she could find no empathy in herself for the larger world outside her doors?

"Forgive me," he gave in, weakened by second thoughts, keen now only to escape the room. "I will endeavour to do better in future."

"See that you do."

CHAPTER TWENTY-THREE

A PICNIC GOES TOO FAR

Thus reminded to do his duty and arrest Tomas, Perry's first action should not have been to pay him a social call. He wrestled with the compulsion for a whole night before yielding to its inevitability and walking down to the pretty harbour-mouth cottage where his victim-cum-ally lived.

This was a fine day, and the washing in the garden gave the place an air of a naval fleet setting out to sea, belling like sails in the brisk wind. He noted that the marigolds by the water butt had been augmented with several sawn-down barrels planted with herbs and flowers, blue and white, that made the white walls and blue door even more appealing. When he knocked, it was Iskander who answered, besom broom in his hands and an air of pride that must have something to do with facing the outer world, however briefly.

Perry was uncomfortably aware that he didn't know how to say *Where is Tomas?* in any language the boy understood, but before he could open his mouth and try anyway, Tomas came hurrying down the stairs, adjusting the knot of his cravat.

"I saw you through the window," he said, beaming like the sun, and Perry had to catch his breath because when he was away he forgot the exact lightning-crackle intensity of Tomas's movement: lithe, precise but not delicate, making the hair rise all over Perry's body from a foot away.

Seeing Perry approach, had Tomas run upstairs to throw on better clothes? Because today he had put aside the long trousers and boots of his sailing gear and donned a dark-blue suit that made his bright hair shine like a flame. It, too, had been dressed neatly, caught up in a long clubbed plait.

Perry dropped his gaze, and yes, there were the cuffs of tight breeches, and silver buttons, and then the long, slender curve of his calves outlined by silk stockings. Such legs!

Tomas's smile turned smug, catlike, and Perry snapped shut his open mouth. "I have a hint on the wreckers. Explain to me which is the Lizard Stone, and which Bloody Mary," he said in an abrupt tone more suitable for an argument.

"I'll show you." Tomas snagged a tricorn from the hooks on the vestibule wall. "I have just completed repairs on my jolly-boat, and I wanted to take her out. What do you say to a short voyage down the coast? We can buy some bread and fish in town and make it an outing."

"I'm meant to be at work," Perry grumbled, though it was obvious to them both that he was not going to say no.

"Well, this is work." Tomas grinned. "No reason why it should not be an excursion too."

"What's happening with the boy Iskander?" Perry asked, as they strolled together into the bakery and forewent bread and fish in favour of pasties with meat at one end and apple at the other. "He seems much at home. Did you free him only to have him become your servant?"

Tomas laughed, tucking the wrapped pasties into his bag. "He fears his people would not take him back, gelded as he is. While he works up the courage to make the trial anyway, he seems to be growing ever more content in my own home. There's even talk of him opening a milliner's. I would lend him enough to make a start in that business if that was his wish, but at present my mother insists he is to be allowed to regain his nerve in peace and not hurried into decisions for which he is not yet ready."

He rolled his eyes, the picture of a man nobly surrendering to the whims of women. "I do what she asks—it's easier."

"Do you think . . ." Even with the persistent awareness of Tomas's presence like the warmth of a small sun on his side, it was a balm to Perry's troubled mind to be able to walk and talk with him. The degree of ease Perry felt in his presence should be frightening, if he allowed himself to think of it, so he did not think of it, just basked. "Do you think we've already failed Barnabas? They will have sold him away by now, surely?"

Tomas's smile faltered. By now they had reached his jolly-boat, barely floating on a foot of water at the bottom of the cliff steps. He placed the food bag into it gently and, stepping in, held out a hand to Perry as though to stabilise him as he hopped across. It was a long, narrow hand just as Tomas was a long, narrow man, and the palm when Perry took it was rough, but accepting its steadying strength was like the first breath at the end of a fever, the first moment when one knew everything was going to turn out well.

"What else is there for us to do but to carry on hoping for news, being ready to act if it should come?" Tomas shrugged in something less than despair, resignation, perhaps. When Perry settled on the coil of rope in the bow of the boat, Tomas raised the sail and, with halyard in one hand and tiller in the other, coaxed her to whisper forward out of the bay. "I admit I have never met a tougher nut to crack than this new organization. The locals are running scared. No one will speak up, not even in private—or when they do, they know very little themselves. Against such an anonymous force as this, what is there to do but hope and wait? A chance will come or it will not—and if it doesn't, we cannot blame ourselves for that."

So easily you, too, wash your hands of responsibility, Perry thought, with a whole-body chill as though he was still in that cave cell, but the thought was unfair, and burnt away in the almost celestial flood of sunlight on water through which they passed, the sea chuckling beneath the hull.

Since he had been looking out to sea—trying to spot the *Swift*—when he had sailed these waters on the *Vigilant,* it was new, and instructive, to see the coastline from this angle. The myriad dark flecks were caves in which contraband could be hidden, if one manoeuvred carefully enough past the rocks showing beneath the surface as mounds of creamy spume. At the very top of the cliffs, the coast path was visible, running in and out of sight like a grass snake, and when they rounded the headland, a white glimmer and a point of brilliant reflection was all that could be seen of the Quicks' house: the admiral's telescope in the window.

About a nautical mile further on, they came upon a grouping of small islands rising from the sea like pillars. The first and the last were the largest, wide enough to have soil on their summits and grass or trees growing from their sides. Tomas lowered his sail and shipped his oars, rowing cautiously up to the first. At a closer examination, Perry could see the ladderlike steps in its side, a ringbolt secured to the rock at its base.

He caught the ring as they approached, and Tomas passed him the painter to tie them up.

"This is the Lizard Stone," Tomas said, slinging the bag across his chest and clambering onto its slimy black shore. After steadying himself for a moment, he began climbing up the precipitous stairs, and Perry had no option but to follow. "The other large one is Bloody Mary. She's the one foundering ships generally strike first. I wouldn't like to try tying up to her, not even rowing."

Curious, Perry examined the stretch of coastline between the two. But from here, nothing stood out to him. He would have to return on foot and look at it more closely now he knew which it was. He returned his attention to the ascent, which was essential—for a stretch he needed to hold on with hands as well as feet.

His arms were aching when he finally pulled himself over a grassy lip into a hollow on the seaward side of the rock. Above it, the stairs continued up, but here a misplaced willow had rooted itself, and its trailing tendrils and fluttering leaves closed behind him like a curtain as he crawled gratefully within. On the other side of the tree, a two-foot sliver of grass curved up into the cup of the hollow, and there sat Tomas with his back to the rock, examining his greened stockings with an expression of regret. He had put down his satchel and there were pies and a stoppered leather flagon beside him.

Affection joined the burning lust in Perry's veins and made it holy. This was a trap, but he walked right on in anyway. Putting a knee down between Tomas's spread legs, he leaned in and kissed the man hard, like they had both been wanting for weeks.

"Oh!" Tomas gasped, and then his hands were in Perry's hair, tilting his head so he could fasten his teeth in the soft skin of his throat, sucking and biting down in little shocks of pleasure-pain that made Perry fumble at his own breeches, desperate.

Buttons—so many buttons to undo with shaking fingers, and each one was a transgression and a thrill. Perry was pulled down to blanket Tomas's slender body and to rub that fine blue suit into the dirt. When he got both flies undone, both overlong shirts untucked, and wrapped his hand around Tomas's prick along with his own, it was with the sense that he had finally arrived at the centre of creation, the still point around which everything revolved. Then Tomas made a sound that was half laugh, half sob, and they went scrabbling for joy as though the earth itself rocked.

Afterward, Perry lowered himself to Tomas's side and tugged him close to his chest in an embrace perhaps more protective than Tomas's sharpness deserved. They lay for a long while catching their breath and drowsing.

"What is it between you and the Quicks?" Perry asked, idly, intending only to fill the time until they could go again. No one could see them here. They could fuck as much as they wanted. Though *fuck* was too harsh a word, perhaps, for a thing that made blowsy roses of contentment blossom in his chest. "Why do they want you gone so badly?"

"The admiral is my grandfather." Tomas sat up to take a pull on the flask and offered it to Perry after, still wet from his mouth. Grog, warming and sweet.

"My father was the admiral's first child. From a marriage he contracted as a young lieutenant. My grandmother was a barmaid. She always maintained that they were married properly, in church, but evidently in time he grew to think their connection was not advantageous to him, and he married Damaris Fairbairn for her money, claiming that my grandmother had only been his mistress all along."

Perry worried at this knowledge for a moment, and then it opened to him in its horrible entirety. "Good God!"

Tomas's wolfish smile bit the jugular out of Perry's good mood. "You understand? Somewhere in my father's papers—which are extensive, for he ran a legal practice for several years—is my grandparents' marriage certificate. Once I have unearthed it, I can prove that Damaris's marriage was never valid. That Lazarus is a bastard, and that the Quick estate should have come to my father and thence to me. My father was content with his life, and would not give me the document when I asked. But now that he's dead—God rest his soul—it wants but time for me to find it. When I do, I can ruin their reputation. I can kick them out of their house, which should have been mine, and I can end their stifling grip on this town for good."

"And replace it with your own?" Perry asked, all the flowers inside him curling up and dying at the thought. This grudge was bigger than he had supposed. No wonder the Quicks were vehement and even scared. No wonder Constance had looked at Perry with such condemnation at their last meeting. He had allowed himself to be seduced by the man who wanted to ruin her.

"I will be a more benevolent dictator than he ever was." Tomas laughed, and abruptly Perry was so cold that he had to scramble back into his clothes, holding himself tight against a storm of new doubts. For that kind of prize, a man would do anything, play anyone as a pawn. What if Perry himself had been—

"Perry? What's wrong?"

"To think I believed you were a good man. Indeed, I almost believed it. And this is your plan? A grab for power and money with no compassion at all for your own family? Am I part of that? Is this"—he gestured around himself, while reordering his clothes with the other hand—"merely a way in which you can steal me from them too? I will go back now. Take me back to the mainland at once."

The perplexity and hurt that had been on Tomas's face when he began this speech had turned into a frozen and steely affront by the time he had finished. Even in Perry's first flood of horror and betrayal, he would have welcomed an explanation, or better still, to be soothed and spoken to persuasively until he could put his suspicions down. But Tomas offered neither of those things, and Perry was not yet willing to ask.

"This is what you choose to believe of me, is it?" Tomas rose and began to dress himself in jerky, aggressive movements. "Fuck you, then."

They sailed home seething, without saying a word.

Cut to the bone by Perry's sudden turn, Tomas's fury drove him to his door like a lash across his shoulders. But when he shut the heavy wood behind him, his defiance ebbed enough to show him despair beneath it. He staggered to a chair in the hall with a sense that something had broken in his back and he could no longer stand. His legs weighed a ton each, his shoulders supported the pillars of the sky. He hardly knew what to make of this feeling, never having had it before, and might have gone to his mother with it, but that she seemed to have gone out and taken Iskander with her.

Tomas repeated Perry's words in his head, trying to rekindle his anger. Anger was what he was familiar with—the kind that put a spring in his step and stirred him to further efforts—not this. He should not be flattened by Perry's distrust, as though the man had pulled the whole earth out from beneath him and left him in the abyss.

This was not supposed to have happened—whatever this was, this sucking despondency. This was not the plan. Perry was to have become infatuated with him. Perry was to have found his own heart incapable of enduring a life in which Tomas did not hold pride of place. Tomas was to have enjoyed his admiration and used his new malleability to thwart the bloody Quicks' attempts to ruin Tomas's life.

Yes, I wanted to steal you from them. Why not? I know how to value you better. We could have been kings of this town together, safe, wealthy, respected by all.

Heartbreak veered back into fury like a treacherous wind. *But I didn't steal you. I treated with you honestly, and see now what that gets me! Fine. Sod your caveats and your scruples. I'm going to do this, and I'm going to do it this instant. I don't need your approval!*

He threw himself to his feet and stormed upstairs, to go through his father's papers. Peder had been a highly sought-after lawyer in his later years, and one of the upstairs bedrooms had been repurposed as a study. Tomas had helped his father make the shelves and cabinets that lined the room, and even with the prospect of finding the marriage certificate, he had not yet been able to make himself deface his father's room with the thoroughness necessary for the job.

Now, however, he needed somewhere to vent his spleen or it would burst, and it didn't worsen his misery significantly to pull out and riffle through all the folders of briefs and evidence, all the letters in his father's handwriting, the very shape of which—a year ago— would have made him want to weep.

He made a fire in the grate, and went through every folder, burning what was no longer relevant, assembling a smaller pile of paperwork to be wrapped in oiled paper and stored in the attic. When a bookshelf was cleared, he comforted himself by smashing it into pieces with a hammer, relishing in the splintering blows as though he could pulverise this sense of loss, anger, and need into pieces so small they could be safely ignored.

How dare he? I don't mind being thought a smuggler and a criminal, for that is what I am, but for him to think me false? Why would I trifle with him when the rumour of it could lose me all my support in this town? I put myself into his hands, and he—

What was so special about Perry anyway? Other than the darkness of his eyes and the richness of his skin? Other than his stupid impulsiveness and an honour that Tomas admired. Perhaps it was that one knew where one stood with Perry. Even when he tried insincerity, the truth of his passions was clear as a window. Honest and trustworthy . . .

And apparently thinks himself better than me.

That thought had Tomas turning to the bureau. He tipped out the drawers, the tray of quills, scattering the sad glass bottles of dried ink and clumped sand. He pulled out every paper rolled up and forced into the pigeonholes and scanned them with a hasty eye before flinging them onto the flames in disgust. Never what he wanted! Nothing ever was.

There was nothing special about the bureau—a thrice hand-me-down bought from a junk dealer. Even if there had been, Tomas might not have stopped, the bar in his hand alive and his fury moving through him like a lightning strike. The pain in his hands and shoulders was like brandy—made him cough and flame up alike, wild and all the more satisfied for the knowledge that it would hurt later.

He smashed in his father's desk as though it was a ghost of grief, and as the writing slope separated from the drawers beneath, a shallow, secret cubby was revealed.

Tomas's seething emotions lurched as though he had run into a sandbank—a sensation of hitting unexpected resistance, a sudden halt that threatened to break his back, and then settling into a new and wary shape. There was a document folded into the compartment, and he feared it with an unexpected fear.

He sidled up to the paper with his hand outstretched as though it might bite. Was it . . .? Was it really . . .?

Tomas drew it out, unfolded it. The heavy black letters were solid and harsh before his eyes, but it still took him three attempts to read them. *Certified copy of an entry of marriage*— and yes. There they were. *Lieutenant Thomas Justinian Quick to Mary Chantrey of this parish.*

Sitting down hard on the remnants of the desk, he struggled not to clench his fists and wrinkle this miraculous survivor. God, it was true! Not that he had disbelieved his father's words, but having the proof at his fingertips was different.

Very different. He would have expected to feel a purer joy, a greater vindication, but his bleak mood combined with this victory to turn it into a burden. *I could destroy them now. Utterly. But Perry would never forgive it.*

Why should I care what he forgives?

But he did. And he could not—God forgive him—go forward from this discovery without sounding Perry out first, without making sure with absolute certainty that he might be losing more than he gained by it.

He would talk to Perry first. When his nerves had had time to calm, and his thoughts to settle. Tomorrow, maybe. They would talk, and then he would see.

CHAPTER TWENTY-FOUR

PERRY SHOULD JUST STAY OUT OF CAVES

The following day, as if reflecting Perry's mood, the weather took a turn for the worse. The wind picked up, but blew steadily shoreward, trapping even the nimble fishing boats in the harbour, while a rolling blanket of dirty-grey cloud closed over the sky and took away the special vibrancy of light and colour that gave Porthkennack's cramped streets and nautical litter their unusual charm.

Trapped beneath the cloud, the summer's heat was sweaty, feverish. Or perhaps that was Perry's undecided mind, which tossed and fretted as if it had an ague of its own.

I am beginning to think I am too soft for this work, he wrote to his mother. Their first exchange of letters had contained only pleasantries and the transmission of his address, but now he needed someone to talk to who was not embroiled in this whole affair. *I had every intention of doing whatever needed to be done to establish myself as a great man in this town. A man of justice and probity, certainly, but also of power.*

He dipped his quill in his inkwell. After he had spared Mary Castille, the gossip network of the town must have been hard at work, for two days later, his landlord had casually mentioned he had a larger, windowed room, available for the same price as Perry's old coffin-like cabin. There was still barely room to straighten his legs or elbows, but a tiny writing desk and chest could be squeezed in, and in the daytime there was all the light he could wish.

But I found myself moved by the plight of the poorest people in my new community, and the example of France teaches us the wisdom of mercy, of equity, lest those who are left with no other recourse rise up and destroy their oppressors.

He pressed the heels of his hands into his eyes, and massage his aching jaw with his thumbs. Which of these two categories did Tomas fall into? If it was true that his birthright had been taken from him, didn't he have every reason to want it back? If he found his paperwork and used it to utterly humiliate and ruin his cousins, was that not exactly what they deserved?

Yet are not the great also human, also to be pitied? he wrote, feeling odd about the concept. But Damaris would not have known when she wed the admiral that her marriage was invalid. Her children and her grandchildren were not to blame for their progenitor's faults. They were proud people, and the shame would destroy them. Who would wed Constance if it was known she was the daughter of a bastard? No wonder she was not sleeping—this threat could undo her whole life.

The words *Why can we not simply help one another?* formed on the end of his pen, but he heard how childish and despairing they sounded and did not write them down.

There had been something in Tomas's demeanour from the start that proclaimed him harsh, sharp, even ruthless, and Perry could not deny that he had found it attractive, reined in as it was by Tomas's Wesleyan faith. It had been exciting to think of the man as someone who could, by nature, be a monster, but who was choosing not to be.

If he did go through with this plan, though? Ruined a family, when he himself had everything a man might need already? It would not be illegal, certainly, but it would be cruel beyond what Perry was willing to accept. It would give the lie to what Perry had begun to find was his sustaining belief that Tomas was, underneath it all, a good man.

And if Tomas put himself in charge of all the Quick's businesses, made himself the magistrate, stepped into every possession and duty he had stripped from Lazarus, and used them to further his smuggling career, like a pirate lord of old?

Perry moved the pressure from his jaw to the bridge of his nose, where a headache was building that almost matched the aching throb in his chest—the one that might be a heart attack, or might just be grief. If that was Tomas's plan, then Perry would be forced once again to become the man's enemy. Sometime over the last month, imperceptibly, his pursuit of Tomas as a villain had become a courtship. They had become allies, then lovers. But all that would have to end if Tomas came into the Quicks' power.

If he did, would he not give you everything you wanted? Position, money, respectability, power to change the world for the better?

Tomas might—he might give all that to Perry as a great man gifts his mistress with jewels and estates. And Perry's pride utterly revolted at achieving his ends by such a method. He would shape his fate by his own hands, or not at all.

A knock on his door interrupted a train of thoughts he had already grubbied with repetition. He capped the inkwell and covered the letter with a sheet of blotting paper and a smooth stone he had picked up in the harbour to serve as a paperweight, and opened the door to the landlord.

"Message for you, sir." The landlord handed him a scrap of newspaper with the words *Talk to me* scrawled on it in pencil. "Mr. Tomas brought it himself. I told him you weren't having visitors, and he give me this and walked off, but—"

The landlord narrowed his eyes. Perry felt his newfound status tremble beneath him. Perhaps this was the point at which he would be moved back into his old room or thrown out altogether.

"You and 'im have a falling out, sir?"

"We never had a falling in," Perry lied without thinking, only to have his conscience and his heart rebuke him in such a deep inward welling of darkness that it took him a long moment to realize that the sky, too, had dimmed, and the distant kettledrum roar was the sound of approaching thunder.

The flags on the customs warehouse were visible from here, streaming out south southwest so strongly they looked as though someone had taken a flatiron to them, starched them rigid. A well-handled ship might just slip from Constantine Bay and run unscathed past Land's End, but any vessel coming from Wales or Ireland, or even the great port of Liverpool, would have to pass Bloody Mary first. The night was drawing in and a storm stood out to sea. Wrecking weather at last.

Abruptly he wished he could talk to Tomas, could allow Tomas to persuade away his dilemma and his scruples. Could at least give the man the chance to explain himself that he probably deserved.

"But if he comes again later this evening, you may tell him that I am going up to the cliffs—to the spot he pointed out. If he will not join me there, then I will speak with him tomorrow noon at his house."

Once the landlord had gone, Perry threw on a sea cloak with a deep hood against the inevitable rain. He buckled on his sword and thrust a brace of pistols into his waistband, powder and shot and chalk in his pockets, and then he ran down the back stairs of the inn and stepped out into an evening of cold drizzle.

Already the light was fading. Remembering his partner's offer of backup, he called on Jowan, but the man had gone over to Boscastle to visit his eldest daughter, and Perry did not trust any of the other customs men enough to consider them.

This is fortunate, he told himself, *a fortunate opportunity for you to face your lingering fears and overcome them.* But it didn't feel anything of the sort as he strode out for the cliffs with his cloak flaring behind him, and a dark lantern lit but shuttered in his hand.

By the time he reached the Lizard, the wind was lashing water against his face like tiny arrows. A grey blur atop the promontory caught his eye—something white went whirling away like a great cartwheel. He stopped to frown up at the disturbance, and a moment's peering through the rain resolved into the sight of Constance Quick clutching her straw hat to her head with one hand, and an easel and paint box with the other. The whirling thing must have been her canvas.

She wore a stylish riding habit, the wide skirts of which were streaming in the wind as relentlessly as the flags on the customs house, catching on the bag of supplies by her feet and billowing out like sails. Surprising that she didn't blow away. Perry snorted. It was foolish of her to try to paint a sunset on a day when the weather had been so set for misery that even he—a landsman—had been able to tell it was going to be filthy.

Yet she'd grown up here. Why had she not been able to tell?

As he watched, lightning ripped through the sky with a sound like tearing linen. His heart leaped and thundered. Hand on her hat, Constance was looking at him, her gaze as piercingly cold as it had been in the pink room. It pricked at him, like it was significant, but he set the feeling aside when the shocking blue-white light revealed a sliver of void behind a holly tree in the cliff barely a man's height up from the path. A cave mouth! One that he had passed beneath a dozen times, not knowing it was there.

Hands on the roots of the tree, he hauled and scrambled himself up. The long line of the cave mouth was bigger from close up, and he wiggled himself into it shoulder first, and found that barely a step inside it widened into a veritable passage.

Putting his hood down, baring his chilly neck to the cave's damp cold, he slid open the shutter on his lantern, took the chalk from his pocket, and marked the wall with a large *E* and an arrow pointing in the direction he would go. He was not going to lose his way again. Nor did he need to be taught a lesson twice.

Feeling accomplished, he walked on into the hill. Where the path split, he chose always the larger passage, and marked each intersection as he passed. He had hoped to listen for any signs of activity, but several of these passages seemed to lead to the sea, and its angry roar, cut through again and again with the *crack* and *boom* of distant thunder and lightning, made even his own footsteps hard to hear.

After almost half an hour of this, he began to doubt that there was anything here to discover after all. What if it was a natural cave, inhabited only by bats? What if he was chasing phantasms?

A deep-green glint in the gloom shone out at ankle level. Perry hunkered down to see what it was. Only a glass buoy in a tangle of old net, but it meant someone had been down here. Something human used this place for good or ill.

He went to straighten up, and a cold circle pressed against the back of his neck, sending a shock of anger and terror down his back like a snowball shoved down a warm coat.

"Don't move or I shoot." A young man's voice, hoarse as though he had breathed in smoke and burned his throat.

Perry stilled, except for the roiling of the humiliation in his gut. In God's name, not again!

He eased himself onto one knee, turning his head just enough to discern the youth behind him. Long legs skinny in seaboots, the shape of his body swamped beneath a wide coat, and his face invisible behind a kerchief, the boy looked and sounded like a lightweight.

A sudden spring to knock the gun away, a fist to the jaw, and Perry could turn these tables easily enough.

He exhaled with nervous relief, gathered himself to leap, and the boy's off hand came round with . . . Perry froze again in astonishment. It was a metal tube with a plunger—a syringe, such as might be used for giving an enema. When it was jabbed into the side of his throat, he was bemused by what was happening. *Could you do that? Could you press a liquid into a person's body through the skin?*

The answer seemed to be yes, though it hurt and bruised as it went in. But why?

A little drunk and dizzy-calm, forgetting altogether that there was a gun pressed against his spine, he lifted a hand to try to bat the tube away. Hilariously, his hand didn't seem to work as he expected, though it mattered not, because a most delicious drowsiness was weighing on his eyes. Suddenly all he really wanted to do was to lie down and rest. He toppled forward, his misbehaving hands encountering wet cave dirt.

Something about that sensation tried to send a spike of panic through him, tried to wake him up, but it wasn't strong enough.

He closed his eyes. A little sleep could do him no harm.

Infuriated with being turned away at Perry's door—having to beg for an audience, no less—Tomas took a long route home across the moor to feel the wind on his face. It tugged fiercely at the loops of his hair bow and chilled his cheek. A cannon blast of a wind, south southeast, that would stretch the sailsmanship of his crew to their limits but, if it could be caught, would be like harnessing the gulls and flying.

He felt the call of the *Swift's* tiny deck. Yes, why not? If he went out in this, it would take him a week just to get back home. Time to think.

He touched the marriage certificate, which he had taken to carrying in his inner pocket, pressing urgently against his heart. The mysterious reluctance, which had prevented him from finding it before, now seemed determined to stop him from using it. He was aware that the desire to sail away for a week or so was merely another attempt of his mind to delay his plans, sabotage his own revenge, but that did not make the desire to avoid the decision go away.

Now that it was within his grasp, his vengeance felt uglier than it had when it had only been a matter of imagination. Quite aside from the fact that Perry might never talk to him again, a part of Tomas's heart was telling him the money and status he would earn by it would sour many a friendship, would change his reputation from one of honesty to one of cruelty.

How much did he care?

Shaking his head to try to clear it, he took another deep breath of the racing wind. It tugged him as always. A trip to France might give him time to settle on a course of action. Outwitting the French coastguards, particularly if there was a fight—the *boom* of cannon and the greasy salty smell of lit powder—that would lift his spirits.

Perhaps, after an absence, Perry would come to find him for a change. Perhaps, if he did, Tomas would cut *him* off, refuse to speak to him. Let him feel the proof that Tomas didn't need him either.

I was fine before he arrived in Porthkennack. I will be fine again without him.

Yet Tomas's thoughts still turned to Hector—to how whole he had felt those years they had spent together. When it had been the two of them against the world instead of Tomas alone? That had been a blessing no money could buy, and one for which he would give up a great deal.

Still without a true decision made, he began the long task of rounding up his crew to put to sea.

When he delivered himself to Anne Lusmoore's cottage, Anne was out. So he sent her youngest brother to tell her to meet him at the *Swift* as soon as possible, and then, having a household of small children to hand and no desire to criss-cross the town himself, he gave them all farthings and sent one to each of the other members of his crew, telling them to assemble on board with provisions and money, and to come urgently, for it was a rescue.

That done, he stood in the cottage's rose be-wound porch for a moment, watching the harbour and the sky. As the sun set, a hazy golden light had gathered beneath the murky clouds, and against it, a large rowing boat pulling out into the open sea looked like a laborious beetle on a marigold. The humped backs of the rowers were black in silhouette before the falling sun, and the tarp between them was snugly tucked over a shape . . . the shape of an unconscious body.

Tomas stiffened. *Barnabas!* And as he did, a three-masted brig sailed out from the cover of the headland—the storm light filling its sails with arcs of lemon. The rowing boat coupled onto its chains. But now, with the bulk of the brig between himself and the sun, he couldn't see what was handed up the side.

He didn't need to see. Somehow he just knew.

Starting forward, he began to run toward the *Swift*. They could still do it. These merchant ships were always short-handed, and therefore slow. And damn him if he was going to let anyone else get away from him today.

"Mr. Quick," a boy called to him as he emerged onto the street. "I been looking for you for hours. Message from Mr. Dean."

Oh. Oh! The heaviness under which he had been labouring fell off as his spine unbroke, his stomach doing something extraordinary and almost nauseating in relief. He tried not to let it show. "Yes?"

"He says he's going up to the cliffs—to the spot you told him about. He wants you to join him there, but if you can't, he'll speak with you tomorrow noon at your house."

So turning him away at the door had been a temporary rejection! A spat even—an invitation to do more next time? Tomas's natural self-assuredness rolled back over him in a spring tide of joy and he grinned so hard his cheeks ached. His inclination was—of course—to rush to Perry's side. Why would the man go after wreckers without taking a party? Did he still think he was invulnerable?

But if Tomas walked up to the cliffs now, he would be abandoning Barnabas to his fate.

The memory of that abject cell recurred to him, Perry as a captive—how strong he had seemed, and yet how he had shivered afterward, undermined. *You love him, you should go to him*, Tomas's instincts told him, but he had spent a lifetime tempering his instincts with reason. *If I love him, I will trust him to know how to do his job, because if I go to him now, Barnabas will be beyond saving when I return.*

"I'll meet him tomorrow, then," he said and flicked the boy a penny as he passed.

CHAPTER TWENTY-FIVE

A RESOURCEFUL SAILOR

"Mate, wake up! Wake up, I need you."

Perry's head was full of a drowsiness so thick it clung like glue, but these words penetrated it, along with a pain in his wrist—very cold—that he really wanted to go away.

He tried to roll over. The world swayed beneath him, rough and white, with a smell of tar and paint.

Somewhere too close to his head, a scuffling noise made him think of rats—there had been rats in the dockyard flat where his family lived when he was an infant, and he sometimes dreamed of them running over his face in the night. If he lay still too long, they would gnaw him.

Groaning, he forced his eyes open just as a bare heel slammed down within an inch of his nose. A thud and "unh" of impact above him; a *shing* and rattle as what sounded like a metal chain was snapped across a wooden surface; and full awareness came back to Perry in a volcanic eruption.

The pain in his wrist was the pain of an iron shackle. Even now, a sailor was hammering a ring bolt at the end of it into a wooden floor. No—not a floor, because the world continued to rock. The lantern above him, which hung from a wooden ceiling held up by crooked knees of oak, creaked as it swung through a regular circle that swept shadows and lights over painted wooden walls that wept with steady trickles of water.

This was the belly of a ship, and he was being chained to the deck.

Outrage had him on his feet in seconds. He grabbed the chain with his other hand and pulled with all his might. The hammering process must have only just begun, because he could feel the bolt wobble and give. Another desperate wrench and it tore out. He grabbed it so he could use it as a whip and raised his head to meet the eyes of the man with the hammer—a scrawny creature, wrinkled and tanned as any sailor, with pale-grey eyes that in the lantern light seemed not to have an iris at all—a pinpoint of black on an all-white background. Creepy.

Seeing Perry straighten up, free, this man raised both hands and backed away toward the hatch into the next deck. Glue still clung at Perry's thoughts. There was something important he should—

"Don't let 'im get out," said the voice which had woken him—a deep voice with an accent that reminded Perry of his mother's. "Hop to it, cap'n, before 'e brings 'em all down on us."

Perry had no experience with a whip, but he had thrown enough hawsers to know what to do with a length of rope. He snapped the chain out in a slithering hissing arc. The sailor stepped back, but the final links snarled in his braces, turning him into its spiral, wrapping him like a constricting snake. Perry yanked and the man came stumbling into his space. The sailor's mouth opened—he was going to yell, bring reinforcements—so Perry got one arm around his neck and clamped the other hand over his mouth and nose, pressing harder through the panicked flailing until the man's body went limp against his own.

Then he lowered it to the deck, shoved its own neckerchief in its mouth and tied its arms behind it with its own belt. Only then did he turn to see who had spoken behind him.

It had not been above a month ago, but so much had changed in himself in that time that he felt jerked into ancient history by the sight of Barnabas Okesi, still in the white duck trousers and ochre pea jacket in which he'd been captured. Alive! Very much alive, in fact, with his own jailer dangling from his capable hands and a light in his eyes, turned loose in his own element.

"I've been looking for you for so long," Perry gasped out. His head was clearing by the second, but he had to say this. Barnabas deserved to know. "To rescue you, I mean."

Barnabas grinned and trussed up his own captive as impersonally as if he were bailing cargo. "Well, mate, I hope you got a plan from here on, because I'm winging it."

Distressingly, Perry's first thought was of Tomas. Had he received the innkeeper's message? Had he come in time to see Perry being carried off? Would he— Something spasmed in his gut like a sob and he had to grind his teeth to keep it in. Would Tomas even care anymore, after Perry had discarded him like a used washrag once they were done?

The thought that Tomas might be sailing after this ship in his speedy cutter, ready to throw open every cage and deliver Perry to the light a second time was probably nothing more than wishful thinking. Unneeded too. Perry was not incapable—he would rescue himself.

"They saw four men come down," he said, working this out aloud. "They expect two to return." He shuffled off his coat, untied his prisoner enough to strip the jacket and trousers from him. "At a distance, if we're wearing their sailors' clothes, they might think—"

"Little coal-black ain't we?"

Perry jammed the sailor's wide tricorn on his head, then retied him and dragged him to where a stack of barrels towered, lashed together against the roll of the sea. "Is there no flour?"

Barnabas actually laughed. "I tell you what there will be—paint. White paint for the cabins. Hold on." He helped Perry wedge their captives in among the barrels, then darted into the bows, returning with a container of white paint. They thinned it with the seawater trickling through the walls and daubed their hands and faces.

Barnabas's face was disconcerting, his coverage uneven and the effect more of a walking corpse than of a healthy white man. "It'll only pass at a distance," Perry concluded. "But it might give us time enough to get to a boat."

They had taken Perry's pistols and his sword, and then had made a cursory search of his pockets, taking all the balls of powder they could find, but one pocket had a hole in it, and when he felt around inside, he discovered several balls of gunpowder had slipped into the inner lining. He tried to press this on Barnabas, because he had sworn to protect the man and it was the only weapon he had to give, but Barnabas shook his head. "I've no gun to put it in, and if I'm hauling out a boat—they're going to see that, you know. Craning a boat over the gunwale is hard to hide. We should just throw ourselves over. Swim for it."

Though chained for a second time, Perry still believed he could turn this situation around on his own. He could change the very world by his own efforts, and it was his duty to do so. He squeezed the gunpowder tight in his hand, consumed with the desire to blow something up. But Barnabas had a point and every right to look after himself. "You go if you can." Perry nodded. "But I want the logbook first. I want evidence to get these people arrested, so they can't do this again. Make as much noise as you can when you go over—draw them away from the cabin for me, and I will come after when I have it."

"You think anyone's ever going to listen to the likes of us?" Barnabas's scepticism suited him. Even drippingly pallid as he was, he seemed the best kind of British tar—active, intelligent, resourceful.

They should. But Perry said, "No. No, I don't. That's why I want irrefutable documentary evidence."

He heard what he had said with a clench around the lungs that felt like despair—so he had already accepted, had he, that the Quicks would never listen to him, that they saw him as Lord Petersfield's exotic pet as Elijah was Damaris's. Very well then, Perry would stop pulling his punches on their behalf.

"Heh." Barnabas shrugged and held out his hand. "Give me the gunpowder after all. I know what to do."

Climbing the companionways, Barnabas behind him, Perry hinged open the hatch as silently as he could and emerged into the shadowy warmth of the lower deck. This, too, was lit only by a pair of lanterns, barely bright enough to delineate the hammocks swinging like huge peasecods fore and aft. A black metal galley by the main mast still gave out a pleasant heat as the hands of the sea rocked the sleepers side to side. Fate was on Perry's side, it seemed—it was dark outside, giving them much less chance of being spotted at once.

Up again then, and out onto the sparsely populated deck of a merchant ship. A figure at the wheel was illuminated by the binnacle lamps, and a black shape, lumpen against the sky, was a lookout on the top yard of the main mast. Voices and smoke drifted from the sail crew, who had settled themselves onto their coiled ropes and were talking with the slow, lazy cadence of folk unmoored from past and future, swept along by a steady breeze through the warmth of a summer night.

Perry and Barnabas leaned on the rail on the other side of the capstan from the crew. "The captain will be in his cabin asleep." Barnabas nodded in its direction, where a faint yellow light shone through the slats of its door. "I'll draw him out. You dash in. Then you're on your own."

"All right." Perry held out a hand, and they shook solemnly. "Good luck."

Cautiously, yet trying to act as though he had every right to stroll the decks at night, Perry slid up the quarterdeck ladder and approached the cabin. How long he had been held unconscious he didn't know, but the storm had passed and the clouds were breaking overhead, enough to allow a silver-blue wash of moonlight through. He flattened himself into the nearest shadow and watched as Barnabas rolled, easy and confident as you pleased, up to the bow signal gun. There he bent and began to cast off the ropes that tied it to the ship's side.

When he hauled it back, the rumble of its wooden wheels against the deck planks made the gossiping crewmen fall silent. Nothing further seemed to happen for a long time, Barnabas hugging the cannon's muzzle, taking out the tompion and shoving the powder down.

The crew had just relaxed and begun to chat once more when the cannon roared to life, springing back on its chains with a *boom* and *twang* as though a giant had released his crossbow. The very ship shuddered under Perry, and a tongue of flame three yards long spat out from the bow like the display of an annoyed dragon.

"What!" someone cried in the cabin. "What the hell!"

Already the ship's sailors were on their feet, running toward the gun. The cabin door flung open, and the captain ran out in his nightgown and cap. "Who is responsible for this?"

Perry slipped into the cabin as soon as the captain's back was turned, but the answer was still audible, even as he shuffled through the papers on the desk for the cargo manifest. "Don't know, sir. It gone off by itself. There weren't no one here. There ain't no one here now."

Barnabas must have jumped the moment he lit the fuse, letting the roar of the gun cover up the splash as he entered the water. Clever.

But now it was Perry's turn. He caught a glimpse of the words *two male slaves*, on a piece of parchment tucked into a logbook, snatched it out, and looked around the cabin for something to fold it into, to waterproof it for the time he spent swimming . . .

They'd be coming back now, if only so the captain could dress before he ordered an examination of the ship. Quickly! Quickly—he needed to be quick.

There, in an open footlocker, the tight-woven waxed linen sack of the post was visible. Perry snatched it, emptied out letters and parcels with shaking hands. *Come on. Come on.*

He wrapped his purloined list into this covering and shoved it into his shirt, where it lay invisibly beneath his waistcoat, tight to his skin.

Movement outside. He ran to the cabin windows, intending to climb out, fling himself from the stern, where the splash would be hidden in the turbulence of the wake.

But the windows would not open. He ran his hands around them, looking for catches, only to cut his finger open on the head of a nail. They had been nailed into their frames—nailed shut, as effective as prison bars. *Shit.*

A voice outside was answered by another. The door rattled and began to open. Perry ran for the curtain around the hole in the deck that was the captain's personal head, but he had barely got a hand on it when the captain burst back inside, two sailors with marlin spikes behind him, and behind them, a man cradling a rifle to his chest with the kind of easy confidence that boasted he could split a hair at night while drunk, and would be delighted for the opportunity to show it.

Shit, Perry took hold once more of the length of chain he had tucked into his pocket. He should have taken Barnabas's advice, should have been long gone, but damn him, damn all of them, he was not going back into the hold without a fight. They would have to kill him first.

CHAPTER TWENTY-SIX

SWIFT TO THE RESCUE

All Tomas's crew bar Temperance Smith were already at the *Swift* when Tomas jogged up, and Smith arrived bare minutes later, when they were heaving the cutter out into deeper water. Tomas leaped aboard as soon as he might, and yelled at his sail crew to work faster as the sheets tumbled slowly down. Trusting him to know when an action was truly urgent, they put their backs into hauling the ropes, and within another five minutes, the *Swift* was gulling up the bay toward the open sea.

But already the light had slipped from citrine to smoky. The trim brig with all her sails set was no longer in sight, even through a spyglass, and if Tomas did not guess her course correctly, she might slip away from him in the night and in the morning be miles away, beyond his reach.

What route would they take? Where were they going? To America, to deliver Barnabas to the Quicks' plantation? To Africa to take on more captives so they might deliver a hold full? Or to the Scilly Isles, where illegal cargoes of every sort were traded with impunity? He had no way to guess, and if he got it wrong...

It was already dark. Now they would be looking only for stern lanterns and the light of the cabin. Tomas bit his cheek, trying to think.

Take a single captive halfway across the world? Not worth it. They will be going somewhere as close as possible where they can trade him on.

"Set a course for the Scilly Isles," he said, running up the ratlines to the top of the main mast for a better look out. "And keep your eyes peeled for lights. If God is with us, we will free that poor man tonight."

"Aye, sir," said Anne, bending over her charts. A moment later she called out a change of course, and he felt the clipper respond beneath him, the heel over of the masts, the tension of the rigging. But the last dregs of sunlight had slipped from the sky now, and the stars barely glimmered on the choppy waves. Darkness enclosed him from one horizon to the next.

Some of his unaccustomed flatness returned. The taste of failure, that was what it must be. He hated it.

"I can't see anything," Bob Ede called from the bows. "Maybe 'e's doused 'is lights? Does he know we're—"

And a glorious plume of red-and-gold flame tore out of a distant cannon, visible in the pitch as the lightning had been visible in the storm. "There!" Tomas called, focusing his glass. Yes, now he could just pick out the dim illumination of a single lantern on the brig's deck, and some kind of scuffle going on in front of the cabin. Could that be Barnabas himself, putting up a fight? Tomas's hopes soared. "A gold sovereign for every man on the crew if you can get us there in under a minute," he cried, and slid down to go pick up the ropes at the bow.

The brig's lookout must have been asleep, or distracted by the altercation on deck, for the *Swift* whispered up to her unseen. Tomas tied them to the anchor chain—for the rowing boat still trailed behind the main chains—and in whispered conference told Bob and Sully to stay on board, holding her ready to fly at his word.

"This is a rescue not a vendetta," he told the others. "I don't deny they probably don't deserve to live, but we deserve not to kill—"

"All right, my lover," said Temperance testily. "Not like you don't tell us this every time. Let's go."

Tomas huffed at the insubordination, but jammed down his hat, tightened his kerchief about his face as a mask, and nodded. "Let's."

Silently, more like pirates than smugglers, his crew eased up the anchor chain and rolled over the gunwales onto the deck, the sound of their bare feet hitting it camouflaged by the din of a brawl.

A *shhhnk* of metal. Someone screamed. Tomas shrugged the fish-priest down his sleeve into his hand and weighed its reassuring heaviness to calm his nerves. Fanning out, keeping to the shadows, he and his crew stalked up behind the fighters.

Was that Barnabas in the centre? There was something familiar about the way he moved, but his face was a livid, melted white that made him look like a pond demon. He was fighting the crew of the ship with a length of chain wielded like a whip, the prodigious swings of it knocking his assailants off their feet, sweeping them into one another, continuously jostling the aim of the man with the rifle.

It was magnificent, seeing him there alone against these dogs, but the longer it went on, the more chance for him to fail. Tomas made a cutting gesture to his crew, and they pounced out of the shadows together.

The rifleman was Tomas's, and the angle at which his face was snugged up to his gun's stock turned his temple perfectly into range. Tomas brought his bludgeon down with a *crack*. The man's finger tightened.

Tomas held his breath, but then the rifleman slackened, the gun fell from his nerveless fingers, and he thudded to the deck, followed by half a dozen sailors and a man in a nightgown.

In the sudden silence, Barnabas Okesi let his chain-whip furl at his feet in a rattle of links. He straightened up, and the garish white paint of his mask resolved all at once into a face that Tomas knew.

With a shock of retrospective terror, he appreciated how much more he would have suffered if he had known this beforehand. "Perry? What the hell?"

Chapter Twenty-Seven

Technical Piracy

*P*erry gave a startled gasp of a laugh and buried his face in his hands for a long moment. Tomas recognised the signs of a man reordering his mind, coming back to himself after the extremities of battle. And what a warrior he was! Tomas fancied himself with a knife, but he would never have been able to keep half a dozen men at bay all by himself with nothing more than a length of chain.

"Sir." Anne plucked at his sleeve, interrupting his swell of pride on Perry's behalf. "We should get them into the cabin before anyone else comes up on deck and sees 'em lying."

He nodded, and they dragged the sailors into the captain's cabin, tying their arms behind them and gagging them with strips torn from their shirts. Perry went at once to the captain's nightstand, where a jug of water hung on a gimballed shelf. Hands shaking, he poured it into the basin and washed the strange tint off his face, though shades of it lingered in his hair, making him look older, distinguished.

Tomas handed him one of the captain's shirts to dry off with, and when their fingertips brushed as it passed between them, a flash of galvanic energy leapt at the point. This time when Tomas smiled, Perry returned it, his gaze heating by degrees into a warmth Tomas could not afford his crew to see.

"Did you find Barnabas?" Perry asked, dropping his gaze as soon as Tomas frowned.

"Find him? He's not aboard?"

Perry shook his head and began opening drawers in the cabin's great table. Pulling out an eating knife, he tried to lever open the shackle on his wrist. "He jumped, less than quarter of an hour ago. I fear for him trying to swim to shore in the night, on this coast."

Something with the same root as indignation rose up in Tomas then, filling him with a fire that was similar to his own rage. He went to kick the unconscious form of the rifleman, and Perry grasped him and stopped him.

"Bastard deserves a kicking," Tomas protested. "If he drove a good man to jump to his death. If he put that ugly thing—" he nodded at the shackle "—on *you*. If more of these devils got what they deserved, then maybe they'd think twice."

"Or maybe they'd hang you too!" Perry shouted it in his face, as always as thankful for a rescue as Tomas would have been himself— in other words, not at all. He didn't blame the man for that. No one wanted to feel indebted, obliged. "This is an act of piracy you're committing here. Or have you forgotten that?"

The accusation startled Tomas into a laugh, wrong-footing his righteous wrath. "Then I suppose you'd better arrest me," he said, grinning. This bickering felt like old and well-worn territory now, like flirtation.

It brightened Perry's face too. "I might be able to overlook it this once. There is a rowing boat attached to the anchor chain. Can you have one of your people take it out and begin to search for—"

"Anne," Tomas called—she would know the tides around here best, where a man might be swept, and she would need someone to row while she watched, "and Dennis, go now and look for our lost sailor. Temperance, Alan, you stay here as witnesses. Abdul to the wheel and the rest of you to the sails. Make sure we don't founder while we're talking this out."

A brief flurry of movement and the cabin emptied until there was almost elbow room, though it was still hard to step on a foot of floor not occupied by unconscious sailors. Though he had asked for them, Tomas begrudged the two of his men who remained. He wanted to hug Perry, or at the very least inquire if hugging would ever be allowed again. But it wasn't the time for working out his personal relationships so he stifled the impulse and only gazed at Perry with perhaps more pleasure than was strictly wise.

"You're the official," he said. "Is there anything else we should do before we get you out of here?"

"Did any of them see your faces? Can you be identified?" Perry asked, and Tomas pressed the scarlet cloth of his neckerchief into his cheeks, covering the delighted smile beneath it. Was this Perry thinking about how to protect him in court? Bless him! This was exactly the sort of cooperation he had been longing for.

Well, his prick stirred in his breeches at the memory of Perry's thighs beneath him, the strong hands around his waist, not the only kind of cooperation, but this was the foundation that would make the other possible. "Not at all. They didn't see us coming and we knocked them out from behind. If we go now, that's all they'll know. They can't go to court with that."

"Then we should go before they wake. Give me five minutes to search—"

"I'll search with you," Tomas interrupted, already turning to the litter of documents on the table. "Temperance and Alan, we won't be needing you after all. Get back to the boat and make her ready to sail at a moment's notice."

He kept his head down over the logbooks as his men left, hearing the thin cabin door snick shut behind them. Then he glanced up and found Perry watching him, a thoughtful look in his eye.

"I didn't know if you'd come after me," Perry said, his voice soft and intimate now he had no audience. "After I rejected you. I hoped, but . . ." He bowed his head briefly before meeting Tomas's eye again, unapologetically. "I knew we had to rescue ourselves. I couldn't count on anything."

Tomas would have liked to have claimed this as a rescue, as a proof of his high moral character, but neither of them liked to be manipulated, and he respected that in Perry. The scheme of holding any relationship between them over Perry's head, forcing him to act to Tomas's advantage, had been a passing one, and it was long over. He snorted. "In plain truth, Perry, I didn't come after you. I got your note even as I was watching what I thought was Barnabas being smuggled off shore. I knew you could handle yourself, so I chose to go to him. If I'd known you were outmatched, I would have—"

"You would have ridden down to the Lizard Stone, and we would both have been lost."

Perry's smile was precious to Tomas; it spoke of forgiveness, a way back, but his eyes still retained a certain wariness that told Tomas not to push his luck.

"The Lord was with me, then," he said and awkwardly looked away, pushing the crew manifest away from the crabbed lists of a lading tally; it was a record of the cargo—where it had been bought from and at what price, where it was destined for, and at what price it should be sold.

A moment of soft silence passed as Tomas turned the pages of this journal, looking for any entry that referred to the captives, and Perry sorted through the many letters lying loose over the books. The sea outside had settled into regular swells, lulling as the rocking of a cradle. The tied-up crew breathed around his ankles, reassuring him he had not yet become a murderer, and the sight of Perry's profile, solemnly intent in the pursuit of justice, even though his person had been traded like so much cattle, made him wonder if perhaps he shouldn't give up the smuggling life altogether, so they would never have occasion to quarrel again.

Somehow when he opened his mouth to say this, what came out was "You know, I could set this ship on fire if you wanted. If you want them all to burn, just say the word."

Perry gave a quiet laugh, and whispered, as if it were an endearment, "You are so full of bullshit. I've no doubt you are as gentle a pirate as you are a smuggler."

"Indeed, for I am no smuggler." Tomas laughed.

Perry rolled his eyes. Fondly, it seemed. "I mean . . . I thoroughly approve of this act of piracy. I am convinced that sometimes the world is so arranged that one must break the law to prevent an evil thing. And I would like to believe that this is the extent of your wrongdoing—that you are a good man whose goodness is not constrained by the courts, but is no less good for all that."

Tomas managed to catch Perry's hand across the table, though groaning by his feet told him there was no time for long speeches. "I hope so indeed," he said, and felt the darkness that had dogged him since Perry had fled from his embrace lift from his shoulders.

If another man had quarrelled with him as Perry had, he would have demanded an apology, an explanation, but Perry needed to give him nothing. He regained Tomas's affections just by standing in the same room. Perry pulled the record book out from under his hand, even as the captain began to chew his drool-soaked gag. They had drawn his nightcap down until it covered his eyes, but once he regained enough thought to scrape his face down the deck, he would certainly dislodge it and see them.

"Come on." Tomas tossed one of the captain's knives onto the floor next to the man so he would be able to cut himself free as soon as they had left. Then he tugged at Perry's wrist. "Time to go."

With a deep hiss of breath, Perry went rigid under his hand, and Tomas knew the man had found something. "What?"

"Clement," Perry gasped, and said nothing more for a long heartbeat while Tomas gawped at him and tried to work out why he was commenting on Tomas's clemency now.

After a moment, as Tomas continued to gape at him in incomprehension, Perry huffed and slammed the book down in front of him, his finger underneath a specific entry.

Two adult male negroes, both healthy, one educated, suitable for overseer duties, bought from C. Quick for ninety guineas.

Pencilled in the right-hand column, *perhaps for Mr. Jeremy Quick in Antigua, if they survive the journey.*

Tomas tried to pull the book back from Perry, an irrepressible need to *tear the damn thing in half* overtaking him. But Perry snatched it up and caught Tomas's grabbing hand in his own. "Time to go," he repeated, urgently, tucking the book into his shirt with his left hand and moving out to haul Tomas toward the door with the other.

"They think I'm the—" Tomas began, incensed, only to find Perry's hand clamped about his mouth as he was manhandled toward the *Swift*. The words howled out indignantly in his head nevertheless. *They think I'm the disgrace to the family name?*

"Ninety guineas!" he hissed, when Perry had to let go long enough to grab the anchor chain with both hands. "That's a fortune to a poor man, but to bloody Clement it's a night's gambling debts. I bet he owns waistcoats worth more than that! He'd ruin two men's lives for pin money?"

He broke off his rant to whistle two notes, high and shrill, that brought his crew down from the rigging and running soft footed to swarm ratlike down the chain after him. A whistle was unlucky at sea, so hopefully someone below would come to investigate before her unmanned sails foundered her.

"Tell me you see now why I have to bring the Quicks down," he demanded of Perry as they thudded into the waiting *Swift*. "Surely you must see now why they have to go?"

But Perry was looking instead at the sodden bundle of something dark that lay in the bilges breathing like a beached porpoise. Some kind of reverse mermaid—too many legs for a man and an impenetrable octopus tangle where its face should be.

"What the hell," Tomas exclaimed, dropping into his boat as though it was enemy territory. "What is it now?"

CHAPTER TWENTY-EIGHT

FINALLY THE RIGHT MAN

The octopus gave a further determined writhe at the sound of Tomas's voice, and as Temperance Smith and Ben Ede cast off the rope that grappled them to the ship's chains, Perry seized a lantern and brought it closer to the creature.

Oh, it was two coats tangled together on top of two bodies. Even as he made this discovery, an arm emerged from the heap, its dainty hand folding the material down and revealing Anne Lusmoore's smugly grinning face. Water cascaded from her hair over her bright eyes as she sat up, someone groaning beside her.

"All right, Captain?" she said, her voice slurred. "I pulled 'im out of the sea like a gannet takes up a mackerel, though he didn't know who I was and he fought me."

"Barnabas!" Tomas exclaimed, ready to crow with satisfaction at the success of this endeavour, but Perry got there before him, stooping to remove the second coat, though the man beneath it tried to snatch it back.

He'd been looking for this man so long, it was a surprise to find him merely another ordinary human being—a youngish man with the weather-beaten skin of a professional sailor, stripped to his smallclothes, presumably to bear less weight as he swam. He was shivering so profoundly that it was visible to Tomas a foot away.

Barnabas knuckled his forehead to Tomas, as a naval seaman might salute an officer. "Water's so cold I thought I'd die."

"We just come back ourselves," Dennis commented, lurching across the deck from where he'd been propped opposite them. "Anne had to go in after him. When he felt himself grappled, he panicked, I think. Leastways there was lots of splashing. By the time I got the boat alongside 'em and they rolled on board, they was both chilled to the bone, barely able to get themselves on the *Swift*. They fell down there, and I put the coats over 'em. Let 'em rest a bit, you know?"

"I do know." The strength-sapping cold of the Cornish waves was barely to be borne under full summer sunshine, let alone at night in the tail end of a storm. "But, Anne, we need you to guide us home. Go into my cabin—you'll find dry clothes and brandy. Take whatever of each you need to be back at your post as soon as may be. Dennis? Bring out a change of clothes for Mr. Barnabas—"

"Okesi." Barnabas sat up, pulling the borrowed coat tighter around him. He watched Anne make her stumbling way back to the cabin, half supported by the sprightly but elderly form of Dennis, and turned a concerned expression on Tomas. "Barnabas Okesi. I didn't realize Miss Anne was a woman. Nor did I think she was trying to rescue me at first. I thought the men from the *Rosalinde* had come to recapture me. I'm sorry I fought her. Will she—"

"She'll be fine," Tomas reassured him. "She's tougher than any boy, as she would be the first to insist. And you? On behalf of my entire town, I regret that you've been subjected to this treatment. I apologise. How are you?"

"Better for this." Barnabas cocked his head to one side. "Some kind of patriot are you, then? An abolitionist?"

"I like to think 'a decent man.'" Tomas shrugged, aware of Perry's gaze on the side of his face like the light of a second lantern. He hoped for Perry's approval and was tempted to show off until he knew he had it. "And in that light, I would like you to help me to take these people to court. Selling freeborn Englishmen into slavery is an abhorrent act. They should suffer for it."

Dennis returned with a bundle of Tomas's clothing. Tomas spent a great deal on nondescript items, so that he would not be recognizable by his garments—giving them away the moment they became familiar. So there was always two or three changes of clothes in his locker. These were a pair of tan breeches that would not buckle around Barnabas's calves, but seemed to fit tolerably well otherwise, with a white shirt and a quilted waistcoat whose warmth restored a healthy undertone of bronze to the man's skin.

As Barnabas dressed, Tomas couldn't help but turn to Perry with a smirk, the thought of his victory—his complete and utter victory—blazing up in his veins like desire. With the evidence slipped down Perry's shirt, the marriage certificate, and Barnabas's testimony, he could deal the Quicks such a blow as they would never forget, and the chain on Perry's wrist had banished some of his earlier doubts. Now Perry would want it too, surely? And if he wanted it, then Tomas wanted it all the more. *I'll give you anything, Perry,* he thought, grinning. *Anything you want. When I am in charge.*

"Using a man's misfortune to bring down your own enemies is also abhorrent," Perry glared. And oh—how could he still be this forgiving? It was admirable from a Christian point of view, but Tomas's feral side wanted to shake him for it.

"I am amazed you will defend them still," he snarled, cold all at once, though already they had swung around the headland and were headed inward to gentler waters and warmer winds. "Did their kidnapping and selling you not harden your heart at all?"

This was unfair! The admiral himself—Tomas's grandfather—had put his father on a ship at age nine to learn a seaman's trade, and that was all he had ever done for his true family, discarding them like a leaky boot. Every slight Tomas had suffered all his life because he was the son of a bastard recurred to him in memory. He deserved the chance to turn the tables, to lord it over them for a change. To make them understand what it felt like having to work for your living while folk sniggered behind your back about your grandmother's virtue.

His own doubts felt distant from him at this moment, almost as though Perry was holding them for him, freeing him to snarl and posture like the hurt beast he was.

"It has not hardened my heart enough to make me willing to turn out a grandmother from her home," Perry insisted. "Damaris was as much practiced upon as your grandmother. Why should she be punished because the admiral was a cad? And you—do you really want to attract the ire of all the magistrate's cronies on your head? It is an open secret that you flaunt the law whenever it suits you. You stand on shaky ground from which to challenge the great and the good in this county. He'll take you down, Tomas. You may push him in to drown, but he'll drag you after him if you do."

"Is that a threat?" Tomas snapped, the fireworks of his invincibility fizzling out one by one, cold and disappointed. He wanted Perry, and he wanted the Quicks gone, and Perry was making it hard to achieve both.

Perry threw the *Rosalinde*'s record book onto the deck with a furious snap. "It is an expression of concern, you idiot! I do not wish you to get into a fight with the Quicks because I do not think you can win. At best you will ruin each other. Just for once—for *once*, acknowledge that you cannot get away with everything, and work in the real world as you have urged me to do. The powers that be will stand with him, not you, whatever your pieces of paper proclaim."

Tomas's straw-blaze of resentment died down, but it had already been enough to leave a thin film of soot over his victorious mood. It was nice that Perry cared about him, but he could show it better by falling in line with his plans, instead of being so damned disapproving.

"As you can see—" he turned a grimace of a smile on Barnabas, who had just finished squeezing the water from his hair and was accepting the flask of brandy from Dennis for a swig "—it's a complicated subject, but your testimony would shed light on it. I can put you up until a trial can be arranged, if you—"

Barnabas shook his head. "No, sir," he said. "I'm obliged for the rescue, but I want to get back to London before the news of the wreck. I don't want my family thinking I'm gone any longer than they have to. And like Mr. Dean says, justice ain't really available for the likes of me. If I come home at all, that's a victory."

The night's work settled on Tomas's shoulders in myriad small aches and pains, fatigue dropping like a shawl over him and—just for a moment—smothering his certainty. Suppose he, too, settled for what he could have; a man could be content with a loving mother and a business that kept him in everything he needed, and a love that might be even better than that which had blessed his youth. Couldn't he?

The crew hauled up the sails. A stir at the bow showed where two men were making her tight to the ring bolt in the rock beneath his house. The town lay sleeping beneath the faint sift of pearly moonlight, but a candle shone from his mother's bedroom window. She often waited up to be sure he came home.

"As you wish." He guided them both up the path to his door. He couldn't argue with Barnabas's choice to go back to his own home. "Come inside until the sun rises, and we'll put you on the morning coach."

He lit his bedroom fire and offered Barnabas a nightgown and the bed. Perry stood by his shoulder as he restacked the kindling, and blew gently on the catching sparks to strengthen them.

"I suppose I'd better be back to my own lodgings," Perry whispered, for Barnabas was tired enough to have fallen asleep the moment he'd hitched the blankets over his shoulder, and neither of them wished to wake him.

Tomas looked up at him, the fire's glow softly warm on his cheek. From down here, Perry was a tall pillar of solidity, even though his fingers trembled and his voice was slurred and weary. Tomas couldn't stand to see him walk away again.

"Stay," he said, more like a plea than an invitation. "The room next to this is in a shambles, but this bed's big enough for three if none of us are lively."

Perry huffed a little laugh and dropped down to hunker next to him. Their knees touched, and both of them gasped at the contact. *I wanted to kiss you there on deck*, Tomas thought. *You were so magnificent.* But Barnabas might not be as asleep as he seemed, and those words could not be spoken where anyone else could hear.

"You would be a distraction that I could not overlook," Perry murmured, reaching out to draw a finger along the line of bare skin where the cuff of Tomas's breeches had parted from the gartered top of his stocking. The tiny touch boiled all the sea's cold away from him. He felt the flush on his face spread all the way to his belly button.

"Are you using my own weapons against me?" He laughed, shaky but delighted. Oh God, he'd never met another man who challenged him like this, who was as stubborn yet as teasing as himself. He had to make this work somehow. He had to. Because right now he wanted Perry more than he wanted anything else, and if getting him necessitated a shift in his own manner of doing business, he could live with that.

"They're weapons, are they?" Perry grinned, his whole face gilded by the fire, his hair shot through with sparks. "I knew it. You've been trying to conquer me this whole time."

Tomas shot a glance at Barnabas, who still seemed to be asleep. "Oh," he said, "don't try to tell me you haven't been doing exactly the same." He leaned closer, bringing his mouth up to Perry's ear and relishing the way it made the other man bite his lip and crane towards him. "You have tried to give me the greater death, but I hope you will be satisfied with the little."

Perry's caressing touch turned into a firm grab at the back of Tomas's knee, the possessive jostle of it promising in its roughness. "Tomas. I've never thanked you for—"

"I don't need thanks—"

"Shh!" Perry insisted, planting one knee so he was stable enough to bring up his other hand and place two fingers on Tomas's lips. "I'm trying to say that I owe you too much to bring you to the gallows. That death threat should not still be lying between us."

I have decided to stop trying to kill you was perhaps not the most romantic thing Tomas had ever been told, but he didn't expect romance. He didn't even expect this. Treacherously—totally without his permission—his eyes welled with tears, and the gasp of his breath was more sob than he would have wanted. Perry's trust seemed to both break and remake him like a hug to a friendless child. Speechless, he kissed the tips of Perry's fingers.

It was Perry's turn to flinch and sneak a worried glance at the third man. He stood up, blinking the glossiness from his own eyes. "But let us not court the noose together. Not now, at least. I should go."

"Stay," Tomas repeated, smiling. The lust of earlier had met his heartfelt relief and produced something brighter, larger than itself. Something that simply wanted Perry under his roof for as long as he could keep him. "Take the bed. I have some papers to look through. I'll sleep in the morning." *When he's gone.*

CHAPTER TWENTY-NINE

THE LIGHT BRINGER IS IDENTIFIED

The marriage certificate crinkled under Tomas's left arm as he waved goodbye to the nine o'clock stage with Barnabas Okesi on it. He had sat with the document in his hands in front of the fire for the rest of the night, looking between the dry brown words on the page and Perry's face, lax and trusting, asleep in his bed.

Perry's words had tossed through his head all night like loose cargo tumbling through the hold in a storm. With Perry quiet, Tomas's own doubts had returned in force, and he was bruised with them this morning, unable to get past the dread of Perry finding him unacceptably cruel.

It was Perry's disapproval that he feared. He would weather any other consequence—even his mother's rebuke.

I would weather his too, he tried to convince himself, as the dust spat up by the iron-rimmed wheels of the coach settled on the doorstep of the Hope & Anchor and whited all their window boxes as if with flour. *He would come around. He would forget his ire and return to me, all the more readily once I had power of my own.*

But Perry was stubborn, and his sycophancy had not yet stretched further than his principles. If he thought he was being bought, he would dig in his heels out of mere pride, and then who knew—

"Put your hands where I can see them. Turn around."

Tomas had heard the footsteps coming, of course. He had assumed they were running for the second coach. Evidently not. Lowering one hand and raising the other, palms empty, he slid his eyes sideways. Perry looked nonplussed, but not afraid, so Tomas turned slowly, still peaceful, to see who had come.

It was Mr. Gwynn himself, Customs Supervisor of Porthkennack, Perry's boss, with a pistol in his hand and two of his men behind him, similarly armed.

"What can I do for you gentlemen?" Tomas asked, the slight fuzz of his sleeplessness clearing as his heart beat hard.

"You've been accused of piracy, Mr. Quick," Jowan Ede offered from his place at Gwynn's left, his face apologetic, but his aim unwavering. "And you too, Mr. Dean. They said you robbed the customs warehouse, Tomas, and Mr. Dean helped you. In an inside job, like."

"Quiet!" Gwynn snapped, glaring at Jowan.

Tomas didn't know whether to be angrier on his own behalf or on Perry's. "Oh." He rolled his eyes. "Let me guess. Lazarus sent you. He's grown bored of waiting for Perry to invent some nonexistent evidence against me and sent you to do it instead?"

Gwynn's jaw locked, and a cold glint came into his bloodshot eyes. "You know how honest I am, Tomas Quick. Just as I know the same of you. Let's have none of your posturing now—we've come to the pinch."

"'Posturing'?" Tomas raised his chin with a sneer. He didn't posture. He merely said things, at times, that he would have been wiser to keep to himself. "Take me before the magistrate, then," he said, fearless because he had the power in his breast pocket to ruin the man. "I have a document here that'll put the fear of God into him."

"Tomas—" Perry cut himself off, but Tomas could assemble the whole argument from that one word: *We've talked about this before. Don't do it.*

Tomas fixed Perry with a stare that challenged him to save his neck from the noose in any other way.

"Sir," Perry responded, speaking to Gwynn with the earnest, upright look that Tomas always wanted to rumple. "You know I was engaged by Sir Lazarus to investigate the smuggling in this town. I also ask you to take us to the magistrate so I can give my report. It's time, I think, for us all to come clean."

Gwynn hesitated.

"He did say 'arrest them,' sir," Jowan put in, plucking at the stained kerchief around his neck. "But he didn't say we was to take them straight to jail. Maybe he *wants* us to bring 'em to him?"

The supervisor's face hardened still further. "He has no business arresting my men anyway," he burst out, walking off toward the cliff path with such a stamp to his gait that it was as though he were trying to kick the earth in the face. "As if Dean weren't the most insufferable do-gooder I've ever come across. Fine."

Tomas had been to jail twice before, waiting for trials at which he'd been acquitted. With his mother and many friends in the town willing to feed him, it had not been too uncomfortable an experience, but he would rather avoid it if he could. The thought that Lazarus might have found evidence against him would not stick—he'd been careful. He knew no one in town would ever speak against him. It would be fine, especially with the blackmail material in the pocket of his coat. He would hate to use that and incur Perry's wrath. But rather than see either of them die? He would burn the world down rather than that.

Their appearance at the Quicks' door caused it to be shut in their faces while the muffled sound of an argument inside faded through the grey stone walls, which were now beginning to be blotched with lichen. Tomas touched the paper beneath his arm and counted the windows, estimating the tax on this mansion that might still be his if he chose it.

"They weren't expecting this, sir," Perry noted dryly to Gwynn. "Expected you to hop to their will unquestioning, like their servant."

If he was aware he might be talking about himself, if he was hurt that his erstwhile protector had thrown him off without even looking him in the face, he didn't show it, but Tomas wondered if this latest betrayal had yet made a dent in his mercy.

A burst of shrieking inside the door—a woman's high voice pitched in fury—and a moment later it was opened by a servant girl with tears dripping into her fichu and her bonnet askew as if she had tried to clutch at her hair.

Damaris stood behind her, in a gown of ivory embroidered with peach roses, a peach stomacher and petticoat picking up the theme, yet failing to conceal her air of almost military command. Her steel-grey hair was scraped back plainly beneath a rabbit-eared cap, the delicacy of which did not soften her harsh face. "Well, don't stand there," she addressed Mr. Gwynn. "Bring them in."

The cost of the curtains in the very pink drawing room might have fed the poor of Porthkennack for a month, but that was not what Tomas noticed first. For the Quick family was drawn up in a circle as though they were watching a play, and at the focus of their regard stood Hedrek Negus, brown and hairy and incongruous like a bear that had wandered in from the street.

Negus put up his bristly chin and met Tomas's astonished gaze with a smirk. "'Tis the man himself."

It felt like he had swallowed his own stomach, everything within turning inside out and falling into itself. His feet went cold as though they remembered that wet morning when he had put a razor to Negus's throat because he had been impatient and too angry for niceties.

"I see you know what this is about." Negus's smile broadened. The world gave a sickening lurch and fell out from under Tomas's feet. *I thought you forgave me. You spoke so reasonably. We parted as friends.*

"Bloke put a knife to my throat, told me not to say anything or I was dead," Negus told the room at large—Lazarus and Damaris in their arm chairs, Clement and Constance on the sofa, a matching pair in periwinkle blue. "But that's why I'm ready to talk. I don't take to being threatened by young upstarts in front of my own door."

Of course, he might have spoken softly because I had a knife in my hand, yet resented it later, as I would have done, Tomas acknowledged, recovering swiftly now the surprise was past. *Yet if this too is a battle, I am not unarmed.*

"As you see." Lazarus cleared his throat. He sat in his chair much as though he were sitting for a portrait emphasizing his casual power, apparently relaxed, one leg tucked beneath the seat, one outstretched. One hand on his hip, the other resting on the arm of the chair. But both hands were in fists. "We have finally found someone willing to testify against you, Tomas. It will give me the greatest of pleasures to sentence you to hang."

"Sir!" Perry objected, "I investigated—"

"You investigated this ruffian as I asked, and you ended up working for him. I know." Lazarus's expression of disgust was so extreme it was possible to see the gums in his snarl. "You cast back my trust in my face. I have never known such a betrayal. I will be having words with Lord Petersfield about the quality of the young men he takes under his wing. He need not think I will spare you for his sake. One law for all—you will hang next to your seducer to drive home the moral."

"That is not what I was about to say," Perry insisted, drawing himself up to his full, impressive height. He turned to Mr. Gwynn. "Sir, in investigating Mr. Tomas Quick, I discovered instead a smuggling ring run by Clement Quick. This accusation is but a ploy to divert your attention from—"

"Clement?" Damaris exclaimed, effortlessly riding over Perry's words. "What nonsense is this? The man would say anything to—"

Gwynn cleared his massive throat, jowls wobbling. "Ma'am," he said ponderously. "Mr. Dean is many things, but in my experience, dishonest is not one of them." He held out a hand to Perry. "Do you have proof? Everyone accusing each other—proof is what we need."

The radiance of Perry's grin felt like the sun kneading the aches out of Tomas's shoulders. He relaxed into it, feeling rescued.

"I do, sir." Perry reached into his shirt and drew out a letter and the *Rosalinde*'s manifest. "This is from a ship that left Porthkennack yesterday. You will see that it took on board a large amount of tea and brandy at prices that cannot be legal and was destined for the Scilly Isles. I don't need to tell you, sir, that all there is in the Scilly Isles is a smuggler's marketplace. These items are being traded in the name of C. Quick, and have been signed for."

"A signature can be forged," Damaris insisted, clutching the arms of her chair as though she intended to rise.

Tomas examined Clement narrowly, hoping to see guilt, but Clement's obvious puzzlement was not reassuring. Tomas's anger might sometimes take him too far, but he read people well enough to say Clement looked like an innocent man.

"In addition," Perry went on, official still, like a man used to giving evidence in court. "You'll see that C. Quick attempted to sell 'two negroes' into slavery. That was myself, sir, and a freeborn English sailor named Barnabas Okesi, who left on the coach to London this morning, but could be subpoenaed to return and give evidence if needed. That is the kidnap and sale of an officer of the customs service, sir."

Gwynn's round face hardened. "So it is," he said darkly while his men muttered behind his back.

"Forgery again," Damaris insisted. "It is a tissue of malice, no more."

Beside Clement, his sister had put her head down sharply, her gaze apparently fixed on her hands. Her nails were remarkably short for a woman's, Tomas noted, registering the twitch of her skirts as she drew her foot beneath her hem.

"When I was captured," Perry went on, a note of enjoyment entering his voice, as though he could feel how the room swayed to his side, "I was attacked from behind with some form of poison in a sharp tube." He folded down his collar to display a bull's-eye of a bruise around the red gape of what resembled a huge insect bite. "I was able to turn and see my attacker for a moment before I swooned. They wore a mask, but the eyes, the blond hair, the slender frame—these things I am prepared to swear to. It was Clement."

"You say this was last night?" Lazarus leaned forward as though breaking himself out of a cocoon of ice. "Clement was here all night. We had a party of friends over to play whist. They will attest it. Now if perhaps we could drop this nonsense and get back to—"

"'C. Quick' is Constance," Tomas said, speaking it out loud even as he realized it. Her shoulders twitched and her back straightened, but she did not look up, which now seemed to Tomas as though she was hiding her face. "Of course. See how similar they are in height and colouring, and the shape of their eyes."

"It's preposterous to think that a young woman—" Mr. Gwynn began, his tone much less convinced than his words.

"Anne Lusmoore works for me as a pilot, sir," Tomas cut in. "When she's dressed for the sea, she's often mistaken for a young lad—and she is as hardy and enterprising as one."

"I did see Constance on the cliff when I approached the cave where I was assaulted," Perry offered in the voice of someone for whom it is all coming together. "She had a large painting bag with her. If she had trousers on beneath her skirt, it would have been a moment's work to throw off the skirt, throw on a fisherman's coat and hat, and then who would suspect her of being a wealthy heiress?"

At last, Constance raised her head. Her face was livid white and her eyes furious. "I was painting," she said, chilly as an iceberg.

"On that stretch of path between the Lizard and Bloody Mary," Tomas said as the scales fell from his own eyes also. "Even though the light had already gone. On an evening with a storm out to sea."

She looked so demure, golden ringlets by her cheeks, her dress the pale blue of a winter sky, and her eyes full of killing cold. By contrast, Tomas felt himself go up in flame. "What else did you have in that bag? A lantern? One light, that's what I saw the night the *Kittywake* foundered. One light, high up on the cliff exactly where you claim to have been painting. My God, you Lucifer! The wrecker is you."

CHAPTER THIRTY

MANY RECONCILIATIONS

"How dare you!" Lazarus leapt to his feet and took two steps forward before he seemed to remember that violence was beneath him. "Gwynn!" he turned to address the supervisor. "Pay no attention to this slander. The both of them are lying. Dean has a heart as black as his skin, and the bastard is as cursed as one can expect from one of his get. I insist that you take them to prison immediately. I will deal with them in court."

"Hold your horses and let me have my last laugh." Negus plopped himself down on the unlit hearth and picked at his teeth with a fingernail. "Still here, ain't I?" He gave Tomas a smug smile. "Like the shadow of your sins. You accusing them. Them accusing you. This'll run and run, this will. If you get out of it with your neck, that's still your fortune eaten up in lawyers' fees. You're done, mate."

Tomas's anger and his victory sucked back out of him like a retreating tide, leaving a barren and salty mud of dread. Because Negus was right. This counter-accusation might take Lazarus off the bench, but he would only be replaced by a crony of his, eager for revenge. Negus knew a great deal about Tomas's business over the years. With his help, a honest prosecutor might yet make something stick, and a dishonest one would not baulk about taking Perry down beside Tomas.

Ruin weighed down his limbs and his spirits with dragging darkness. For a long moment all he could do was breathe and fight the despair.

Mr. Gwynn fidgeted with the ends of his cravat, exchanging reluctant glances with his men. Jowan Ede was red as a blood moon. "After I just got him broke in right."

"Wait." Damaris's voice fell into the atmosphere of clinging doubt like an anchor—heavy, barbed. "This pointed tube of poison? Was it a device that would be easily thrown away?"

Perry frowned up at her, perhaps wondering what her game was. "It seemed a specialist thing—expensive. A little like a brass spyglass. She used it as if she had used it many times before."

"Then, gentlemen." Damaris folded her hands against her stomacher, back straight as a fire poker. "I suggest you search my granddaughter's room."

"Grandma!" Constance burst out, and Lazarus at the same time cried "Mother!" But Gwynn nodded, and his escort hurried to the stairs that led up to the private rooms.

"I have lived all my life in an unflinching adherence to the law and to the bounds of public decency," Damaris declaimed. "My honour is unswerving, and I will not bend it even for my grandchildren. If Constance has done this, she will not hide behind me."

The old woman's face was bloodless, her lips pressed thin, but the rubies on her fingers trembled like settling embers, for somewhere under her armour of pride, she was shaking.

A reluctant admiration for her kindled in Tomas's breast. She, too, was honest, then, though her honesty was terrible.

Clement pulled a cigarillo from a silver pocket case and attempted to light it from a candle on the mantel. His hands were more noticeably shaking than his grandmother's, and he choked when he tried to inhale. Constance, by contrast, had walked over to open a window. She looked sick, but her hand was still toying with the drawstring of her skirt, ready, perhaps, to shuck it off and climb through to freedom. Lazarus had his head in his hands like a child hiding from a thunderstorm, his knee bouncing under his elbow.

Bloody Hellfire, Tomas realized. *I have no need to ruin this family. They are achieving that all by themselves.* He yearned to reach out to Perry and hold his hand while they waited. To somehow be able to say to him, *Perhaps I do understand your mercy after all.* But that was not permitted to either of them. So he simply edged sideways until his shoulder brushed Perry's and took what comfort he could from that touch.

A rattle of leather heels on the oak staircase, and Jowan burst in, carrying a glossy teak box opened to reveal a polished brass tube and plunger with a hollow metal spike on the end and two ampules of fluid beside it. One empty.

Swift as a jack out of a box, Constance dropped her skirts and scrambled out of the window. Tomas heard her feet crunch down in the gravel outside and take off in a sprint. After a moment of stunned silence, Jowan and his colleague followed, but they were already too late. She would be over the cliff and into the caves at any moment, and they would not find her there.

Silence fell in the wake of their sudden scrambling departure. Lazarus's foot tapping stopped like the watch of a dead man. "We are ruined," he groaned. "My daughter a wrecker! A pirate! I shall be the laughing stock of the bench. I shall never show my face in public again."

He lifted a glittering gaze to Tomas, dry eyed but full of an anger that Tomas recognised as akin to his own. "Are you happy now, Mr. Quick? You cannot possibly bring our name into more disrepute, so you may as well keep it now. Keep it. I care not."

Tomas's skin prickled as a great emotion he could not name moved beneath it. He plunged his hand into his pocket and touched his father's marriage certificate, folded lengthways like a lawyer's brief. Now was the time. He could say *I do not need your permission, sir, but you will oblige me by moving out of my house at once.* But now Perry's compassion was at work in him too. He watched Damaris watch him—she was iron haired, iron hard, a terrible old woman. But was he the kind of man who could use the day of her grandchild's disgrace to tell her that all her life she had been living in sin with the admiral, that her son was a bastard and her future was one of ridicule and litigation? He had no doubt that she would fight for the last penny of her personal fortune, rather than let it pass to him, but her money and the admiral's had been entwined for decades. Unpicking exactly what she was owed would take many an appearance in court, brazening out the public ruin of her virtue. What would Tomas's mother say if he put her through that?

He turned to Lazarus, feeling the balance of the room rock beneath his hand, needing a delicate touch. Pity in him felt like fishhooks in the gut, and he didn't like it at all. "Do you still intend to kill me? And this upright gentleman, Mr. Dean, who has done nothing but be honest with you? Would you destroy him too?"

"I would see you both hang," said Lazarus, wearily. "But now is not the time for me to anger Lord Petersfield, nor to invite further calumny amongst the rabble of the town, who have an inexplicable liking for you, Tomas. The joy of this hunt has rather gone out for me."

"Hm!" From the hearth, Negus huffed a startling laugh. "Slippery bastard," he said, grinning at Tomas. "Well then, I don't mind. Had my revenge looking at your face, young man. Though you may want to apologize to me—to stop it happening again."

"Wait." Mr. Gwynn took off hat and wig and rubbed a large handkerchief over his perspiring face and pate. "Hedrek, are you saying you were willing to bear false witness against Mr. Tomas here on account of a personal quarrel? Because that's a crime too."

"I am not." Negus laughed. "I'm saying I've had my fun, all's fair, and I'm going home now. The whole lot of these Quicks is loony as a full moon, and the further away I get from them, the better I be."

Suiting his actions to his words, he strode across the room, jerked the door open—revealing the housekeeper caught with her ear to the planks—shouldered past her, and was gone. *The old reprobate probably never meant to go through with it at all*, Tomas realized, with a rising sense of joy and relief. *Probably knew I would never cut his throat either, but wanted me to feel the threat.* A fondness of Hedrek's mere existence came over him like respect. He *was* going to apologize. That was a man who it would be well to be friends with in future.

This sense that difficult people were somehow irreplaceable and invaluable made him sigh, the tension going out of his shoulders as he returned his gaze to Damaris. Lazarus was bent over himself, crushed, and at some point Clement—like the ornamental ghost he was—had left the room without anyone really noticing. But Damaris was upright and cold as ever, facing the future of shunning and mockery like an icebreaker facing a berg. Tomas could respect that too.

"Would it comfort you if I changed my name?" he asked, more gently than he had ever spoken to her before. "I am not ashamed that my father chose to call himself by his mother's surname . . ."

He was halfway through the sentence before the weight of it caught him up. Was he really saying farewell to the revenge of a lifetime just because he felt sorry for her? Sorry for her for being caught up in a doom that was none of his doing? Perhaps if she had been a better parent, a better grandparent, Constance would not have grown up thinking she was entitled to murder sailors for profit.

Again, his hand strayed to his pocket, but before he could touch the parchment, Perry's hand was on his back, in between his shoulder blades like a congratulation. This mercy, though it would cost him a great house and a fortune, would gain him the man he loved. After that, it was easy to shove the certificate back down, unused, and finish, "So if it would take some of the sting from this bleak day for you, I am prepared to call myself Tomas Chantry from now on, if you ask it from me one more time."

"And have the town think you were now ashamed of the name of Quick? I think not." Damaris's eyes flashed like light from steel. "I have spent all my life trying to make this family respectable. But the admiral was a hellion, and the blood carries the taint, sure enough. Keep the name, and may God have mercy on us all."

Tomas left the house with Perry's hand nestled in the small of his back, on the excuse of guiding him. And indeed he was in something of a daze, buffeted by thoughts that changed direction and strength like a summer squall. Had he won? Had he defeated and deposed the Quicks and emerged triumphant over all? Lazarus would certainly not be magistrate for much longer. No more would they be able to lord it over Porthkennack in the appearance of moral rather than financial superiority. Was that the prize he had been chasing all these years?

"Well, Mr. Dean." Gwynn paused outside the Quick's porch to mop his shaved head again and regard Perry with a complaisant look. "I 'ope you've understood now how delicate matters stand in this county. 'Ow what's needed in a customs man is a sense of balance, of justice, and not just an aptitude for counting crates. When you do send that report back, I 'ope it will reflect the subtlety of the job, young man. The humanity."

Perry caught Tomas's eye and tipped up the ends of his glorious mouth in a smile that felt too intimate to be shared. "I have been well taught, sir," he agreed. "I will strive to do you proud."

When Gwynn nodded in satisfaction and stomped away, Perry linked his arm with Tomas's, and squeezed Tomas's elbow into the dip of his waist. "Thank you," he whispered. "You had the chance and every justification for your revenge, and you gave it up. Was that for me?"

Of course he'd noticed. He was as observant as he was kind. *I had my eyes on a greater prize*, Tomas thought. But that was not quite right, for Perry was no object to be attained. Tomas squeezed back. "I, too, have had a very wise teacher," he said. "Now let's go home."

CHAPTER THIRTY-ONE

LETTERS HOME

o my esteemed patron Lord Petersfield, Perry wrote some weeks later, sitting at a folding desk battered from many years at sea. Through the window, the last flaming brands of an apricot-gold sunset gilded his papers almost as much as the single candle lantern he had already lit and set by the bed. The tide was in, and in the harbour all the small craft nodded brightly, the pooling amber radiance picking up their many colours and smoothing over their dirt and defects. It looked like the idyll he currently felt it was.

I must thank you again for your great condescension in choosing me for this task of investigating the alleged corruption in the customs service in Porthkennack.

He dipped his pen and brushed the triangle of remaining feather on its end against his lips, deep in thought. The drag and tickle on his mouth made him smile, anticipating his plans for the evening. But the letter must be finished first.

You may wish to make inquiries among your staff to uncover those who cannot meet a decent standard of discretion, for when I arrived here, my purpose was already known to everyone involved. My chance to establish myself as a run-of-the-mill colleague to whom hearts might be opened in confidence was therefore lost before I even began.

Notwithstanding this disadvantage, I pursued my inquiries diligently. I found a small degree of laxity amongst the officers with whom I served—a jug or two of spirits might be consumed, if the keg was broken, rather than transferred to a new container and returned to the warehouse. One or two men are old and somewhat inclined to skimp on their daily rounds etc. etc., all very much in the common way of backwater departments in sleepy towns.

I did not find any evidence of large-scale corruption among the customs officers of the town, but—as you will see from the pages of the local newspaper I enclose—I did flush out a wrecker, a human trafficker, and a major player in the local network of smugglers. This enterprising young woman ran a gang comprised of strangers to the town, who might be paid off after a couple of jobs before they became recognizable. To enable these strangers to identify each other, they would each wear a cormorant feather somewhere about their person, either singly in their hats, as a cockade, or perhaps dangling from an earring.

Going in men's raiment, Constance was mistaken for her brother Clement by those with whom she dealt face-to-face, and thereby she was always provided with an alibi at the best or a scapegoat if it should come to it. Meanwhile, the knowledge that the head of this new smuggling ring was the child of the local magistrate meant that the local people— even if they knew her name—were in despair of their knowledge being believed or acted upon, should they say anything. And, indeed, I believe Sir Lazarus would have gone to any lengths to keep the matter quiet if he had not been so taken by surprise himself.

I see now why you warned me of the dangers of pride and the corrupting influence of high station, for once the wrecker's name came to light, so too did a number of incidences of favouritism and corruption in the legal practice and the business ventures of her father, the magistrate. Give you joy, sir, that your instincts that something was very wrong in this small town were exact and correct.

He dipped his pen again. A scent of soused mackerel and samphire drifted to him up the stairs. They had eaten dinner hours ago, but the smell lingered. The sound of Iskander and Zuliy playing trictrac by the fire downstairs was a homely babble of words he couldn't understand and comfortable ceramic clicks.

I have always been and will continue to be indebted to you for your interest in my career,

Here came the words that he dreaded—that he had to pull out as one had to pull out an arrowhead. He thought back to Tomas, the struggle to be merciful, to settle for anything less than absolute victory, written plainly on his vivid face as he faced and forgave the woman who had disinherited him. That must have cost Tomas a great deal. So Perry could not do less.

but this example of corruption in high places has given me a revulsion for the ambitions I once cherished.

"But see how oft ambition's aims are cross'd, and chiefs contend till all the prize is lost!" as Mr. Pope puts it.

I have seen this for myself, and now my desire is only to stay here and do what good I may in Porthkennack. Perhaps ere long, through hard work and dedication, you will see me rise to the place of supervisor here, but I can no longer see my future anywhere other than in this place.

For delivering me here and for so many other things, I remain, sir, your most humble servant.

Peregrine Dean, Esq.

He shook sand over the ink to dry it, and read it back, waiting for the sense of defeat that would surely come, but the sun slipped a fingernail lower and the first star made a pinprick in the sky, and he understood gradually that what he felt was relief. Thankfulness.

Smoothing down a fresh sheet of paper, he smiled at the bead of ink on the end of his quill.

My dear mama,

You will be glad to hear that I am out of that poky little room of which I spoke last time. I have taken lodgings in the house of Mr. Tomas Quick, whom I also mentioned in my last. The points of contention between us having now been settled, I am happy to say he is an excellent young gentleman and we have become fast friends.

I am now established in my position and understand better the internal tensions and stresses both of my department and of the town, into which I, as usual, walked as though handing down judgement from above. They tolerated me nevertheless and have quite won my good opinion one and all.

I know it is a sudden change in me to have given up my political ambitions and thrown myself into small-town life so cheerfully, but my aim in pursuing personal power was always to do good with it, and I believe I can do good here, in prosecuting those who deserve to be punished and in showing mercy to those who do not.

Since my pay has finally come through, I have kept back a portion for lodging and food and am sending the remainder, in the hopes it will bring you all cheer.

I hope to hear from you soon,
All my love,
Perry

Even as he was folding and sealing this letter, the door between his room and Tomas's swung silently open. He looked over his shoulder to see Tomas beneath the lintel, clad in nothing but a long shirt, his feet bare and his ruddy hair outshining the sunset in the light of the candle in his hand.

Perry's mouth and prick flushed, tingling. The hem of the shirt rose on either side, exposing Tomas's endless slender legs and just a hint of buttock. Throwing himself to his feet, Perry closed the shutters over his window with a snap, then darted to lock the bedroom door.

That done, they were safe. Iskander had the next room along, but spoke no English and was already deep in plans to return to his own country. Zuliy—who slept across the corridor—would do nothing to hurt Tomas, and still retained a Turkish attitude to the question of sex. Perry had never imagined being in such a situation—a place where he could rise and kiss his lover with the expectation of bed and not of disgrace. Who would have thought this luxury was available to the honest working man as much as to the rich?

"Done with the letter writing?" Tomas asked, padding over to raise a golden eyebrow at the name of Lord Petersfield on the direction. "Is that it? The 'I want to stay here forever' letter?"

In white linen as Tomas was, svelte and sudden in his movements, topped with fire, he was as intense a presence as he had been when the sight of his face had changed Perry's life that first day. Some elemental thing of lightning and flame. "I would have given up much more for you if I could," he vowed, sliding a hand up one tantalizing leg, lust and adoration mingling into something he could only think of as amazed gratitude. How had he been found worthy to be given this?

"Oh"—Tomas grinned, mockingly—"don't try to pretend I haven't made the larger sacrifice here." He pushed the banyan down Perry's shoulders until it tangled at his elbows, all but imprisoning him, and walked him backward until his calves hit the bed. "You'll find I love you very much more than you love me."

Perry half sat, half fell onto the bed, still struggling to free his arms so he could touch as Tomas climbed into his lap. "That's not true," he protested. "I can beat you in any contest, even one of adoration."

Tomas leaned down and caught Perry's lips between his own, biting down on the lower, the combination of pleasure and pain racking Perry's body with desire. "Is that so?" Tomas laughed, blue eyes ablaze. "Prove it."

Explore more of the *Porthkennack* universe:
riptidepublishing.com/titles/universe/porthkennack

a PORTHKENNACK HISTORICAL

A Gathering Storm
Joanna Chambers

Count the Shells
Charlie Cockrane

a PORTHKENNACK CONTEMPORARY

Wake Up Call
JL Merrow

Junkyard Heart
Garrett Leigh

Broke Deep
Charlie Cochrane

Tribute Act
Joanna Chambers

House of Cards
Garrett Leigh

One Under
JL Merrow

Foxglove Copse
Alex Beecroft

Dear Reader,

Thank you for reading Alex Beecroft's *Contraband Hearts*!

We know your time is precious and you have many, many entertainment options, so it means a lot that you've chosen to spend your time reading. We really hope you enjoyed it.

We'd be honored if you'd consider posting a review—good or bad—on sites like **Amazon, Barnes & Noble, Kobo, Goodreads, Twitter, Facebook, Tumblr,** and your blog or website. We'd also be honored if you told your friends and family about this book. Word of mouth is a book's lifeblood!

For more information on upcoming releases, author interviews, blog tours, contests, giveaways, and more, please sign up for our weekly, spam-free newsletter and visit us around the web:

> **Newsletter:** tinyurl.com/RiptideSignup
> **Twitter:** twitter.com/RiptideBooks
> **Facebook:** facebook.com/RiptidePublishing
> **Goodreads:** tinyurl.com/RiptideOnGoodreads
> **Tumblr:** riptidepublishing.tumblr.com

Thank you so much for Reading the Rainbow!

RiptidePublishing.com

ALSO BY

ALEX BEECROFT

ABOUT THE AUTHOR

Alex Beecroft was born in Northern Ireland during the Troubles and grew up in the wild countryside of the English Peak District. She studied English and philosophy before accepting employment with the Crown Court, where she worked for a number of years. Now a full-time author, Alex lives with her husband and two children in a little village near Cambridge and tries to avoid being mistaken for a tourist.

Alex is only intermittently present in the real world. She has spent many years as an Anglo-Saxon and eighteenth-century reenactor. She has led a Saxon shield wall into battle, and toiled as a Georgian kitchen maid. For the past nine years she has been taken up with the serious business of morris dancing, which has been going on in the UK for at least five hundred years. But she still hasn't learned to operate a mobile phone.

In order of where you're most likely to find her to where she barely hangs out at all, you can get in contact on:

Twitter: @Alex_Beecroft
Her blog: alexbeecroft.com/blog
Her website: alexbeecroft.com
Tumblr: tumblr.com/blog/itsthebeecroft
Facebook: facebook.com/alex.beecroft.1
Facebook Page: facebook.com/AlexBeecroftAuthor

Or sign up to Alex's newsletter, and you'll receive *Under the Hill: Bomber's Moon, Buried With Him, The Wages of Sin,* and *Lioness of Cygnus Five* absolutely free: alexbeecroft.com/alexs-newsletter

Enjoy more stories like
Contraband Hearts
at RiptidePublishing.com!

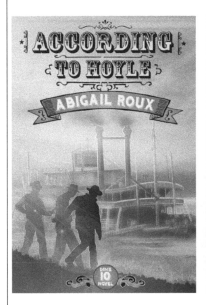

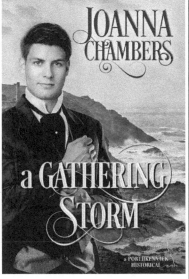

According to Hoyle	*A Gathering Storm*
The line between heroes and villains is narrow.	The storm is gathering. Will their fragile bond survive it
ISBN: 978-1-62649-215-8	ISBN: 978-1-62649-561-6